I0599214

THE CITY BENEATH THE SEA

By

Ricardo S. Dubois

Edited by: Angela Hooper
Back photo courtesy Dwight Moore

THE CITY BENEATH THE SEA

THE CITY BENEATH THE SEA

DEDICATION

As we grow, we all become products of our own life's experiences. Good, or bad we carry with us the emotion scares of situations and experience that we are either taught or learn on our own. After half a century of life I've come to learn that it is often so easy to silo individuals into groups. Gays, Blacks, Mexicans, Muslims, all fit into nice neat silos. Silos which prejudices and stereotypes can easily be heaped upon. It is not until you find a friend in one of these groups that the silos you created, no longer have a perfect order. Your friend no longer fits into the stereotyped silo, and you are forced to view individuals in that silo a little different. Ten years ago I met such a man that I would come to view as a friend. He opened my eyes up to many things, and forced me to approach people a little differently, looking beyond their skin color and into the content of their character. This book forced me to view the events of hurricane Katrina through many different eyes, and this would never have been possible if it had not been for my friend, shattering so many of my prejudices and stereotypes. So this book is dedicated to my friend, my brother, Leon.

THE CITY BENEATH THE SEA

THE CITY BENEATH THE SEA

CHAPTER ONE

Somewhere in the Gulf of Mexico, a WC-130 turbo prop was being bounced around by the high winds and turbulence.

Captain Ron Holmes of the U. S. Air Force Reserve was at the controls; he was calm, cool, no sign of fear or discomfort on his fifty-year-old wrinkled face as he piloted his craft into the belly of hurricane Katrina.

Over the years, Holmes had taken this flight many times, escorting National Oceanic and Atmospheric Administration research scientists to take vital readings of one of the deadliest forces of nature. Through the years, scientists had learned more and more about hurricanes, due in a large part to the efforts of brave pilots like Holmes.

"Hang on!" Holmes said over the PA, "We're going to start to punch our way through, It might get rough."

"Rougher than this?" questioned one of the research scientists in the back of the plane, who had been fighting not only to keep his seat, but also his lunch.

The warning came none too soon as the plane bounced about and daylight gave way to darkness, as they entered the outer edge of the storm.

Looking around at the other occupants of the plane, it did not take long to differentiate between hurricane veterans and first-timers. Usually, the appearance of uneasiness was enough of an indicator. If that failed, the beads of sweat on their forehead and the close proximity to a barf bag was a dead giveaway. The look of fear on the young scientists faces when everything went dark was unforgettable. With only the red cabin light illuminating the cabin, it gave each person a surreal appearance as they entered the hurricane, and the turbulence became more violent.

THE CITY BENEATH THE SEA

Holmes fought with the controls of his plane; an uneasy look began to come over him, though he tried not to show it to the rest of his crew. If there was one thing a captain was supposed to be able to do, it was to instill confidence in his crew, regardless of the circumstances they found themselves in.

"Whoa!" Sean the co-pilot said, as they hit an exceptionally hard patch of turbulence. "She's turned into a rough one!"

Sean Cooper, though younger than Holmes, was no stranger to flying in bad weather; in fact, he had flown into many hurricanes with Holmes. But something was different this time, he didn't quite know what it was, and couldn't put his finger on it, but something was beginning to give him a bad feeling.

"I've got a bad feeling about this one," Sean said as he looked over to Holmes for reassurance. Holmes, however, had an expression, a look that for the first time, did not instill confidence in those around him. "Anyway to get out of this?" Sean asked, sensing danger thick in the air.

"No, we're committed, either we'll make it or we won't," Holmes said, for the first time giving a faint clue that they might be in trouble.

Flashes of lightning struck about them, momentarily filling the cockpit with light, forcing them to refocus their eyes to the darkness after each strike.

Then after a few minutes, which when you're in the belly of a storm seems like hours, the plane smoothed out, with the wind not howling as before.

The scientists in the rear of the plane began to think it was over; they had successfully ridden through their first storm. While they began to give each other high fives and congratulatory pats on the back, one of the Reserves broke the news to them.

"That was only half of it," he told the bewildered scientist.

"Half!" they repeated, almost in unison.

THE CITY BENEATH THE SEA

"We're in the eye of the storm right now," the pilot explained. "We should be hitting the other side soon; tighten your seatbelts, this party is just getting started," he said, trying to brace the men for what was coming up ahead.

"Did you know this was going to be my last hurricane flight?" Holmes asked Sean.

"No I didn't, why didn't you say something before now?" Sean asked.

Having known Holmes for some time, and knowing he probably was getting close to retirement, he really had no idea how close he actually was. It just wasn't something they talked about.

"I didn't want to jinx the mission," Holmes said, offering an explanation that only created more questions.

"So why are you telling me NOW?" Sean asked, the uneasiness he had been feeling for some time beginning to swell inside of him.

Holmes just smiled; the smile someone smiles when they know something you don't.

CRACK!

The sound was deafening, as lightning struck the plane, just as the plane left the eye of the storm and dove into the other side.

Being struck by lightning was nothing unusual, the loud sound apart; usually no other problems arose in an airplane built to withstand almost anything Mother Nature could throw at her.

This time, for whatever reason, it was quite different. It was almost like the storm was sending a signal; saying that she was a force to be reckoned with.

As Holmes and Sean's eyes adjusted to the sudden blast of light, only then did they realize how much trouble they were really in.

Somehow, someway, the storm had knocked out all their instruments and communication systems. There was not a problem with the plane flying, and if they could see where they were going, it would not be a problem at all.

Being inside a hurricane in total darkness, without instruments to tell you if you were climbing or diving presented a very big problem.

"So much for not jinxing the flight!" Sean said, as he fought to get the instruments back up. He checked fuses, switches, backups; nothing helped.

"Without instruments, and with the storm knocking us around, we could go nose first in the Gulf!" Holmes said, informing his co-pilot of what he already knew.

"I say we pull up; if the lightning strike and storm didn't turn us around, we should go right above the storm," Holmes explained.

"And if it did, we'll go head first into the gulf," Sean said confirming his understanding of the situation they now found themselves in.

"One thing is sure," Holmes said, the sense of urgency apparent in his tone. "We can't stay in this storm long without instruments. If the plane gets thrown sideways in here, the storm will rip us to shreds."

"I guess it comes down to a fifty-fifty guess," Sean said, he too realizing their options were limited.

"You want to call it or should I?" Holmes asked, turning to Sean.

"It's your call," Sean said, relinquishing the choice to Holmes.

"Well, if I choose wrong," Holmes said, "it'll be over pretty quick. I just want you to know it was a pleasure serving with you."

"Same here, Captain," Sean said, taking a moment to shake Holmes' hand.

"Well, here goes." Holmes pulled back hard on the wheel as the plane nosed in a direction he believed to be upward. The turbulence violently increased to a point far greater than anyone had ever experienced. It literally felt as though the plane was going to be torn apart. Then the vibrations and jarring of the plane began to subside as the plane broke out the top of the storm.

"Yoo hoo!" Holmes yelled when he shot out of the storm. "We made it!"

Looking towards Sean, it was obvious he was still a little shaken up by the whole situation.

"You OK, Sean?" Holmes asked, "We made it!"

Obviously shaken up a great deal by what he had just experienced, he searched for words he could not find for a few moments, until finally, he spoke.

"Whew!" Sean finally said. "The old girl almost broke our hearts!"

"I think this is just a prelude to what's ahead," Holmes said. "Before she is through, she's going to break a lot of hearts."

Sean nodded in agreement as Holmes turned the plane on a homebound course.

THE CITY BENEATH THE SEA

CHAPTER TWO

Evan King brought his baby blue Cadillac to a smooth stop in the nursing home parking lot. He was no stranger to St. Nita's; in the last couple of years he had spent quite a bit of time there. Opening his door, he slowly exited his vehicle; the fifty-plus years of hard work and hard living had begun to take its toll on his six-foot frame. Aches and ailments he had never experienced before began to become more and more a constant companion, rather than a temporary inconvenience.

First impressions would be somewhat deceptive when meeting Evan. Impeccably dressed and good-looking, he concealed his years far better than most African American males his age. His charm and personable demeanor, and the pride and confidence with which he carried himself offered no clues to the insecure and tormented man that concealed itself inside. Giving no-one, not even his closest family, any clue to the demons he wrestled with on a daily basis.

Reflecting back often on his earlier years, Evan knew the pain and discomfort he had often put not only upon himself, but also on the ones he loved. A compulsive gambler and a hard drinker; he had put his wife through years of hell, and emotionally scarred his only daughter.

It ultimately took the death of his wife to make him begin to turn his life around. He found God and was saved, and put all his vices to the side. He often wished he could have done it when his wife was still alive, but he had come to accept that God had a reason and a purpose for everything that happened in this life. More and more, he had come to trust God and allowed him to be the driving force in his life.

Slamming the car door shut, Evan headed inside St. Nita's. From the outside, St. Nita's did very little to try to maintain a presentable appearance. The twenty-year-old sign that boldly advertised their location was faded, and in need of replacement; not to mention the peeling paint and rusted sections of the post that supported it, which had long since lost its ability to illuminate like it was originally designed to do.

The grass, though not excessively long, was far from well-manicured, and the edging was non-existent, with grass encroaching several inches onto the sidewalks.

First impressions aside, St. Nita's was relatively clean on the inside, and it did staff competent personnel. It was not what Evan would have wanted for his mother, but then again, it was not his decision. His mother, Sarah King, requested that she be housed there, after shopping the various nursing homes in the area.

Despite her family's objections, she left her home when she realized she could no longer care for herself. This was a difficult decision for her, having spent most of her adult life in the same house, but she knew it would be for the best.

Growing old, you sometimes reflect upon the memories you will be leaving behind. One thing Sarah wanted was to never be a burden on her family; that was not something she had ever wanted to be remembered for.

Evan walked down the hall without hesitation, the path etched not only in his memory, but also on the well-worn tiles that echoed his approach with each step he took. Arriving at his destination, Evan knocked on the door and waited.

"Come in," a voice from the other side of the door replied.

Evan entered and saw his mother, Sarah May King, sitting up on the bed. Eighty years old and looking every bit her age with gray hair and wrinkled skin, but she was still quick-minded although feeble. Bedridden for the most part, she was only able to negotiate short distances with her walker.

"Evan!" Sarah said, her face lighting up as he entered.

"Hi, Momma, how are you?"

"Come give your momma a kiss," Sarah said, stretching her arms out to her son.

Evan walked over to his mother and kissed her on the cheek, as Sarah wrapped her arms around her son, giving him a warm embrace.

"How you doing, Momma?"

"Ok, all things considered," Sarah began to explain. "My legs are giving out, can't walk much anymore. Doctor was supposed to come in and look at me."

"What do you think it is, Momma?" Evan questioned, his tone one of concern.

"Can you keep a secret?" Sarah asked, her voice low in a whisper. "I don't want it getting out around here."

"Sure Momma," Evan responded in the same soft whisper, leaning closer to his mother for her to reveal the secret to him.

"Come closer, I don't want to scream it out," Sarah whispered.

Evan moved closer to his mom, putting his ear only a few inches from her lips.

"I'M OLD!" Sarah cried in a normal tone, which brought a smile to Evan.

"You got me," Evan said, pulling up a chair next to Sarah's bed.

"Are you Pastor of that church yet? Sarah questioned, already knowing the answer.

"No, still associated Pastor."

"When they gonna get rid of that preacher? You're better than he is. The time you took me to church, I nearly fell asleep. Everyone just sat there; the Holy Spirit didn't move anyone. No hand raising, no speaking in tongues, no one fainting in the aisle. Shoot! I thought I was in a white church."

"He just has a different style, Momma, that's all," Evan said, trying to explain why her experience in church was so different than what she was used to.

"Well, you all should get together and assign a name to his style," Sarah countered, then paused for a moment as though pondering a thought, then revealing it a moment later. "And I have a suggestion," she finally said with a big smile on her face.

"What's that?" Evan asked cautiously, not knowing what to expect next.

"Somonex!" she said with a giggle.

"Now, Momma," Evan said, trying to fight back a smile.

"Ok, Ok, I'll move on. How's your brother?" Sarah asked. "He don't come by much anymore."

"He's fine, I'll see him and Janelle tomorrow. They're having a barbeque, you want to come?"

"No, my legs aren't working well lately, and you and your brother are getting too old to be picking me up and down, but do tell him to come see me," Sarah said, her voice soft and sad.

"I will, Momma," Evan said, assuring his mother the message would be delivered. "You want me to read to you?" Evan offered, knowing how she liked it.

"Would you?" Sarah exclaimed excitedly, "I love it when you read my bible to me."

"Sure Momma, I'd be glad to."

Evan picked up the bible from the nightstand and opened it to a passage he had come to know as one of her favorites over the years, and began to read. After a while, Sarah slowly faded away to sleep, her face peaceful and serene. This was the image Evan would often see in his mind when he thought of his mother. An image of peace and tranquility.

Returning the bible to the table, Evan touched his mother's hand, then leaned over and kissed her goodbye. There was no way for him to know this would be the last moment he would ever share with his mother.

THE CITY BENEATH THE SEA

CHAPTER THREE

The sound of jazz could be heard, as LaToya Williams stepped out the door of her government funded apartment. The sound was distant and faint, but unmistakably jazz.

She reflected back on how she once dreamed of being a musician, performing jazz, the music that spoke to her soul.

Soon, the reality of her situation came back to her. She knew any opportunity for her dreams had long since passed with the birth of her first son, Jamal. Only sixteen at the time, she thought she was in love. James was a handsome man, he promised her the world and a life she often dreamt of. Away from her crack-head mother and daily abuse at her hands, away from the poverty and despair.

Her mother was a second-generation welfare mom who had got caught up in the hopeless cycle of poverty. It was easy, the government made it easy. While thinking they were helping, in reality they were destroying any ambition people may have had. Human nature is such that most individuals will often take the path of least resistance, the easy route. When dealing with people's lives, the easy way chosen by most people has devastating long-term consequences.

LaToya knew if there was any possible way, she could break the chains of this modern day enslavement that white politicians call welfare, and make something of herself, she would find it.

She thought James was her ticket out of the projects, unfortunately he was soon to be the instrument that would guarantee she would never escape. He pursued LaToya relentlessly, with a love and affection she had never known from a male figure before. Having never known her father, James was the first male she had ever connected with, felt close to and trusted. Finally, she relented and gave James what he had worked so hard for. Soon after, he disappeared, leaving her devastated and pregnant. LaToya had become another statistic on the hit and run syndrome that infected the black community. What she had sworn would never happen to her began to tear apart her dreams piece by piece.

LaToya knew that education would be the only key that would release her from the chains and the life she cursed. Education would give her the wings to rise above her current lot in life. So, when LaToya had to drop out of school, she knew any hopes for a better life had all but disappeared, just like her baby's daddy.

Soon, LaToya found herself in the position she cursed and swore she would never be in. She was now a third-generation welfare mother. The government gave her an apartment in a housing unit, along with a monthly check.

For many of her friends, and people she knew, this was all they had wanted in life. Many of her friends, unlike her, intentionally sought to get pregnant and enter into the system. For someone with no ambition or desire to achieve anything other than to produce babies, the system was indeed generous. Housing, food stamps, free medical, formula, food substitutes for the children. Plus a monthly check that would arrive in the mailbox like clockwork.

It was this regular source of income that would often attract the wrong people to LaToya. Young men with no goals or future; dropouts, many on drugs looking for a sugar mama to provide for their basic needs.

It was here where LaToya, though older and wiser with a now two-year-old son, would make yet another mistake which would almost cost LaToya her life.

At first, Sweet was charming, with a bright smile, strong body, and a butt so tight you could crack walnuts on it. LaToya immediately fell into lust with

THE CITY BENEATH THE SEA

Sweet, and it did not take her long to fall head over heels with him.

But the careful façade Sweet had put forward did not last for long. After he had moved in with LaToya, she soon found herself pregnant again. What she thought would be good news for Sweet had the opposite effect.

Thrown into a fit of rage that only escalated at each passing moment, Sweet began to beat up his pregnant girlfriend. Her cries and screams only fueled his anger as he slapped her.

"You whore! Who's the daddy? I know it's not me because I can't have children! Who've you been messing with?" Sweet yelled at the top of his lungs.

"No one! I swear!" LaToya pleaded, but there was no talking or reasoning with Sweet; his anger blinded him, making him unable to think rationally.

"You gonna tell me or you won't tell no-one nothing again?" Sweet yelled, as he picked up the hot iron from the floor where it had been knocked down.

He began to approach LaToya with it. Realizing his intentions, she tried to run, but was thrown back in the corner by Sweet's powerful arms. She screamed and pleaded, but it was as though she were trying to negotiate with the devil himself. It was as though Sweet could hear nothing she was saying.

Backed into a corner, she crumbled to her knees, waiting for what she knew was her inevitable fate. She thought of her two-year-old son; she could hear him crying in the background. *What will happen to him?* she wondered. *Will he even have a chance at a decent life?*

LaToya could feel the heat of the iron as it neared her face, and she realized only then that he was not going to bludgeon her to death with it, but his intent was far more evil. By burning and disfiguring her, he would accomplish far more in his mind. His time incarcerated would be much less than if he did kill her, plus her face would be a walking, living advertisement to what happened to people who messed with him.

The hot iron singed LaToya's flesh, she screamed and squirmed in an effort to escape, but LaToya was hopelessly pinned in the corner. Using his heavy body and powerful arms, Sweet was able to render LaToya helpless. He could smell LaToya's melting flesh; a smell that would turn the stomach and sicken most people, but it somehow intrigued him. Like a fragrant perfume would appeal to normal people, who would seek to sneak another smell.

LaToya felt the iron move to another place on her face. A place that the nerve endings had not yet been destroyed, a place where she could once again relive the agony that brought her right to the edge of consciousness. She began to think about death, surely that would have to be better than the hell she now found herself in.

Why doesn't he just kill me and get it over with! she wondered, as the iron once again found fresh flesh to burn and scar.

As Sweet pushed the iron onto her face, finally, mercifully, the surge of pain shooting through her body proved move than she could stand. LaToya lost consciousness, relinquishing her fate completely to Sweet.

It was then, when all hope seemed lost for LaToya that the NOPD burst through the door. Late as usual, but in this case, just in time.

Seeing the police burst through the door, Sweet was determined not to make it easy for them. He immediately attacked the two officers, delivering blow after blow upon them, bloodying their faces and almost rendering them unconscious. Then suddenly, Sweet felt a sudden jolt, his body went limp and he lost all control, collapsing to the floor at the mercy of his assailants.

THE CITY BENEATH THE SEA

Sweet had not seen the third officer enter the room, and it was he who, luckily for the other two officers, administered the Taser to Sweet. It was only then that the two officers were able to bring the fight to an end.

As the two officers handcuffed Sweet, they could not resist the opportunity for a little payback, each taking a turn at delivering a couple of blows to his face.

No amount of damage the two officers could have administered to Sweet's face would match the damage LaToya would have to live with for the rest of her life.

LaToya looked in the mirror at her scarred face and remembered, as she was once again brought back to the present.

She worried now, more than she did in the past. She had come to terms with her scarred face, but what worried LaToya more was the fact that Sweet would soon be released from prison. She wondered if he would try to finish what he had began, or try to see his four-year-old son, who he must have begun to realize was really his.

As scarred as she was, LaToya knew her options were limited. She had no money, no way to escape. The only line of defense that stood between her and Sweet was the police, and she knew they could not be with her all the time. If Sweet wanted to hurt her, there was nothing anyone could do about it.

But she knew she had to try, if only for her children. So she had gone to court and filed a restraining order against Sweet, whose real name was Leonce. She knew it would not stop Sweet, but maybe the police would respond just a little sooner knowing there was someone violating a restraining order. Maybe, just maybe, that would make the difference.

Hearing a knock on the door, fear was the next emotion to follow, as LaToya trembled in fear.

THE CITY BENEATH THE SEA

Has Sweet got out of prison and found me? she wondered. They were supposed to let her know when he was to be released.

Almost paralyzed with fear, it took a few more moments for LaToya to respond. Slowly, she moved to the door and the peephole. She heard voices as she neared, peering through the keyhole confirmed what she already suspected. Two young white police officers stood outside her door. She paused and listened, eavesdropping on their conversation for a moment.

"I hate coming here," the first white officer said, as he nervously looked around. "Every so often, an officer is killed in one of these slums."

"Your tax dollars at work, my friend," the second officer said, somewhat amused by his friend's apprehension.

"It wouldn't be so bad if they kept them up, they tear the hell out of them and expect us to build them new ones. Lyndon Johnson's great society, is this what he had in mind? Put all the animals together in one zoo so they can kill themselves," the first officer concluded, looking out and around the projects.

"Maybe, but the problem arises when we have to respond to this hell hole," the second officer added.

The first officer lowered his voice a bit, but LaToya could hear him just fine.

"I don't know about you, partner, but I'm not sticking my head in here at night until they run out of ammunition," the officer said, with a faint laugh.

"I'm with you, partner," the first officer agreed.

"Come on, no one's home," the first officer said, "They are probably giving away government cheese somewhere."

Both officers laughed and began to walk away.

"That reminds me, you know why Negros can't take group photos?" the racist cop asked his partner.

"No."

THE CITY BENEATH THE SEA

"Because when the photographer says cheese, they form a line."

The two racist officers laughed as LaToya opened the door and stepped out.

"You looking for me?" she asked, standing tall, strong, and confident, not the least bit intimidated by the two officers.

The two officers turned around and headed back to LaToya.

"You're lucky you caught me, I was just about to head out for my free cheese," LaToya said, unable to resist taking a shot at the two officers.

The two officers looked at each other, knowing they had been overheard. Knowing there would be nothing they could say, they chose to ignore LaToya's reference to their conversation, and instead, conclude their business as quickly as possible.

"LaToya Williams?" the second officer asked.

"Yes."

"We were sent to notify you of the release of Leonce Haynes. Since you have a restraining order on him, we're required to make notification in person before his release. If he comes around, notify us immediately; day or night, and we'll be here as soon as humanly possible," the officer said in his most sincere a tone possible.

LaToya listened to the words and the way they were delivered with heart-felt sincerity, and wondered how these white devils could be so convincing. If she had not overheard them moments earlier, she would have been lured by their serpent tongues into a false sense of security.

The second officer finished and turned to walk away. As he turned, LaToya read the patch on his arm. 'To Protect and serve,' but in her mind LaToya added another line. 'To protect and serve white people.'

As the two police officers walked away, LaToya could not help but take one last shot at them.

THE CITY BENEATH THE SEA

"One more question, Officer," LaToya asked.

The two officers stopped and turned to her, ready to address her concerns.

"Yes?"

"You said to call if he comes here, right?"

"Yes."

"Do I call before or after the ammunition runs out?" LaToya asked. Not waiting for a response she knew would never come, she walked away.

The two officers' facial expressions changed, they now knew the extent of which their conversation had been overheard.

"Have a nice day, ma'am," the first officer said, and they both walked away.

THE CITY BENEATH THE SEA

CHAPTER FOUR

Leonce Haynes, nicknamed 'Sweet' by his friends because of his love for candy, moved toward the processing counter. His six-foot-three inch height and broad shoulders dwarfed the two white deputies that escorted their handcuffed prisoner. His brown cleanly-shaven head shone, only adding to the aura of his menacing appearance.

At the processing desk, Sweet came face to face with Leslie Cooper, a no-nonsense correction officer who had been in the system for over twenty years. Over the years, Cooper had seen scum like Sweet come and go, and return again. A never-ending cycle of reprocessing the same people over and over again. But what especially got to Cooper about Sweet was how he was able to intimidate anyone who crossed his path. Even after five years of incarceration, Sweet still maintained a strong affiliation with the street gang he formed, and many people believed he still ran it throughout his five years of being incarcerated.

Unlike some gang members, who for the most part proved to be mostly talk, the reputation that surrounded Sweet was of a ruthless man, without conscience, and was capable of anything.

Cooper, like many on the force, suspected Sweet of many crimes and even some murders. Though try as they may, they were never able to connect Sweet to a single crime. Even when the rare occasion would arise when there were witnesses to his crime and he would be arrested, his loyal gang would swing into action, blackmailing, or threatening any and all witnesses against him. If it had not been for the unfortunate mishap with his girlfriend, Sweet would have never served one day behind bars.

Arriving at the processing desk, Cooper pushed an envelope towards Sweet.

THE CITY BENEATH THE SEA

"Your personal items. Sign for them," Cooper said, sliding a clipboard towards him.

"You know, Sweet, your luck is gonna run out. Eventually, your gang won't be able to scare off every witness. You'll be back," Cooper said, his tone hard and abrasive.

"Maybe your wife will testify against me after I do her," Sweet said to Cooper, staring him hard in the eyes.

Cooper lunged at Sweet, but was restrained by the other officers.

"You come near my wife and I'll kill you!" Cooper yelled, fighting to break free of the arms that held him away from Sweet.

"Yea, whatever! I'll keep in touch, you're in the book right? Name, address, telephone number!" Sweet said with a big smile, as he picked up his remaining belongings and headed out the door.

Exiting the prison, Sweet turned down the street, heading in the direction of his old gang.

While in prison, it had been hard for Sweet to maintain control of his gang, but with the help of the loyal men he left behind, his control of the gang had remained firmly in place.

Most men released from prison after serving a long period of time usually want one of two things as soon as they can possibly find them. The first being sex, the second being booze. In Sweet's case, the overriding craving that consumed his thoughts and desires was not a drink or a woman. Sweet wanted candy.

Only having to walk a couple of blocks to the nearest shops, Sweet did not waste any time getting there. Soon, after only a few minutes walk, Sweet entered a convenience store. He sought to satisfy the cravings he had suppressed for the last five years. Sweet turned into the convenience store and disappeared inside.

THE CITY BENEATH THE SEA

Going directly to the candy aisle, Sweet proceeded to stuff his pockets with candy, creating large bulges in his pockets. As he turned to leave, the unexpected happened; he was confronted by the Korean shopkeeper behind the counter.

"You pay for candy!" the shopkeeper demanded, shaking his finger at Sweet.

Almost out the door, Sweet stopped and slowly turned to the storekeeper, a look of disbelief on his face.

"What did you say?" Sweet asked, surprised at the audacity of the shopkeeper to even try to stop him.

"Candy! You must pay for candy!" The shopkeeper repeated himself, reiterating his previous statement.

Sweet stepped up to the counter and gave a hard, menacing stare at the owner.

The owner swallowed hard, an uneasy look came over him. He wondered if he had chosen the wrong person to try to confront.

"If I pay!" Sweet said, his voice strong and forceful, with a menacing tone.

Sweet swiped the counter clean, sending boxes and articles to the floor.

"You die!" Sweet yelled.

Sweet stared hard at the shopkeeper. His look blank with no emotion, no compassion. A man capable of doing anything, anytime, to anyone.

"Ok! You no pay! You leave!" the shopkeeper said, unwilling to antagonize Sweet any further.

The shopkeeper was well aware of the street gangs that had been tormenting the neighborhood, stories were never in short supply when it came to the activities of the New Orleans gangs.

"I thought so!" Sweet said, recognizing the fear in the shopkeeper's eyes.

Sweet left; in his wake a trembling shopkeeper began to clean the mess created by Sweet.

CHAPTER FIVE

Les Moore concentrated, as he held his bowling ball in front of him. He knew this bowl would decide the fate of the tournament.

Eying the pins, Les slowly but deliberately began his approach. His partner and teammate, Paul Stall, anxiously waited in the background, he too knew what was at stake.

Not everyone watching was wishing Les the best. Charles Cunningham anxiously waited too. If Les did not get a strike, he and his partner would win. Charles had worked hard, training all year for this moment, now it all came down to one final bowl.

With a power swing and release, Les sent the ball sailing down the alley toward the pins.

Following the path predetermined in Les' mind, the ball was catapulted forward, spinning rapidly as it headed towards the distant pins. The path was straight at first, then at the last possible moment, a strong curve brought the ball around and struck the pins with a violent force, ricocheting them against each other, leaving none standing.

Les jumped up in celebration, Paul joined in the celebration, slapping hi-fives in the air then jumping up slamming each other's chests together. Les pointed to the D.J. booth overlooking the lanes, getting the D.J's attention.

"Hit it!" Les yelled, as the D.J. nodded his head in understanding and began to play M. C. Hammer's "Can't touch this".

Les and Paul began to dance, acting up while the rest of the lanes watched, shaking their heads and bagging their balls.

Les' wife, Quiana, along with Gina, Paul's fiancée looked on in disbelief as Les and Paul made fools of themselves.

THE CITY BENEATH THE SEA

Quiana sharply contrasted her very white, blonde haired, blue-eyed husband. An African American female, with a strong sense of who she was, and pride in where she came from, no one, including her, would have ever dreamed she would have fallen in love with a white man.

Having met at LSU, Les struck her immediately as someone different. His oversized heart and strong sense of compassion immediately appealed to Quiana, and in a relatively short time, she found herself in love with Les.

They both knew what lay ahead for them, bi-racial marriages were still looked upon with disdain in the south, and Les, for the first time in his life, was experiencing what it felt like to be discriminated against.

It was always very subtle, not even noticeable to most people. A look, a feeling of avoidance. To Les and Quiana, it was always a constant reminder that they were different. Even Les' parents, strong, southern Christian Baptists, cut off all contact with Les once they met Quiana. Apparently, their Christian values and compassion did not extend beyond their own race. To this day, they had never seen their grandson, Timmy.

Despite everyone and everything, Quiana and Les' love survived. They were a living testimonial to what love could conquer.

"Please tell me he'll grow up after we get married," Gina asked, somewhat embarrassed by Les and Paul's display.

"He's dancing with my husband," Quiana said, "and you ask a question like that. They've been like this since their days at LSU. Two frat boys who never grew up."

Gina smiled in understanding, as Timothy turned to his mom with excitement.

Only eight years old, Timmy was energetic, inquisitive and most of all, he idolized his dad.

THE CITY BENEATH THE SEA

"Mommy! Daddy won?" Timmy asked, his voice excited and anxious for the answer.

"Yes Timmy, Daddy won!" Quiana said, elevating her young son's excitement even further.

"Ya Hoo!" Timmy yelled and began to bounce around. He then ran out onto the lane and joined in with Paul and Les in their celebration dance.

"Like father, like son," Quiana said, with a smile to Gina as they both shook their heads in disbelief.

Breaking off his dance with Les, Paul ran up to Gina and gave her a big kiss.

Gina had the looks of a super-model. With long brown hair and a shapely figure, she would often turn heads in whatever room she entered.

"Come on," Paul said, taking Gina by the hand. "We've got to get our trophy."

Paul Stall, unlike his partner of ten years, was short with brown, thinning hair. Looking at Gina, people would often wonder how anyone with Paul's less than average looks could have possible landed anyone like her. What Paul lacked in looks, he more than made up for in personality. Having met Gina during a routine traffic stop, he knew the first time he saw her that she was the girl for him. His quest would not be an easy one though; having to ask her out no less than ten times before she finally agreed, either out of total exhaustion from repeatedly saying no, or curiosity about what type of person could not take no for an answer. Regardless of why, Gina did give in and this was all that Paul needed, he quickly swept her off her feet, and before long, they became inseparable.

Gina was led away by Paul with Quiana following, as Les and Timmy headed for the large banner on the distant wall.

The banner, almost eight feet wide and four feet high, hung on the wall as a centerpiece. On the banner, in letters as large as the banner size would accommodate, were written:

THE CITY BENEATH THE SEA

Fraternal Order of Police
3rd Annual Bowling Tournament.

In front of the banner, a rather large trophy stood, waiting to be awarded by the President of the FOP.

"I'd like to thank you all for participating in this year's tournament. I think we all had a great time," the President said, taking the podium as the crowd applauded his words.

"And the winner of the third annual Fraternal Order of Police bowling tournament," the President said, pausing as though no one knew who had won and he was just trying to build excitement and anticipation.

"For the third year in a row goes to Les Moore and Paul Stall."

The crowd applauded as Les and Paul walked forward to accept the trophy and hoist it high above their heads.

Leaving the bowing alley, Les, Quiana, and Timmy headed for their car. Quiana was holding the trophy, which was almost the size of Timmy, while Les was carrying Timmy on his back.

They both looked to the sky; the night was calm and pleasant, giving no indication a hurricane was heading in their direction.

"You just about packed?" Les asked, as he bounced Timmy on his back.

"Almost. I wish you would reconsider, we could stay here, we'll be just fine. We've ridden out storms before," Quiana said, once again trying to change her husband's mind.

"Not with me, you haven't," Les said, his voice determined and non-compromising.

"And the reason being?" Quiana questioned, obviously wanting a better explanation for why they had to evacuate.

"Do we have to go over this every time we have a storm?" Les asked, his voice a little frustrated, as though worn out from giving the same explanation over and over again. Then he smiled, which only agitated Quiana a bit.

"Baby, you're probably right, just another storm. A little street flooding, a few missing shingles, no big deal. But if it's more, I don't want to be called up and have to worry about you and Timmy. What's my motto?" Les asked, waiting for Quiana to reply.

Quiana rolled her eyes and shook her head, not answering him.

Getting no response from Quiana, Les turned to Timmy. "Timmy, what's our motto?"

"Prepare for the worst! And hope for the best!" Timmy answered without hesitation.

Les held his hand up and Timmy gave him a high five.

"Alright, we'll leave in the morning. We should be able to beat the contraflow," Quiana said relenting to Les's decision.

"That's my girl!" Les said, giving her a hug as they continued to walk towards the car.

"We're going to see Aunt Kirra in Baton Rouge?" Timmy asked, having picked up on the conversation.

"You and Mommy are, Daddy's got to work, protect the city from bad people," Les explained to his young son.

Les opened the door to his Explorer and placed Timmy inside, as Quiana got in the passenger side. Once Timmy was safely secured in his seat, Les walked around the car, looking up at the sky as he went, a wondering look on his face.

THE CITY BENEATH THE SEA

CHAPTER SIX

Outside the New Orleans Community Center, Melanie Lewis, exited her vehicle. Melanie, a very attractive African-American female, looked much younger than her twenty-eight years. With her arms full of books, she struggled to maneuver them to get to the meter, her average height and slender build, becoming a disadvantage.

Having successfully accomplished her balancing act while she fed the meter, it wasn't until Melanie turned to head into the community center that disaster would finally play its hand. As she turned, Melanie collided with Evan King, scattering the books on the ground around them.

"I'm so sorry!" Melanie said, realizing what she had done. "I didn't see you!"

"No problem," Evan said in a reassuring tone. "Let me help you."

As Evan helped to pick up the books, he began to notice they were all children's books, spanning a range of grades.

"These are all children's books," questioned Evan. "Are you a teacher?"

"I'm a counselor at the community center." Melanie began to explain the purpose of the books. "A lot of our teens have trouble reading, these books sometimes help."

"I see," Evan said, as he continued to pick up the books. From the corner of his eye, he noticed a young black male approaching them, and kept a cautious eye on him.

Sweet saw the collision coming and could only smile once it had taken place. *Stupid people!* he thought as he continued down the street, unwilling to expend a hand to help anyone.

THE CITY BENEATH THE SEA

Evan watched cautiously as Sweet passed by, years on the street had taught him to always be aware of his surroundings and never be caught offguard. It was only after Sweet walked by that he was able to once again lower his guard and focus on helping Melanie.

Seeing how Evan watched Sweet with such a heightened awareness led Melanie to believe he knew him.

"Did you know him?" Melanie questioned, curious by Evan's behavior.

"No ma'am, but I've known plenty like him," Evan offered what he thought was an explanation, but only puzzled Melanie further.

Melanie, although raised in New Orleans, was far less streetwise than what one would think. Having been raised by foster parents after her father, a dockworker, tragically died, she had always excelled in school, and with the help of her foster parents, she had worked hard to achieve her goals. Her exceptional good looks did not hurt either. Receiving a full scholarship to Loyola, she went on to receive her Master's degree, at LSU.

She returned to the city she loved and the people she sought to help, to somehow make a difference in their lives. Employed as a social worker, her eyes had been opened to the problems and despair that she had been fortunate enough to have been sheltered from. Independent in both her thinking and life, she was slow to anger, but quick to express her views. Though not extremely streetwise, she was a formidable opponent in every other arena you would find her in.

"Well, good luck Ms.?" Evan said, as they stood to their feet and he handed her the books, only now realizing he did not know her name.

"Melanie," Melanie offered, as she accepted the books from Evan. "Thank you. I didn't get your name," she asked.

THE CITY BENEATH THE SEA

"You're welcome, my name is Evan King," Evan said, heading down the street.

Melanie once again loaded down with books headed for the entrance of the community center. Reaching the front doors of the center, she cautiously negotiated the massive doors open and disappeared inside.

No sooner had she cleared the doors, help once again arrived just in time.

The director of the center, Jessica Larose, a forty-something Caucasian female with only average looks, had devoted herself unselfishly to the community center and those of the community it served. Often asked if she would ever marry, she would reply, "If I got married, I'd have less time to help out here."

As Melanie once again teetered with her load, on the verge of spilling them once more, Jessica was ready to lend a hand, removing some of the books from Melanie's death grip grasp.

"Thank you, Jessica, I almost dropped them for the second time," Melanie said, being able to relax a bit.

"No problem, glad to help."

"Can you get these to Elise for me?" Melanie asked, referring to her aide, who had been so instrumental in helping the young adults to read.

Jessica paused for a moment before responding, almost unwilling to share with Melanie what she already knew.

"You don't know?" Jessica asked, a little surprised that she would have to be the one to break the news to Melanie.

"Know what?" Jessica asked, caught totally offguard by her question.

"I had to let Elise go," Jessica explained.

"Why?" Melanie asked, shocked by the news and a little angry.

THE CITY BENEATH THE SEA

Elise had been a godsend since she was hired, and no one person had done more for the local youth than her.

In an area infested with drugs, gangs, and hopelessness, the community center was the only beacon of hope most of the children had. Now with Elise's dismissal, the beacon had become just a little dimmer.

"We talked about this, Melanie," Jessica began to explain. "If our budget was going to be cut, you were going to lose your assistant."

Melanie stepped back, remembering the conversation she had had days earlier with Jessica, though never realizing it would actually ever happen.

"I know, but I didn't think it would happen so soon. I didn't even get a chance to tell her goodbye," Melanie explained, her voice saddened by the news.

"I know, but she was pretty broken up about it," Jessica explained.

"We were beginning to make a difference! Then they cut our funding," Melanie said, her demeanor going from one of sadness to anger. "I hate thinking like this, Jessica, but I'm beginning to believe that there are people out there that don't want us to succeed. It's as though they want to keep us in our projects on a minimum wage, and in the service industry to serve them."

"I don't think you're too far off the mark," Jessica agreed. "This is the third program that's showed progress, only to be slowly dismantled. They fund failures and torpedo successes."

"It's funny how much coverage and publicity these programs get for the politicians when they start," Jessica said, remembering all the hoopla the program had received when it first opened. "They open up with a bang! Then die with a whimper. The only thing the poor people remember is their politician brought some pork home."

THE CITY BENEATH THE SEA

"This is so sad," Jessica agreed. "You and Elise were beginning to make a difference in some of these peoples' lives. Speaking of which, Birdie is in your office."

"Thank you, Jessica," Melanie said, as she turned and headed towards her office. Angered by the recent events, she could not let that get in the way of what she was still expected to do. That was to make as big a difference as possible in as many lives as possible, and one of her biggest challenges was waiting in her office.

Entering her office, Melanie found Birdie behind her desk with his feet propped up.

"It's about time! I've been waiting for thirty minutes!" Birdie said, his tone though rude and harsh had little effect on the emotionally hardened Melanie.

"Well, considering our appointment was for three and it's now just three, I don't see how that's my concern. Now, if you give me my desk back, maybe we can begin," Melanie countered, though her tone was not as harsh, but strictly business.

Birdie, as he was known on the street, was a seventeen-year-old African-American, with a cocky personality and a willingness to bully anyone he sensed weakness in. On parole at seventeen, Birdie was well on his way to being a career criminal, with a large rap sheet, and an attitude to match. As a condition of his parole, Birdie was required, though reluctant, to see Melanie once a week, and from the very beginning, he had not made it easy on her.

Obviously anxious, Birdie paced about the room, it was only now that Melanie noticed he had been beaten quite severely.

"What happened to you!" Melanie asked, coming from around her desk to get a closer look at him. "You're all beat up! What happened to you?"

"I got jumped in!" Birdie said, confirming what Melanie had already suspected.

THE CITY BENEATH THE SEA

"Birdie! One of the conditions of your parole is not to be associated with any gangs," Melanie reminded Birdie, but the words slid off him with little meaning or concern.

"Yea I know! And the other is to come see you once a week, so what! You gonna turn me in?" Birdie demanded, his tone threatening.

Sidestepping the question, Melanie knew she could not let Birdie gain control of their meeting.

"The gang you're so fond of is just going to land you back in prison, is that what you what?" Melanie asked, her voice angered and elevated by the latest revelation.

"I want! I want to be able to eat!" Birdie began, previously suppressed emotion springing forth in his words. "I want to be able to go to the store and buy things. I want to walk down the street and not worry about being shot! That's what I want! But the man won't let me get those things!"

"First of all, you need to stop blaming your problems on others," Melanie said, quick to bring awareness to Birdie assigning blame to others. "There's no one out there trying to hold you down. Birdie, if you stay in school, you will eventually be able to get all those things."

"Who you kidding, lady, I graduate and get a job at McDonalds, so what!"

"You could go to college."

"College! Lady, what planet you come on?" Birdie said, agitated by the suggestion of such a lofty goal. "Then what? Get hired into some white company to meet a quota while they continue to step on the necks of my brothers! No thanks, I'll take my chances on the streets."

Birdie started to leave, then turned back to Melanie as he reached for the door.

"You're a pretty woman, Doc. If you ever want to stop pitching for the man, why don't you come see us."

THE CITY BENEATH THE SEA

With a wide smile, Birdie left Melanie's office. Melanie leant back in her chair, disappointed by Birdie's choice. But she realized that that's what it ultimately came down to was choices. Good or bad, we made the conscious decision to choose.

Unfortunately, as Melanie had seen way too often, the consequences of bad choices were sometimes dire.

Reaching over to her radio, Melanie turned it on, hoping a soft song may relax her, or change the dreary mood which had begun to overtake her. But instead of music on the radio, the voice of a newscaster could be heard, repeating the order that the Mayor had just issued.

"Mayor Nagin has called for a mandatory evacuation of New Orleans. This unprecedented announcement comes as Hurricane Katrina continues to bear down on New Orleans," the announcer concluded the announcement, stunning Melanie as she turned off the radio and left her office.

As she headed for the exit, Melanie ran into Jessica, who apparently had not heard or was not concerned about the recent announcement from the Mayor.

"Leaving already?" Jessica asked, and Melanie stopped to talk with her.

"My session was pretty short, also it looks like Katrina is heading right for us. The Mayor has called for a mandatory evacuation. Did you know about this?" Melanie asked, knowing Jessica kept more abreast of current events than her.

"They do that every time we get a storm," Jessica said, playing down the importance of the announcement. "We have always survived."

"This is mandatory, Jessica, I don't remember a mandatory evacuation ever being called before. Do you?" Melanie asked, hoping she would be proven wrong.

THE CITY BENEATH THE SEA

"I can't say I remember a 'mandatory evacuation' now that you mention it," Jessica said, searching her memory for another similar event, but unable to recall one.

"Regardless," Melanie finally said. "I want to make sure I've got what I need at home to hunker down for the storm."

"Like my mom used to always tell me. Put water in the tub and an axe in the attic, and you'll be fine," Jessica said, imparting Melanie with one last bit of wisdom before she left.

"I've always wondered about the axe part," Melanie said with a smile. "The water would have to get ten feet high, pretty unlikely huh?"

"I know, street flooding is all we've ever seen," Jessica agreed. "But old people usually know what they're talking about."

"Good advice," Melanie said, as she started to leave. "I guess it couldn't hurt. I'll see you in a couple of days." Waving goodbye, Melanie left the building, heading home, then like thousands around the city, braced herself for Katrina's fury.

THE CITY BENEATH THE SEA

CHAPTER SEVEN

LaToya emerged from her apartment to find Big Mama sitting in her chair outside her apartment, which was usually the case.

Big Mama, who came by her nickname honestly, was well over 350pounds, and she loved sitting in front of her apartment talking and watching the people and cars on the nearby Canal Street pass by, from her first floor vantage point.

"What's up, Big Mama?" LaToya asked, walking up to her.

"I should be asking you, Little Momma, but you know me, I like to mind my own business. Those two white police officers knocking on your door the other day would rouse the curiosity of most folks, but not me, cause I mind my own business. When I saw those two white cops coming up here, I ducked into my house," Big Mama explained.

"Why? You didn't do nothing," LaToya reasoned with her.

"I never do, but my philosophy has always been to _"

LaToya cut her off and finished her sentence for her. "Mind my own business," LaToya said, her smile wide.

"That's right! Whatever people want to do to each other, that's up to them, I figure if I don't talk to the police, it can't come back to me," Big Mama said, explaining her philosophy.

"Well, I'm glad you changed your policy when you called the police for me. You saved my life," LaToya acknowledged.

"Yea, baby, that Sweet, he's a bad man, they should keep him in prison. Is that what the two white policemen was here for?" Big Mama asked, her curiosity getting the best of her.

THE CITY BENEATH THE SEA

"Yes, Sweet is being released," LaToya explained, her soft reserved tone speaking far louder than her words.

"Already! He put two cops in the hospital, not to mention what he did to your pretty face!" Big Mama complained, preaching to the choir.

If anyone knew what Sweet was capable of, it was LaToya. She had carried around the constant reminder of his rage for the last five years, and was reminded on a daily basis every time she looked in the mirror.

"I know," LaToya said, trying to help Big Mama understand, "but he pleaded out and his time is done."

"No matter!" Big Mama said, going on to another subject as was usually the case. Big Mama always had a problem with staying focused. "I heard they're evacuating the city, maybe they evacuate his ass out of here too!"

"Evacuate?" LaToya repeated, hearing the news for the first time.

"Yea, a mandatory evacuation, I swear to God that crazy white woman we got for governor don't have the sense God gave a June bug," Big Mama began on a rant that experience had taught LaToya may last a while. "The only reason she's Governor is because the white folk didn't want a man of color in the state's white house."

"What did she do, Big Mama?" questioned LaToya, unable to glean any meaning from her tyrant.

"She said, if you stay, write your social security number on your arm so they can identify the bodies. Scaring folks like that, if I ever see that woman in person, I'm going to slap the false teeth out her head." Big Mama raised her fist to emphasize her intent.

"You don't think there's nothing to worry about?" LaToya asked, seeking the wisdom of the wiser Big Mama.

"Baby, let me tell you," Big Mama began, her tone more reserved, more reassuring. "I'm almost fifty years old, lived here all my life, I've seen the worst of the worst. I've lived through Betsy, I've seen it all. They just trying to scare us poor folk so we can run to the white man to protect us from the big bad storm.

"You think so, Big Mama?" LaToya asked, not fully convinced by Big Mama's reasoning.

"If they were serious about evacuating us, they would have buses here for us to leave on. You see any buses?" Big Mama asked, looking out to the street.

"No," LaToya agreed.

"I don't know about you, but the end of the month ain't got here yet, and I ain't got my check yet, and I can't go nowhere without my check." Big Mama concluded her explanation with her head cocked back and her arms crossed, confident in her summing up of the current situation.

"You're probably right, Big Mama, there's nothing to worry about," LaToya agreed with Big Mama, but deep down she knew something was different about this time. She couldn't put her finger on it, couldn't reason it out fully. Something in her gut told her this storm, unlike the others, would be different.

LaToya disappeared inside her apartment, locking the door behind her, leaving Big Mama alone on the porch. Big Mama continued to mumble to herself after LaToya had left.

"Hum! You can scare the young ones, but you aren't scaring me, I aren't going nowhere!"

Inside her apartment, LaToya pondered the words 'mandatory evacuation,' she too had been through storms in the city, but never recalled a mandatory evacuation. "Did the governmental officials know something they weren't telling them?" she wondered.

Ordinarily, it would not have been a problem in the past. She knew she was a survivor and would have been able to survive in any situation she found herself in. But that was then, when she did not have two small children depending on her.

THE CITY BENEATH THE SEA

She went to her children's room and peered over them as they slept so peacefully. They had no way of knowing the internal struggle their mother was going through to try to make the right decision for them. LaToya knew she had a greater responsibility than others did without children. It was her responsibility to ensure their safety because no one else would.

LaToya picked up the phone, looking at the wall where she had written a number some time ago, she quickly dialed the number.

"Greyhound," the voice on the other end of the receiver could be heard, though very faint.

"Yes, when's your next bus leaving town?" LaToya asked, a hint of desperation in her tone.

"All our buses have departed and we're not expecting any arrivals. There's a mandatory evacuation in place you know," the clerk informed LaToya of what she already knew.

"I know, that's why I'm trying to get a bus!" LaToya retorted, her demeanor less cordial than before.

"I'm sorry, ma'am, all our buses have gone."

"How the hell are we going to evacuate if there are no buses?" LaToya questioned, not really expecting a answer to her problem from a bus clerk.

"I'm sorry, ma'am, I can't tell you," the clerk concluded and hung up the phone.

LaToya hung up the phone momentarily and headed for her purse; searching inside she removed her wallet. Inventorying its contents, she was surprised to realize only six dollars made up her entire cash on hand. Placing the six dollars on the counter, she headed for a coin jar she kept over the refrigerator. Retrieving the dusty jar from its out of the way spot, she poured its contents on the counter and began to sort and count it out.

Soon, the frustrated look on her face made it clear she had not yet reached whatever goal she was trying to achieve, a heavy sigh culminated her frustrated attempt.

Then as though a light went on in her head, LaToya was re-energized with a look of hope as she headed towards her children's room. Quietly, so as not to wake her sleeping babies, she tiptoed past them towards the two piggy banks on the dresser. With the banks safe in her hand, she returned to the kitchen to spill their contents on the counter.

Once again, she quickly counted the money out to the last coin. Only then did she reach for a phone book tucked away in the drawer.

Scanning the pages, flipping them as she went, she finally found what she was looking for and lay the book on the counter open to the page, and quickly dialed the number.

"Car Rentals," the voice on the other end of the line announced.

"I need to rent a car, do you have any available?" LaToya asked, her voice strained and desperate. She knew this would be her last hope if she was going to leave the city.

"Yes, ma'am, we do," the clerk informed her of the good news.

"Thank God!" LaToya said, as though a weight had been lifted from her.

"They're going fast, would you like to secure one?" the clerk asked, moving her towards the sale.

"Yes!" LaToya said, jumping at his words without delay.

"Ok, and what credit card will you be using today?" the clerk asked, ready to close the transaction.

"I don't have a credit card, I'll pay you cash when I get there," LaToya explained, as she began to feel the desperation begin to sweep over her like an enormous wave, unable to divert or change its inevitable course.

THE CITY BENEATH THE SEA

"I'm sorry, we cannot rent our cars without a credit card as security," the clerk though polite, began to project a sense of abruptness.

"I've got the money, I'll pay cash," LaToya pleaded, trying to persuade the clerk of her good intentions.

"I understand, ma'am, but our policy states a credit card must be used as security. It's the same with every other car rental place, if there is nothing –"

LaToya cut the clerk off before he could dismiss her.

"Listen, mister, I've got two small babies. They are evacuating the city. I need to get them out of here, what am I supposed to do?" she pleaded, tears beginning to form in her eyes as the desperation of her situation began to cause her emotions to spill over.

"I'm sorry, ma'am, but there is nothing I can do. I do have other calls I need to take, I do wish you luck, but I can't help you. I'm sorry." The clerk hung up the phone, slamming closed the last remaining option LaToya had to escape.

Dropping to her knees, she began to breakdown and cry. She knew that no matter how bad it got in the city, she would have to be here to face it alone with her two small children.

After a short cry, LaToya was able to muster a little strength and pull herself together. Down but not out, she was not giving up without a fight.

Gathering some bags, she stuffed them with whatever snacks and food she could easily carry and would keep for a few days. She next grabbed a small suitcase and began stuffing it with clothes for her children.

Going to the bedroom, she began to wake Jamal and his little brother Jameal.

"Wake up, Jamal, we're going on a little trip," LaToya explained to her groggy-eyed child. "You remember the Superdome, Jamal?"

THE CITY BENEATH THE SEA

"We're going watch football, Mama?" Jamal asked, unable to grasp the urgency of their situation.

"No, baby, we're going to spend the night there, there's a storm coming and I want us to be safe."

"Ok, Mommy," Jamal said, giving his mama a big hug.

THE CITY BENEATH THE SEA

CHAPTER EIGHT

The slow curling of smoke, as it slowly rose from the backyard offered no clues as to the skill of the chef preparing the barbecue, only that it was being prepared.

Stan King, brother of Evan, labored over the grill trying to dodge the smoke that had begun to make his eyes water.

Unlike his older brother, who concealed his age so well, Stan proved to be just the opposite. His face was lined with wrinkles, visual reminders of a hard, stress-filled life.

"You got those drinks yet, Janelle?" Stan said, calling into the house.

Just then, Janelle exited the house with two hurricane glasses.

Janelle, Stan's wife, could not be more different than her husband. Unlike Stan, who projected a gruff, grouchy, stay-away personality, Janelle had an infections smile, and was always warm and bubbly, a person who people would naturally migrate to.

Passing the glasses over to Stan, Janelle retreated back to the house.

Walking up to Evan, Stan handed his brother one of the tall glasses, filled with a red-colored drink.

"Fine weather for a Hurricane party. Look, there's not a cloud in the sky," Stan said, looking upward to the clear skies.

"You're an old Navy man, you know how deceptive the weather can be," Evan said, knowing as did Stan, how quickly weather changed. Even with the most advanced instruments available, weather could still, and often did rear its ugly head of unpredictability, and often proved everyone wrong.

"You'd never believe a Hurricane is bearing down on us," Stan said, eying the weather once again.

THE CITY BENEATH THE SEA

"Ah, it's going to miss us, they all do; a few missing shingles, a little street flooding and it's business as usually. No big deal," Stan continued, unable to know if he was trying to reassure his brother or convince himself.

"Now you want to talk about a hurricane," Evan said. "Remember Betsy? If we can survive her, I know we can survive anything," he announced, a sense of confidence carried forth in his words.

"So I take it you're not going to evacuate?" Stan asked, up until now not being privy to his brother's plans.

"Evacuate!" Evan said, surprised at the mere suggestion from his brother. "And spend the Hurricane in my car at some rest stop! You remember the news from the last hurricane? Contraflow! What a joke! Works great till it hits the Baton Rouge bottleneck. Then it starts backing up. No sir, I'll be just fine in the Lower Ninth Ward, thank you, always have been."

"Yea, you're right, we're gonna ride it out too. What are they calling this one?" Stan asked.

"Katrina."

Janelle came out the house, a concerned look on her face.

"Stan! Mayor Nagin was on the TV calling for a mandatory evacuation," said Janelle, unable to contain her concern.

"Mandatory!" Stan repeated, then turned to Evan. "You ever hear us being mandated to do anything?"

"No, but you think they would have done it before now if they were going to do it. The storm is not that far out, you can't evacuate a city this size that fast," Evan added, very aware of the logistics of trying to evacuate a city the size of New Orleans.

"How you set for supplies? You got enough for a couple of days?" Stan asked, the consummate worrier.

THE CITY BENEATH THE SEA

"I'm the big brother, remember. You act like this is my first rodeo," Evan said with a smile. "I know how to prepare for a hurricane."

"Just checking, just checking," Stan said, in full retreat.

Turning to Janelle, he saw the concern on her face and tried to reassure her.

"Don't worry, Baby, they just want as many people they can to evacuate. It makes them feel like they 're doing their job," Stan concluded his attempt to reassure his wife, but by the look on her face, it had little effect.

"You don't think we should evacuate?" Janelle questioned one more time.

"Evacuate where?" Stan began to reason with his wife. "We've got no place to go. No family in another city. The only family we have is Donald in New York, and we sure aren't driving there."

"Just thought I'd ask," Janelle said, beginning to finally accept her husband's decision. "I'll get the beans."

Janelle left, going back in the house to retrieve the beans.

"What about Mom?" Stan asked, remembering his mother in the nursing home.

"Just came from there earlier, talked to the administrator, he assured me they had a plan to evacuate if they had to," Evan communicated what he had learned with his brother. "They were going to bus and ambulance everyone to Baton Rouge."

"That's good, I guess that's one less thing to worry about."

"She asked about her grandson, how is Donald?" Evan asked, knowing how his brother did not like to brag about his son voluntarily.

"Haven't heard from him in a while," said Stan, "He's pretty busy."

"He made partner yet?"

THE CITY BENEATH THE SEA

"Yes, he did. First African American lawyer in his firm to make partner." The pride in Stan was starting to show, but underneath something was troubling him.

"You're pretty proud of him, so what's bothering you?"

"You know I am, given where we come from," Stan said, acknowledging the humble beginnings he and his brother had come from. "It's like he went to the moon and back."

"So what's the problem?" Stan asked.

"It's just that I always hoped he would come home, this is where his people need him. Not New York!"

"Well, you know yourself you can't make their decisions for them. They need to find it within themselves, what's right for them."

"I know, but I can wish, can't I?"

Just then Evan grabbed his chest, a startled look on his face.

"Evan! Janelle! Call 911!" Stan screamed, his voice panicked, seeing his brother having a heart attack right in front of him.

"No! It's not my heart!" Evan finally said, overcoming the surprise of his cell phone vibrating in his pocket.

Evan removed the cell phone he had placed in his top pocket, flipping the phone open as he did.

"Hello," Evan said, then listened as the person on the other end communicated the message only Evan could hear. "Ah, Uncle Stan and Aunt Janelle will be disappointed, but they will understand. Ok, baby, thanks for calling."

Evan replaced the phone in his pocket, looking at his brother, the startled look still on his face.

"Damn phone! I forget I have it on vibrate and when it goes off, it scares the life out of me," Evan said, explaining to Stan the reason he acted the way he did.

THE CITY BENEATH THE SEA

"Scares YOU!" Stan countered, "You just shaved a couple years off my life!"

"Scares the hell out of you!" Stan said, "You just shaved five years off my life!"

Both men shared a laugh then Evan shared with Stan the phone conversation he had just finished.

"Kisha gave me the phone in case something happens, I'd have a way to communicate. She worries about me," Evan explained.

"What's all the commotion out here?" Janelle said, as she came out the house holding a pan of beans.

"I thought my brother was having a heart attack. Instead he gave me one."

"That was Kisha," Evan said, "they're going to evacuate, so they're not going to make it."

"Maybe that's best with the kids and all," Janelle said, understanding her niece's predicament. "They're doing alright?"

"Oh they're fine, don't see them as much since Debbie died, it's been pretty hard on Kisha, her and Debbie were very close."

Evan paused for a moment as though hesitant about how much he was willing to share, then offered more information to his brother and sister-in-law.

Stan and Janelle could see the anguish in his face as he spoke, they both knew there were some deep-seeded issues between him and his daughter.

"I'm trying to connect with her, but it's been hard," Evan finally said, almost choking up as he did, so much suppressed emotion wanting to surface, but as was his nature, he fought it back.

"Don't worry," Janelle finally said, trying to give him some sense of hope and solace. "She'll come around, she's only got one dad."

"I know," Evan said, trying to convince himself that Janelle's words were true.

"Well, let's eat," Stan said, ready to devour anything put in front of him.

THE CITY BENEATH THE SEA

Going to the grill, Stan retrieved a tray of chicken and brought it back to the table, handing it to Evan first.

The wind was beginning to pick up with occasional gusts, which brought their thoughts back once again to the Hurricane that was bearing down on them.

"Looks like we're starting to see the outer bands of the storm," Evan said, looking up to the sky, which had begun to change dramatically since he first arrived at his brother's house.

"I sure hope their projections are right, and it misses us," Janelle said, the concern evident in her voice.

"And if it doesn't, what's the worst that can happen? A little roof damage, street flooding? We're going to be fine," Stan said, reassuring his wife once again.

Serving the chicken and beans, the three of them sat down on the patio and began to eat, trying to divert their attention from the weather and the concern of the approaching storm.

"You know you're welcome to ride it out with us if you want," Janelle said, offering Evan the opportunity to stay with them.

"Thank you," Evan gracefully refused, "but I'm going to ride it out in my own bed."

"You're just as stubborn as your brother," Janelle said, becoming more and more frustrated by their 'more macho than you' routine.

"Where do you think he gets it from?" Evan said with a smile and a wink.

The three of them continued to eat their meal, finding it harder and harder to ignore the increasing intensity of the winds, as the gusts began to become stronger and more frequent.

"Those outer bands are getting closer," Stan said, finally stating what the others already knew.

THE CITY BENEATH THE SEA

"Yea, it looks like I'm gonna have to get going," Evan said, eyeing the trees swaying in the wind.

Rising from his chair, Evan started towards his car, followed by Stan and Janelle.

Reaching his car, Evan unlocked the door to his brand new, baby blue Cadillac, his latest acquisition and his pride and joy.

"Yes sire, Evan, I surely do like your ride," Stan said, admiring his new automobile.

"You need to get yourself one," Evan said, as he opened the door.

"Yea right! On a janitor's salary."

"You only live once."

"Yea, but I prefer not to live in the poor house," Stan said with a smile. "How does she handle all those potholes in the Lower Ninth?"

"They've fixed a lot of them since you've been down there. If you come to church more often, you'd know that," Evan countered with a zinger of his own.

"Alright, bro, alright. Give me a hug," Stan said, not wanting to trade any more barbs with his brother.

Stan hugged his brother, there was no way for him to know this would be the last time he would ever see him alive.

As Evan drove off out of sight, a gust of wind came up, shaking the trees around them, reminding them again of the night that lay ahead of them.

"Let's get inside and hunker down," Stan said, putting his arm around Janelle and walking her back to the safety of their home.

THE CITY BENEATH THE SEA

CHAPTER NINE

Captain Errol Ferrell watched as his desk sergeant handed out the duty roster for the night.

From the back of the room, Ferrell beamed with pride. Even with a hurricane bearing down on the city, all his men had reported to work. This, of course, was nothing new for the Algiers police force. Loyalty ran deep, in large part instilled by Ferrell himself on each recruit he would handpick to join his force.

Since running for Sheriff fifteen years ago, Ferrell had seen plenty of changes. Some for the better, some for the worse. Looking out among the sea of officers, the few black faces were easily identified among the otherwise lily-white force. This, in Ferrell's opinion, was the beginning of the end for the rock solid cohesiveness in his force.

Mandated by affirmative action, Ferrell was forced to accept African American officers, regardless if he liked it or not.

"Accepting them is one thing," Ferrell reasoned, "keeping them was quite another."

The African American officers did not know it when they were recruited, but their days on the force, at least the Algiers police force was numbered, and the irony of it all was they would be the ones requesting transfers.

Ferrell's carefully orchestrated implementations of harassment and bad assignments made the officers realize they were not welcome. Nothing too obvious, nothing they could put their finger on, or prove. Ferrell got as close to the line as anyone could without crossing it. If there was one thing Ferrell was trying to avoid, it was a discrimination lawsuit. But anyone who knew Ferrell knew he was too smart for that. The most blatant signal that black officers were not welcome came when back up was requested.

THE CITY BENEATH THE SEA

White officers, loyal to Ferrell, would either not respond, or show up only after the black officers had the situation well under control. Each black officer knew it was only a matter of time before they would roll up on a car load of desperate men, and without backup, they would face injury or death. This technique proved the most effective in Ferrell's revolving door approach to new black officers, as they would check in, then check out as soon as possible, and most importantly, they would tell their black friends Algiers was not the place to be if you were black.

Having little use for blacks, Ferrell would often find himself in trouble for the occasional verbal slips that he felt was harmless, though other people took exception to.

Once, while addressing the issue of black-on-black crime, Ferrell had said, "If those people want to kill themselves, there's nothing I can do about it."

The same approach, however, was not taken when on a rare occasion, a black person committed a crime on a white person. These people were pursued relentlessly until apprehended, and in some cases, the method of their apprehension was brought into question.

The last time a black-on-white murder occurred, the person responsible coincidently never saw the inside of a jail cell. The officers on the scene were forced to use deadly force when the accused pulled a weapon, initiating a chain of events that would leave the accused with ninety-three bullets in his body. There were even reports of some officers stopping to reload.

Racial tension was always high in Algiers, but for the most part, Ferrell was able to keep the black population in their place. He often would say to his friends and white officers, "I don't have a problem with black folks, as long as they know their place."

Taken from a mold most people thought was long since destroyed, Ferrell's racist views and approach to justice was not only tolerated, but rewarded as election after election, he was re-elected by the predominately white population who had migrated from New Orleans to Algiers.

New Orleans, rich in both cultural and racial diversity, had long since relinquished its crown as the Jewel of the South. The great liberal experiment of the sixties and seventies tore at the fabric of society, leaving it in rags. A once proud people who swore never to be enslaved by chains again, were enslaved once more, not by chains, but by government programs.

As crime increased, the white migration increased, many moved across the river to Algiers, and the west bank, others to the north shore.

With increased minority population, minority representation increased. Politicians were elected to perpetuate the failed liberal policy.

Knowing what New Orleans had become, the residents of Algiers were determined not to let it happen to their city, and if Ferrell had to walk the line, and when no one was looking, cross it, well, as the ballots showed year after year, it was alright with the residents of Algiers.

As the desk sergeant concluded his assignment distribution, the officers began to file past the Captain. Each shook his hand, and smiled, much like the subjects of the king files by and pays homage. Even the black officers dared not risk disrespecting Ferrell, as they too smiled and shook his hand, as they headed out to their assignments. As the last officer filed by, Ferrell headed back to his office. This was where he would await Katrina's landfall. With his family safely tucked away with family in Shreveport, Ferrell saw little reason for him not to be on the job with his men.

Walking down the hall, Ferrell's pronounced limp was obvious to even the casual observer.

THE CITY BENEATH THE SEA

Where some would merely write the limp off as arthritis, or a knee injury, only those who knew Ferrell over the years knew of his prosthetic leg.

Many years ago, while he was a patrolman in New Orleans, Ferrell and his partner responded to an armed robbery. With guns drawn, they entered the liquor store, where a shotgun blast blew away Ferrell's leg. His partner was not as lucky, receiving a shotgun blast to his face, taking it completely off, killing him instantly.

Laying on the floor of the liquor store just, barely hanging on to consciousness as his life's blood pumped out of him, Ferrell's last conscious memory was of the two black males laughing as they ran out the liquor store.

Apprehended quickly, the two men were convicted of murder, but what ate away at Ferrell was the fact that one of the men, the one he was sure had blown his leg away, was able to strike a deal with the DA.

For his testimony against his accomplice, he would be given a lesser charge since his action did not actually result in the death of an officer. Only the one who killed his partner would receive the death sentence.

The other would be eligible for parole in ten years. Despite his objections, Ferrell's pleas for justice fell on deaf ears.

After years of rehabilitation, Ferrell was lucky enough to be able to remain with the force, accepting a desk job in the city of Algiers police department, migrating to the west bank with his family, like so many others had done before him.

As Ferrell limped out of New Orleans, the city he once loved so much, now only held bitter memories. One thing he did not leave behind was his desire for justice! *The man who took my leg will pay!* Ferrell thought, and knew what he was going to do. He just had to wait ten years to be able to do it.

Ferrell knew it was just a matter of time before the disease of the city would reach Algiers.

THE CITY BENEATH THE SEA

With crime beginning to rise out of control, and on the heels of black-on-white murders, Ferrell was at the right place at the right time for his style of strong-armed justice.

Encouraged by friends and family, Ferrell ran for Sheriff, narrowly defeating the incumbent, mostly on the commitment he would clean up the city and reduce crime.

This commitment he would waste no time in implementing. Spending weeks combing over personnel records and arrest records, Ferrell was able to come up with a dozen officers that shared his commitment to law and order, even if the rules had to be bent.

Being white was just a part of why these particular men were selected. The weeks of extensive research Ferrell had done previously had identified these twelve disciples, as they would soon be referred to, for their excessive use of force when it came to minorities. This was the indicator Ferrell keyed in on that made him believe in this group of men. He knew if he told them what he wanted to accomplish, then give them a loose rein, they would achieve what he asked for. So what if the civil rights of a few minorities had to be trampled on. To Ferrell, the end would justify the means.

Within a very short time, the twelve disciples had established themselves as a force to be reckoned with, and feared by the black community.

Little got by the watchful eye of the twelve disciples. The brutality they would inflict on blacks if caught committing a crime was the greatest deterrent of all. In fact, a trend was soon established where many of the black criminals in Algiers would take the ferry to New Orleans to commit their crimes. At one point, the twelve disciples were more feared than the Klu Klux Klan.

With a loyal base of officers in place, they were able to recruit more and more officers, until, with the exception of a small segment, the force had become an extension of Ferrell's arm. A steel fist he had no reservations in wielding when he found it necessary to do so.

While Ferrell cleaned up the city, and the years passed, the burning desire for justice that had almost once consumed him had never died out. As Sherriff, Ferrell was able to know when his attacker would be released, and when he least expected it, he would be made to pay!

Through the years, Ferrell kept up with the appeals of the man who killed his partner. One after the other, year after year, until finally after ten years, he was executed. Ferrell made sure he had a front row seat.

Then, almost three months to the day, the man who shot Ferrell was released. Ferrell could now have his revenge and it was going to be sweet.

Ferrell knew he could not be too hasty, he would have to think it out, stalk his prey, know his habits, then and only then would he strike.

After about a month of learning his habits and routines, Ferrell was able to get the man he patiently waited ten years for alone. Under the pretence of an arrest, Ferrell put him in the back of his car. Then driving to a secluded location in New Orleans East, Ferrell executed the man who had almost killed him, and buried his body in the mash. After five years, they still hadn't found his body.

THE CITY BENEATH THE SEA

CHAPTER TEN

The Royal Street Police Station found itself particularly busy this time of day. Late evening in the heart of the French Quarter, officers were entering and exiting the two storey white structure. Late evening and early morning were the only times when the police presence actually doubled, as the night shift reported to work and the day shift prepared to go home.

The station, housed in a renovated building every bit of two hundred years old, blended in perfectly with its surroundings. So much so in fact, if it were not for the tell-tale presence of several police cars and scooters, one could walk right by the station and not give it a second thought.

Inside, Les entered the locker room, heading toward his locker. Several other officers were either preparing for their shift, or leaving for the day. A couple of officers in no great rush even had taken time to take a shower, and now they strolled around the locker room talking to other officers clad only in a towel.

"You got lucky, Les!" an unseen voice from the opposite side of Les's locker called out, in a voice loud enough for the rest of the locker room to hear.

Les immediately recognized the voice as Charles Cunningham. Charles had joined the N.O.P.D. the same time Les had, and from the very beginning, a bitter rivalry had ensued, on that neither of them knew quite how it started or why. Regardless of what it was, from who wrote the most parking tickets, or training scores, Charles had been obsessed with outdoing Les.

Viewing Charles' obsession with humor and bewilderment, Les often sought to avoid Charles as much as possible. This was not to say he would not respond in the event he needed back up. This was his job, and he often had to put personal feelings aside. Les approached Charles cautiously, and viewed him as being very unpredictable. In his past dealings with him, Les often found Charles would be easy to talk to one minute, then when his insecurities kicked in, would accuse him of going behind his back. Les had been able to deal with Charles only by being cordial and polite, but simply did not go out of his way to make friends or find any common ground. Charles was a small and petty man, who was often jealous of the success Les had been able to achieve thus far in his career.

In recent years, the one area that had became a festering sore throughout the year for Charles was the annual bowling tournament, which Les and Paul had been able to win the last three years in a row. This was what Charles was alluding to now.

"Excuse me?" Les said, wanting to make absolutely sure he didn't misunderstand Charles's meaning.

"I said you got lucky!" Charles said, turning the corner of the lockers.

"You mean with the tournament or your sister?" Les asked, as the other officers burst out into laughter.

"Funny guy!" Charles said, trying to shake off some of the embarrassment he felt. "If you're so funny, why are you a cop?"

Just then, Paul walked up to his locker, having heard the beginning of the exchange as he walked into the locker room. He too immediately recognized the voice and knew it to be Charles. Like Les, Paul was no friend of Charles, but unlike Les who sought to avoid him, Paul sought out every opportunity he could find to exchange barbs with him.

"Because your sister likes cops," Paul said out of the blue, erupting the locker room into laughter once more.

Charles began to turn red, his anger ready to erupt at any moment. He clenched his fists, which both Les and Paul caught from the corner of their eye, though they pretended not to notice.

THE CITY BENEATH THE SEA

As expected, Charles did not lash out and was only able to return the witty response of, "Screw you guys!" as he walked off.

"Like your sister did," Les said softly, only loud enough for Paul to hear, bringing a smile to his face.

"You seen the news?" Paul asked, as he opened his locker, which was right next to Les'.

"No, I slept in and came straight here. Quiana and Timmy went to Baton Rouge to her sister's, why?" Les asked, always feeling uneasy when he was not informed.

"The storm didn't turn like they thought; they say we're going to be directly in the path," Paul began, reaching in his locker for his shirt. "The Mayor has called for mandatory evacuation."

"Didn't he already call for that?" Les asked, a little confused by Paul's new information.

"That was voluntary, him and the Governor upped the anti to mandatory," Paul explained, bringing his partner up to date. "You ever heard of a mandatory evacuation before?"

"No, it's the first time," Les said, pondering the severity of the upgrade.

"They must know something we don't," Paul finally surmised, unable to make sense of it himself.

"Maybe," Les agreed, in the fog over the situation just as much as Paul. "How's the highways holding up? ContraFlow working?" Les asked, knowing the problems they had in the past with contraflow.

"As well as can be expected I guess, what genius came up with contraFlow anyway?" Paul asked, having become frustrated with the many flaws that it had experienced in the past.

Contraflow was a system designed to convert interstates from two-way traffic to one-way traffic, thereby facilitating a quicker evacuation from the cities and low lying areas. On paper, the plan looked great, but once the realities of bottlenecks, accidents and breakdowns were factored into the mix, it wasn't the case. In many cases, Contra Flow had become synonymous with a parking lot.

"Just another day in the Big Easy," Les said, closing his locker with a smile.

"Will you be serious?" Paul snapped back, his tone and inflection one of concern. "This could be bad, really bad!"

"You know what I say, prepare –"

"I know!" Paul said, cutting Les off before he could finish and completing the sentence for him. "Prepare for the worst and hope for the best."

"Gina left?" Les asked, trying to understand some of Paul's underlying concerns.

"No, she's going to stay," Paul said, the anxiety in his tone was clear that he was concerned. "She said unless the whole apartment complex comes down, she would be ok."

"Slidell doesn't have much in the way of levees, she's not concerned about flooding?" Les asked, trying to understand her reasoning for staying.

"She's on the second floor, you know her, hard-headed woman."

Les smiled in understanding, while sympathizing with his frustration.

Les and Paul left the locker room followed by the other officers heading into the duty room.

The duty room was a large, unassuming room with only the basic amenities. Enough chairs for each officer, and a podium in the front where the duty officer would address the group, and hand out assignments.

As they entered the room, the duty officer was also entering, and he wasted no time, as he headed for the podium.

"For those of you who haven't heard," the duty officer began. His voice carried easily throughout the room without the assistance of a microphone. "It looks like Katrina is heading for us. The Mayor has ordered a mandatory evacuation, and it continues as we speak." The duty officer paused only long enough to catch his breath then continued to inform his men of the situation the city now found itself in.

"The Superdome has been deemed the refuge of last resort. We're not expecting many people there though, if the roads are any indication, it looks like most people are heeding the warning. As with any emergency, there will be those trying to take advantage of the situation, so be on the lookout for looters. Any questions?" the duty officer asked, offering the opportunity to any officer to ask clarification. After a few moments, the duty officer looked out to his men once more, offering his final words. "Ok, be safe out there," he said, then left the room, soon followed by the rest of the officers.

Outside, the clouds had begun to form and the winds had gradually increased, as Les and Paul patrolled the once busy streets. Many people had left the city, heeding the warnings of the Governor and the Mayor, but many still remained, walking about on their porches, either unconcerned or unaware that a storm had put New Orleans in its crosshairs.

Within the comfort and safety of their patrol car, Paul removed his cell phone and placed a call to Gina.

"Hey, baby," Paul said, when she answered.

"What do you mean, who is this?" Paul said, in response to her obvious joke, which even brought a smile to Les.

"I'm just kidding," Gina said, as she sat on her second floor balcony, overlooking the harbor and the sailboats starting to gently move about, the full force of the storm not having shown its ugly face.

"I'm good," Gina said as the pushed the sliding door to the apartment, returning inside. "The wind is starting to pick up though."

THE CITY BENEATH THE SEA

"Well hunker down, this thing should pass quick, I'll be home soon," Paul said, closing the phone and returning it to his pocket.

"Quit worrying, she'll be fine," Les said, offering some reassurance, to his worried partner.

"Yea right! This is coming from a man so worried he ships his family out of town every time a strong wind kicks up," Paul said, referring to Les' cautious nature.

"Just in case," Les said, countering Paul's observation.

"Just in case of what?" Paul questioned, trying to understand Les' deep underlining concerns.

"In case I can't get to them," Les finally said, though reluctant at first. "I worry about a lot of stuff out here, I don't want them to be one of them," Les confided to his partner. "What if the levees overflow?"

Paul tried to process this new insight about his partner that had somehow been concealed until now. Paul had always viewed Les as overly confident, and had never known him to be worried about anything. This revelation was a shock to Paul, seeing another side of his partner.

"Man, you've been worrying about that for years," Paul said, trying to reassure his partner his fears were unfounded, like he had done so many times before for him. "First of all, we never had a storm surge that high, second, you ever seen the size of the pumps we have to pump the water out? Right off the interstate, there's that big pumping station with thirty-six-inch pipes discharging into the 17th Street canal. I tell you what, if they can't handle a little flooding, nothing can."

"And being below sea level, that's exactly what they have to do," Les said, agreeing with his partner, yet bringing another aspect of the characteristics of the city to the forefront.

"What do you mean?" Paul asked, confused that his articulated argument did not give at least a

THE CITY BENEATH THE SEA

temporary abeyance to any protracted argument his partner may have wanted to counter with.

"New Orleans is below sea level, we are literally the city beneath the sea. Every single drop of water that falls into the city has to be pumped out," Les explained.

"And the problem is?"

"No problem as long as the pumps run, if they don't; there's the problem," Les said, continuing to educate his partner on the topography of the city.

"Your argument is moot," Paul finally countered the only defense he could quickly assimilate.

"How so?"

"The pumps aren't going to fail," Paul said with confidence.

"You're probably right," Les conceded. "But I always like to…"

"Plan for the worst and hope for the best!" Paul and Les said in unison, bringing a smile to each of their faces.

"What say 100 bucks our friend does it again?" Les said, referring to a situation they had experienced over and over in the past.

"NO way!" Paul argued, "After we caught him the second time, I'm sure he won't be stupid enough to do it again."

"Hundred bucks?" Les offered, displaying his confidence in the stupidity of the criminal they were referring to.

"You're on!" Paul agreed, equally as confident.

Les turned the patrol car around, heading into the belly of the city.

THE CITY BENEATH THE SEA

CHAPTER ELEVEN

Jamal headed to the bathroom while LaToya began to dress his younger brother, Jameal.

Her thoughts were of her children, she worried, something inside of her was driving her, as though trying to steer her actions and decision. It was nothing she could put her finger on, but something was compelling her to leave, and she had decided to follow her instincts.

Jamal returned from the bathroom, pulling his little shirt down as he entered the room.

"Ok, Jamal, Mommy laid out your clothes for you, can you get dressed like a big boy?"

"Sure, Mommy, I'm a big boy!" Jamal said, as he began to remove his shirt and change his clothes, while LaToya finished changing his four-year-old brother.

"Ok, Jamal," LaToya said, as she finishing changing Jameal. "Mommy needs to go talk to Big Mama real quick, you watch your brother for me, can you do that?"

"Ok Mommy."

LaToya left the apartment, heading for Big Mama's. Not seeing her outside, as was usually the case, she began knocking on the door.

"Who is it?" a rough, harsh voice on the other side of the door called out.

"It's LaToya."

The door to the apartment opened, as Big Mama answered. "What is it, baby?"

"Big Mama, I'm taking the children to the Dome, I don't want to risk staying here," LaToya explained to her friend.

"You scared this old building will come tumbling down?" Big Mama asked, trying to understand LaToya's fear and motivation for leaving.

THE CITY BENEATH THE SEA

"No, I'm scared of the water, if we flood, we won't be able to escape," LaToya said, revealing her biggest fear.

"I understand your concern, baby, especially with little children," Big Mama said.

"Come with us," LaToya asked, "you won't be safe here if it floods."

"No, baby, this is my home come hell or high water, the only way they gonna get me out of here is in a box," Big Mama said.

"Don't talk like that," LaToya said, not willing to even entertain the thought of losing Big Mama.

"I'm sorry, baby, you go do what you think's best for your children, Big Mama's gonna be just fine."

"Are you sure?" LaToya questioned, not completely believing her friend.

"Yea, baby, Big Mama will be waiting for you when you come back," said Big Mama, trying to reassure LaToya. "Now you go, take care of them babies."

LaToya left Big Mama, not knowing if this would be the last time she would see her if the worst case scenario happened.

Returning to her apartment, LaToya quickly gathered up Jamal and Jameal and left what had been her home for so many years.

Holding the youngest on her hip, LaToya pulled the wheeled suitcase along. "Hold on to the suitcase, Jamal, and don't let go. Ok."

"Ok Mommy."

Slowly and with a lot of effort, LaToya and her two sons began their trek to the distant Superdome.

As LaToya neared the dome, she began to see more and more people like herself, heading in the same direction; some carrying suitcases, while others carried their few possessions in garbage bags, or whatever they could find. Eventually, what started out as a slow

THE CITY BENEATH THE SEA

trickle of people soon gave way to a mass exodus of humanity all converging on one place; the Superdome.

In the distance, lines had already formed to process the masses. Police and National Guardsman could be seen trying to orchestrate some order to the symphony that was quickly becoming chaos.

Minutes rolled into hours as LaToya patiently waited in line. Slowly, step-by-step, she inched closer and closer to the Superdome entrance. Each step, each inch brought with it a renewed sense of hope, all she could think of was getting into the dome, whatever it took, no matter how long.

She knew once inside, she would be safe, and the most important thing to her right now was safety. She wanted to feel safe. After that, she would address the other needs of herself and her children. .

Slowly, almost imperceptible a gust of wind could be felt as it whirled and sliced through the high-rise buildings, reducing much of its original force as it collided with the towering obstacles.

The sky's darkening hue, moving quickly, was a visual warning of what was to come. Suddenly without warning, the heavens opened up, releasing the droplets it had guarded so closely moments earlier. Some in the crowd produced umbrellas of various types, shapes and colors, some unpacked raincoats. The less prepared, and less fortunate resorted to plastic bags and newspapers, in an effort to try to ward off the chill of the rain.

LaToya, being less fortunate than all of the above mentioned, had nothing to protect her and her children from the pouring rain. Covering Jameal with a blanket the best she could, she pulled Jamal to her legs as the rain continued to pelt their bodies, soaking their clothes to the skin.

LaToya cried, feeling the chill of the rain, knowing her children felt the same cold. For the first time in her life, she was helpless to protect her children and it tore at her heart. Little did LaToya know that this was just a prelude to the horror that lay ahead.

Trembling in the chill of the sudden downpour, LaToya began to consider giving up. Exhausted, her body racked with pain, with her youngest screaming in her arms, helpless to do anything to alleviate his discomfort, it was at this point, LaToya began to consider and possibly welcome death. For the hell she found herself in had slowly but methodically stripped her of her will to go on.

Then when all hope seemed lost, and she could go no further, or wait no longer, hope began to appear. The once stagnate line began to move quickly as the streaming mass surged forward, toward and into the Superdome.

"Thank God!" LaToya thought, walking toward the dome, a renewed burst of energy coming over her. She had no distant thoughts or goals, her focus was just to put one foot in front of the other, to keep moving hoping the strength of her and her children would somehow hold out. Crossing the threshold of the dome and finally out of the rain, a sense of relief came over her, she had been able to accomplish the first major hurdle; she had gotten inside the dome.

Her excitement was to be short-lived, however, when she realized the salvation she had hoped for would once again be postponed as the line had not disappeared, but merely relocated inside.

Guardsmen, stationed to search both people and belongings before being allowed to enter the Superdome, would be the final hurdle LaToya would have to face before being granted access to the facility. Once inside, she could change into dry clothes and sleep in safety, knowing the Superdome could withstand the worst Mother Nature could throw at her.

As crowds moved forward to be processed, the guardsmen conducted their methodical search with such a blatant sense of insensitivity that only a blind man several feet away could remain oblivious to their actions. Trash bags, which had been the only means of transporting the few belongings many were able to salvage, were ripped open with their contents scattered about with little respect either for the contents or the person who owned it. For the most part, the people didn't complain; they just picked up their belongings in their arms the best they could and retreated to the safety of the dome. This scene was repeated over and over, as person after person traded their last bit of dignity and self-respect for a safe place to escape the storm..

Finally, LaToya stood before a guardsman who roughly grabbed her suitcase and opened it, searching the contents. Finding no contraband, he turned his attention to her, searching her, along with her crying children for guns, knives, drugs and other contraband that would either contribute or inhibit the Guard from maintaining order inside the massive facility.

But through all the indignations LaToya was subjected to, none tore at her heart more than when she saw Jamal with his hands behind his head being searched.

He tried to be brave and fight back the tears, which were right on the surface, but only held at bay by his sheer will and determination. Even though he was able to restrain his emotions admirably, an occasional tear did escape him.

It was as though he was being treated like a criminal, his only crime was being born poor. This scene, this mental image was much more than LaToya could take and she began to cry.

Finally reunited with Jamal, she dropped to her knees and hugged his still wet clothes, trying to reassure him that this nightmare would soon pass.

Taking her suitcase, with Jamal and the Jameal in tow, LaToya headed into the Superdome's massive

THE CITY BENEATH THE SEA

arena. The sight that greeted her was nothing like she had imagined.

Thousands of people had now gathered inside the dome, seeking shelter and safety, transforming the shining athletic arena into a refugee camp, the size of which this city had never seen before. There were old people, young people, and some very pregnant women, along with old men and women in wheelchairs, some on oxygen. There were those who cried out for assistance, while others suffered quietly in their own personal misery.

The scene was loud and confusing; making it difficult to focus on one thing with so many distractions to divert their attention. Once inside, a sense of abandonment came over them, as they quickly realized they were left to their own devices. It would be up to them to find a spot to settle into, with no cots to compete for, the only viable real estate left was floor space, and as LaToya looked out over the thousands of bodies scattered throughout the dome, she quickly realized that too was rapidly diminishing.

Never in her life had she ever been thrust into such a situation. She had always been able to trust the government to help her. Only now did she realize she was going to have to help herself.

Negotiating the crowded floor, LaToya looked for a spot she could stake a claim on; but would have to walk still even further until finding one. Still chilled from the rain, and tired, fortune once again shone on LaToya as she found an out of the way spot on the dome floor. Feeling relatively safe as she evaluated her surroundings; other ladies, some old, some young, only an occasional man could be seen. This she knew would offer her the best hope for the safety she so desperately sought.

As LaToya began to settle in, she observed what the others around her had done. Some had stretched out blankets, in some cases along with tarps, to try to

THE CITY BENEATH THE SEA

put a barrier between themselves and the cold hard concrete floor. There were no blankets, if there ever had been any, they had been quickly scooped up by any one of the thousands who now crowded into the dome, which at a quick glance of the interior would estimate a number close to twenty thousand plus people. No one could have planned for the area of last resort to have been resorted to in such a big way.

LaToya opened her suitcase and removed some clothes for Jamal, stripping off his wet clothes and replacing them with dry ones. Amazing enough, they had remained relatively dry, despite the deluge which had engulfed them earlier.

"Ok, Jamal, sit here while I change your brother," LaToya said, placing Jamal against the wall. Jamal never once complained, nor did he cry, he sat in silence, just overwhelmed by what was happing to them. Absorbing and processing each and every experience, which he would relive in his mind for the rest of his life.

THE CITY BENEATH THE SEA

CHAPTER TWELVE

"Your honor," the young defense attorney began. "My client is not denying the events that transpired on that fateful day, only the circumstances that led to them."

Trying to put the best spin on an almost impossible case, Donald King presented his argument before the judge. His client, charged with a forth DWI, faced jail time. To complicate matters more, the accident he was involved in while driving drunk landed a State Trooper in the hospital, paralyzed.

While most attorneys would throw up their hands in defeat and beg for a plea, Donald was composed and confident. He had rescued other cases from the jaws of defeat, this one would be no different. Even if he had to employ some less than ethical tactics.

Ethics, however, was never something Donald seemed to have a problem with. The thirty-year-old African American had not risen to become the youngest partner in the prestigious Harrington law firm by being afraid to cut corners.

Now, however, with one of their richest client's son's life hanging in the balance, many eyes were on the case. Some wanted to finally see Donald fail, for the first time, be humbled by his failure. Others followed the case, knowing he wouldn't fail, but unable to see a way out for the brash hotshot attorney.

As Donald continued to present his argument, he was polished, charismatic, with a touch of sophistication, which would lead many to believe he had lived a privileged life, but this couldn't be farther from the truth. Donald argued for his client with passion and determination, the empty courtroom resonating with each word he spoke.

The empty courtroom that carried Donald's voice so well stood in sharp contrast to what most people would expect from such a high-profile case. This, however, was no accident, only one of the many well planned and executed moves of a brilliant defense attorney. Anticipating problems with emotional outbursts that he felt could only hurt his client's chances of a fair trial, Donald had successfully petitioned the Judge for a closed hearing. This left only the players who currently found themselves in the room; the Judge, the Assistant District Attorney, the accused, and of course, the defense attorney.

Convincing his client not to have a trial by jury was no easy sell; by agreeing to put his fate in the hands of the Judge was thought by many to be ill-advised. But Donald, never being one restricted by 'in the box' thinking, was able to get his client's permission, on what some thought to be a risky gamble.

But to Donald, who approached his cases much like a master chess player would his board, always two moves ahead of his opponent, the empty courtroom was just another maneuver to move him closer to his ultimate victory.

One of the people who cautiously watched, and calculated Donald's every move was Assistant District Attorney, Susan Herrington. The blond-haired, blue-eyed beauty with an air of sophistication was often underestimated, to the detriment of the attorneys and clients she prosecuted.

Young, aggressive, and tenacious, Susan approached every case she prosecuted with a do or die attitude, failure not being an option. This approach and ultimate conviction rate had earned her a reputation as one of the hardest hitting prosecutors the office had to offer. Ambitious and smart, Susan had always proven to be a formidable opponent every time she and Donald met in court, though often frustrated by the end result.

Time and time again, Susan had been successfully out-maneuvered by Donald. Just when she thought she had him against the ropes, and was about to deliver a knockout blow, he somehow duped his way out of it.

This case, however, she felt more confident in than any of the previous cases she had ever faced against the highly skilled barrister. Even someone with the legal skills of Donald King, even he would not be able to save his client. This would be the case that Donald, probably for the first time in his life, would be able to experience what defeat felt like.

"My client was having an adverse reaction to prescription medication," Donald argued, trying to persuade the less-than-sympathetic Judge.

"Your client was having an adverse reaction to alcohol?" the Judge countered, slamming the door Donald had opened squarely in his face. "When he was arrested, he had three times the legal limit in his system."

Donald momentarily retreated, not able to contradict the counter-argument the Judge had presented.

"Now, unless you can show me, through medical records, what exactly your client had in his system and how it had an adverse affect when introduced with alcohol, I'd say you're dead in the water," the Judge continued, waiting only for a moment for a response he knew would not come. "Do you have anything else to offer?" he asked, as he prepared to put an end to the proceedings.

"No, your honor," replied Donald, his response soft though not sheepish or shy.

"Does the prosecution have anything else to offer?" inquired the Judge, making sure all arguments in the case had been made.

"Your honor," Susan began, her words strong and forceful. "Only that this was the defendant's fourth DWI and leniency should not be taken into consideration. We're requesting the maximum sentence possible by the court."

"We're not in the sentencing phase. Did you just get out of Law School?" the Judge chastised the bewildered attorney, catching her offguard, putting her in a defensive position.

"No, your honor, I –"

Susan was cut off before being able to articulate her position by the impatient, no-nonsense Judge.

"Then save your concerns for the sentencing phase," directed the Judge. "Can you do that?"

"Yes, your honor," Susan conceded, a bit embarrassed at how hard the Judge had come down on her.

"After taking all the facts of this case into account," the Judge began. "I find the defendant guilty. Sentencing will be two weeks from today."

"Your honor," Donald immediately called to be recognized.

"Yes?"

"I would like to request that bail be continued until sentencing," requested Donald, not the least bit surprised by the verdict, and almost giving the impression he had anticipated it.

"So ordered," the Judge immediately agreed.

"Your honor!" Susan called out, surprised and caught offguard by the ruling.

"Yes," the Judge said, giving Susan a patronizing look.

"I object to continued bail, the defendant is obviously facing jail time and has sufficient recourses to flee the country," Susan argued her impassioned plea.

"Did you not just hear me rule?"

"Yes, your honor, but it was so fast."

"Listen, young lady, in the future you need to be a little more up on your game. My court is not a classroom. Do I make myself clear?"

"Perfectly, your honor," Susan humbly acknowledged. "But the people request that the defendant surrenders his passport before the court."

THE CITY BENEATH THE SEA

The Judge obviously getting a little angry at this point, gave Susan a hard look. His wrinkled brow and down-turned lip were clues that signaled his frustration and anger. Yet the Judge refrained from the angry outburst he had contemplated and was able to talk himself out of.

"Very well, the defendant will surrender his passport to the court, that's all," the frustrated Judge said, slamming his gavel down with a force reflecting his anger, then disappeared into his chambers behind the bench.

"What the hell? I thought you were going to get me off!" Donald's client protested.

"Shhh! Be quiet!" Donald cautioned his client. "Give me a second, will you?"

Folding his arms across his chest, anger beginning to boil inside of him, Donald's client turned away for the time being.

Walking over to Susan, Donald extended a congratulatory handshake.

"Good job! You got us good!" Donald said, acknowledging Susan's obvious victory.

"One more drunk off the streets," said Susan, loud enough to make sure his client heard.

"Did you make the reservations?" Donald leaned over to Susan, asking her in a whisper.

"Rotella's at seven," Susan replied, also in a whisper.

"I'll meet you there," said Donald, then returned to his client as Susan began to walk out of the courtroom.

Then as though she had an afterthought, she stopped and turned back to Donald as though reflecting back on the recent events and trying to make sense of them. Something was wrong, though she was not able to put her finger on it. Maybe it was in the way Donald so graciously conceded defeat, or maybe it was the inflection of his voice, which seemed to lack a sense of sincerity. Whatever it was, she had learned to be suspicious of Donald in the courtroom.

"You're not going to pull another rabbit out your hat on this one, are you?" Susan asked, referring to the previous times Donald had grasped victory from the jaws of defeat.

"You heard the Judge, guilty, what else can I do?" Donald said, putting his hands up in the air as though helpless.

Susan smiled and left the courtroom, a look of uncertainty about her still remained.

Donald, now alone with his client was able to reveal his well-orchestrated plan.

But to Ken Franklin, Donald's client, all he wanted at the moment was to wrap his hands around Donald's throat.

Son of a wealthy businessman, Ken had been raised with the proverbial silver spoon in his mouth. Raised by maids and nannies his whole life, Ken had grown up with a sense of entitlement.

Though intelligent enough to know the rules of society, Ken was arrogant enough to believe that they did not apply to him. If history was any indication, he would be right. Ken had continuously found himself in trouble with the law; with several DWIs, and sexual assaults, which his father had to pay dearly to make go away. Ken continued on his path of doing whatever he wanted whenever he wanted, undeterred.

Facing mandatory jail time, this was the first instance that ever got Ken's attention, but deep down, he knew his dad would fix this one too.

After hearing the verdict, a sinking feeling came over Ken, his arrogance finally checked, if only for a moment, as he now faced the real possibility of going to prison.

"I thought you were going to fix this!" Ken said, his tone somewhere between anger and pleading. "My dad paid you a lot of money to make this go away."

THE CITY BENEATH THE SEA

"Listen! You were drunk! Hit a State Trooper, who is still in the hospital, paralyzed. There is no way in hell you're ever going to be found anything but guilty. No matter how much money your dad's got!" Donald said, explaining to his client the reality of his situation.

For the first time, Donald sensed fear in Ken. As long as he had been defending him, he had never once seen anything but arrogance, and a better than thou attitude.

Now, his client fought back tears as the reality of the situation began to overtake him.

"I can't even leave!" Ken yelled. "That bitch made sure of that when she got my passport!"

As much as he would have loved to have prolonged his client's internal torment, time would not permit, and he would have to bring what he had found so amusing to an end.

"However," Donald began, "the Judge is a reasonable man, and your dad has displayed how generous he can be to the Judge, and I got you a suspended sentence with no jail time."

"Alright!" Ken said, reverting back to his arrogant persona, which only moments earlier had all but disappeared. "That's better!" Ken said, then began to leave the courtroom, not even bothering to thank Donald as he left.

"Do me a favor?" Donald asked before Ken could walk out of the courtroom.

"What's that?"

"Stay out of cars when you drink," requested Donald, though his plea fell on deaf ears.

"Yea, whatever!" Ken said, his unrepentant tone cutting Donald like a knife.

Outside the courtroom, Donald ran into Mason Grayson. Mason and Donald had quickly become best friends when Donald first arrived in New York. Never having lived in a city the size of New York, Donald was somewhat a fish out of water, but with Mason's help, Donald was quickly able to assimilate.

Having first met Mason outside his apartment building while hailing a cab, Mason displayed his acute awareness and sensitivity to injustices around him when he saw the problem Donald was having hailing a cab. Reaching out to Donald, Mason offered to share a cab. From that chance meeting, a friendship developed that had grown ever since, so much so that Donald had asked Mason to be the best man at his forthcoming wedding.

"Donald!" Mason called from down the hall, attracting his attention, as Mason walked up.

"Boy, do I have some news for you!" Mason said, bursting from the seams with excitement.

"You just accepted a job as a Federal Prosecutor, and you will be based out of Baton Rouge, a town only sixty miles from my hometown," Donald delivered the pre-emptive strike, revealing the fact that he already knew the good news.

"Man!" Mason said, obviously frustrated. "It hasn't even been announced yet!"

Mason had always been amazed at how much of the pulse Donald often had for the legal community. Regardless of what was going on, or with whom, Donald seemed to have the inside track on the information. Mason often speculated the paradox of Donald's legal career. Did he know a lot of people because he was a great lawyer. Or, was it because he knew the right people that he became a great lawyer?

Whatever the case, there was no question, Donald had become an attorney with few equals.

"Since I'm leaving, I guess you wouldn't give me a going away gift by telling me who your inside source has been all these years?" Mason asked, but knowing Donald as long as he had, and his proclivity to playing his cards close to the chest, Mason already knew the answer.

THE CITY BENEATH THE SEA

"Come now," Donald said, "one could assume all those years of sleeping with legal assistants finally paid off, but a proper southern gentleman such as myself does not kiss and tell."

"I knew that was coming," Mason smiled.

"When you leaving?" Donald asked.

"As soon as the movers pack, I'm out of here," Mason explained. "But don't worry, I'll be back for the wedding.

"Since you're going south, maybe you could get some sun," Donald said, eyeing his blonde-haired Caucasion friend, "you're so white, you're almost glowing." Donald burst out laughing at his own joke, getting only a smile from Mason.

"Very funny, but seriously, if there's anything I can ever do for you, let me know," Mason offered, wanting to maintain his friendship with Donald.

"I will, and I'll be coming down there soon, maybe we can catch an LSU game," Donald said, "Nothing will indoctrinate you to Baton Rouge better than a night at Tiger Stadium."

"I'll look forward to it," Mason said, shaking Donald's hand, then headed down the hall.

THE CITY BENEATH THE SEA

CHAPTER THIRTEEN

Donald stood before a group of six men, all dressed in martial arts uniforms. Each man's belt indicated his rank proficiency. The brightly lit Dojo, with its padded floor and mirrored walls was a place of respect to those who had left behind so much sweat and tears within its walls.

The hanging bags remained motionless at full attention, just like the men who stood before Donald.

Donald's black belt with five strips signified his rank as a fifty-degree master in the art of Tae Kwon Do, Korea's ancient martial art.

Clapping twice, Donald bowed, followed by his students repeating the gesture, before Donald began to speak.

"Business is like the martial arts. Some of you are businessmen, some are attorneys, CEOs. Business is like the martial arts because both require hard work, sacrifice, defensive tactics. Both require summing up your opponent by what kind of commitment he can bring to the table, and in both, it is never wise to underestimate your opponent."

Donald paused for a moment before continuing, using the opportunity to look into the eyes of the members of the class. All grown men in their early to late forties, each very fit, and strong.

"Put your sparring gear on!" Donald yelled, as his class rushed to don their gear; protective padded mitts and boots, along with protective headgear that would offer some degree of protection to the combatants.

One at a time, the class began to form lines on the Dojo floor, having secured their sparring equipment. They formed two lines down the middle, with each student facing another student. The evenly-spaced class did not have to sit anyone out, each had an opponent, each ready for combat.

THE CITY BENEATH THE SEA

Donald positioned himself to the side to oversee the action, and to prevent anyone from getting too aggressive, which would sometimes be the case when the adrenaline began to flow. Fortunately, injuries were rare, each student sharing and demonstrating a mutual respect for each other.

"Bow!" Donald yelled, from the end of the lines, and his students bowed to their opponent as a sign of respect.

"Sparring stance!" yelled Donald, and the class jumped into a combatant stance, with a loud yell.

"Begin!" Donald yelled, allowing the students to begin sparring.

Utilizing combinations of punches and kicks, some roundhouses, some spinning kicks, others more basic. The class fought their opponent, each trying to land a kick or punch while their equally skilled opponent attempted to block it.

After several minutes of sparring, the initial rapid pace at which the students had started began to slow as fatigue set in.

"Stop!" Donald yelled, bringing the students to a halt and rushing to reform their lines.

"Bow!"

The class bowed in unison, giving each other the sign of respect they had earnt.

"Good job!" Donald said, congratulating his class. "You all did well. If any of you would like to stay and help me with my workout, I would be grateful. If not, class dismissed."

The class relaxed and milled around, but no one left. The entire class was ready to help Donald in his workout. Sparring with a master in Tae Kwon Do was the highlight of many in the class.

Retreating to a far wall, Donald opened his oversized black bag and removed his padded gloves and boots, to protect his students. As usual he did not worry about putting on a headpiece.

THE CITY BENEATH THE SEA

Returning to the center of the Dojo, Donald stood ready. His class began to surround him, ready to attack. Though many in the class were quite skilled and would ultimately present a challenge in sheer numbers against him, none were naïve enough to believe their skill could come anywhere close to Donald's.

A student lunged at Donald without warning, only to be repelled by a sidekick he never saw coming, catapulting him backward. Using the initial assault as a diversion, another student swung at Donald's head, barely missing him as he ducked below the punch, then delivered a punch of his own to the student's ribs.

A well-placed kick to Donald's back sent him forward towards the ground, leading some of his students to believe the advantage would be theirs once he fell.

To the dismay of his students, he ducked and rolled, returning to his feet a short distance away, prepared for whatever else his students were ready to deliver.

Seeing two students running towards him, Donald retreated towards the large hanging punch bag as the students followed in hot pursuit. With only a small lead, and the students breathing down his neck, Donald leapt up towards the chain hanging from the ceiling, supporting the bag.

Clasping the chain and using his momentum to his advantage, he spun himself around the bag, turning towards his pursuers. As he neared, he delivered a kick to the head of each of his pursuers, dazing them momentarily and removing them from the fight.

While Donald retired student after student from the fight, his best student now stood before him. Also a black belt, though lower in rank, the student possessed great skill and would offer him a proper challenge.

The two warriors begin to circle each other, slowly, deliberately; each not wanting to make the first move, giving an advantage to his opponent.

THE CITY BENEATH THE SEA

Suddenly, the student exploded with a front kick, followed by a spinning kick. Both missed their target.

The class now encircled the combatants, in awe of the demonstration they were about to witness. But the demonstration the class had hoped for would not last long. As Donald's student spun again with a kick, Donald anticipated the move, ducking, then kicking his student's leg out from under him, causing him to fall hard on the padded mat, momentarily knocking the wind out of him.

Donald stood, extending his hand out to his fallen student to help him up. The rest of the class approached, they all bowed to each other as a sign of respect.

THE CITY BENEATH THE SEA

CHAPTER FOURTEEN

The bright neon sign proudly displayed in front of the restaurant removed any question as to its identify. The gaudy sign portrayed just the opposite of what Rotello's was. A five-star restaurant with a waiting list of a week or more for a table. Catering to New York City's most discriminating palates for over twenty years, it had become more of an institution than a restaurant, where the movers and shakers of the city came to be seen more than to be feed.

From celebrities to politicians, you never knew who you could spot when you were in Rotello's

Inside, the elegant decor immediately elevated its perception as being something special. With Venetian crystal, and silverware, a service second to none in the city, few restaurants could compare to Rotello's.

As Donald entered the restaurant, it appeared every table was taken in the popular restaurant, but he looked around the immediate area for Susan.

"Can I help you, Sir?" a maitre d' Donald had never seen before approached him with a less than cordial tone.

"I'm looking for someone," Donald politely informed the man and he continued to look for Susan.

"Are you sure they can afford to be in here?"

Donald turned around, ready to confront the man when the regular maitre d' approached.

"Mister Donald!" Francois called out in a cheerful greeting, "Come with me, Ms. Susan is already here, she's at your usual table."

Donald followed the second maitre d', after Francois gave the first maitre d' a hard look as he went.

"Please excuse the new man," Francois said in a whisper, "he's the owner's brother-in-law, but I don't think he'll work out. He..." Francois paused as though struggling to find the right word to properly describe his co-worker, then finally he did. "Let's just say he doesn't have a way with people," Francois finally conceded, as he escorted Donald to his table.

"You can say that again," Donald agreed, as he followed Francois, bringing a smile to his face.

"Here we go, Mr. Donald," Francois said, as he arrived at an out-of-the-way table where Susan was already seated.

"Hey, baby," Donald said, as he leant over and kissed her on the lips. "Sorry I'm late, it's getting harder and harder to squeeze my workouts in. Your dad can be a real slave driver sometimes."

"Donald!" Susan exclaimed, embarrassed by his remarks about her father and the choice of his words.

"You know what I mean," Donald said, trying to smooth over words.

As he sat next to Susan, he noticed her engagement ring on her hand, something that had been strangely missing in the courtroom earlier in the day.

"I see you're wearing your engagement ring," Donald said, eying the diamond he had purchased and put on her hand only a month before.

"Of course."

"You weren't wearing it in court today."

"Donald, we've talked about this, me being an Assistant District Attorney, and you bringing so many of my daddy's cases to court, it could be seen as a conflict of interest." Susan tried to explain, but only exposed yet another nerve, as Donald's expression changed to one of surprise and disbelief.

"Your daddy's cases!" Donald repeated her words, the agitation evident in both his tone and inflection.

"You know what I mean," Susan said, trying to play off her comments.

"No, I don't, I'm a full partner in your daddy's firm, I would think they're our cases."

"You're right, I'm sorry," Susan said, tying to defuse the situation the best she could.

THE CITY BENEATH THE SEA

Donald was interrupted from pursuing the line of questioning as their waiter walked up.

"Are you ready to order, or do you need more time?" the waiter asked politely.

"I think so, I'll have the veal," Susan said, handing the menu back to the waiter.

"And for you sir?"

"Bring me a steak, medium."

"Very good, Sir."

The waiter left, and Susan and Donald were able to return to their conversation. Susan skillfully changed the subject to something that suited her.

"Mommy found a designer that could do her dress for the wedding, isn't that exciting?" Susan asked, but seeing very little reaction from Donald, realized he did not share in her excitement. "Well, anyway, Mommy asked the designer if she would be able to design one for your Mom, and she said yes! Isn't that great?" Susan concluded, hoping this revelation would muster at least some response from Donald, but the look and response was one she was not expecting.

As Susan shared the news with Donald, his expression became withdrawn, unresponsive. Susan suspected something was wrong, and hoped it wasn't what she feared.

"You did tell them about us, didn't you?" Susan asked, her tone less than polite.

"Not yet."

"What do you mean, not yet! The wedding is only nine months away!" Susan began to explode, but caught herself, bringing her voice down to a harsh whisper.

"I know," Donald acknowledged. "I'm supposed to go down there in a couple of months. I was going to tell them then."

"Ok, I'll go with you."

"No!" The word burst from Donald's mouth without even thinking, then realizing how it must have sounded, tried to amend his remarks. "I mean, it's probably best I ease them into it, you know they're from the old school of thought."

"You mean the school of thought that thinks races should marry within their own race," Susan persistently pressed the topic.

"Yea, something like that."

"Look around you, just about every race is represented, and we're not the only bi-racial couple in here," Susan said, bringing to Donald's attention what he had already observed when he was escorted to his table.

"Yea, but this is New York, not New Orleans, I like to think of ourselves as more progressive up here," Donald explained, but failed to alleviate any of Susan's anxiety. "I'll talk to them, then I'll bring you down," Donald said, trying to find a compromise they both could live with. "They'll love you, they've just got to get used to the idea, that's all."

"All right," Susan reluctantly agreed, still a little anxious about the whole situation. "I love you."

"I love you too," Donald said, just as their food arrived.

THE CITY BENEATH THE SEA

CHAPTER FIFTEEN

In a Baton Rouge bar, William Flyer sat having a drink with a friend. This bar, however, was unlike any bar most heterosexual males would be caught dead in. Anyone who just walked through the door could see something was amiss. Maybe it was the two men dancing together on the dance floor, clasped together in a loving embrace, taking the moment to exchange a passionate kiss. Or maybe the men in dark corners holding hands and doing god knows what would give the uninitiated a clue as to what kind of bar it was.

But one thing was sure, when you entered this bar, there was no mistaking it for anything other than a gay bar.

As William chatted with his new friend, he occasionally glanced at the TV over the bar, and the storm that was bearing down on New Orleans, only sixty miles away.

The thought of being called up for duty began to occupy his thoughts, as he watched helplessly, unable to affect the outcome. But without a doubt in his mind, he would ultimately play a role in the aftermath of this storm.

A captain in the Louisiana National Guard, William struggled with the military's don't ask, don't tell policy towards gays. The thirty-five-year-old officer had served his country in Desert Storm and Iraq, with commendations for valor. No one would ever have suspected the tall, blond-haired, blue-eyed officer was anything other than an all American male. William, however, knew it would only take one slip up. If the military found out about his sexual orientation, he would be discharged; it was that simple, regardless of what he had done in the past. The one blight on his record would destroy an otherwise promising career.

THE CITY BENEATH THE SEA

William's struggle was not unique; he knew other gay men in the military, enlisted men who were not prepared for the close quarters and open living conditions of a military compound. Most were identified quickly the first time they tried to shower, and were unable to control their arousal urge. Similar to what a heterosexual male would face thrown into a shower with ten beautiful, young naked women, these were the easy ones the military could weed out early. What posed the biggest challenge to the military was the people like William; officers who had been able to go unidentified for so many years. These were the people who the military would love to identify.

As William put his arm around his new friend's waist, escorting him out the bar, he wondered how bad the storm would truly be. Having lived in New Orleans for two years, the city held both fond memories of friends he met in the city's large gay community, and also of the tragic heartache he had tried to run away from five years earlier.

As the hours passed and the storm had not yet made landfall, Ferrell roamed the halls, making an occasional visit to the booking office. It was during one of these visits a young African American male was brought in to be processed. Seeing Ferrell, the black man began calling out to him.

"You in charge?" the man yelled.

He was obviously not from around here, the mere asking of the question gave that away. Because if there was one person the black community knew, it was Sheriff Ferrell.

"Yes, son, I'm in charge, what seems to be the problem?" Ferrell asked, his tone soft, his words sincere, as though he wanted to help.

"This officer beat me!" the man complained, as he tried to pull away from the young officer.

THE CITY BENEATH THE SEA

Ferrell looked over to the young officer, recognizing him as the son of one of his original twelve disciples.

"Is this true, Officer!" Ferrell asked in a stern voice, as though demanding to know the truth.

"No, Sheriff, the man fell while fleeing apprehension," the officer offered an excuse for why his apprehended suspect was beaten.

"You're lying!" the man yelled, not willing to stay silent over the injustice that had been perpetrated against him. "Look at the welts!" the man said, motioning to his back and his torn shirt. "They were done with a night stick."

Ferrell examined the welts with great care before finally nodding his head in agreement. "Yes, they do appear to have come from a night stick," Ferrell admitted.

"Now!" the man said, with conviction, feeling vindicated. "What've you got to say about that?" he demanded.

"Well," Ferrell began, then paused, as though trying to choose his words, but his words had already been chosen. "I say you shouldn't have fallen on the officer's night stick," Ferrell said with a smile.

The black man was shocked by Ferrell's response, while the white officers just smiled, knowing what was coming.

It was common knowledge around the white officers that Ferrell took some sort of sadistic pleasure in toying with apprehended suspects. Making them believe he was on their side initially, all the while waiting to slam the cell door shut on them.

Ferrell smiled as he headed back to his office, amused at his torment of the prisoner.

Melanie was awoken by the storm, having fallen asleep on the couch. Any hopes she might have had of

THE CITY BENEATH THE SEA

sleeping through it had now passed. Storms had always worried her, even as a little child; she remembered her dad having to come to her room and reassure her before she would finally submit to exhaustion.

Hurricanes also brought back memories that Melanie would rather try to put behind her. It was during the preparation for a hurricane that Melanie's father lost his life. As a dockworker, it was routine for the workers to secure any loose objects and prepare as best as possible for the approaching storm. While attempting to move a drum, Melanie's father fell off the dock and into the Mississippi. Pulled under by the strong currents of the river, her dad drowned. His body was not found until five days later, downstream at the mouth of the river near Venice. So every time a storm came to the city, so did the memory of the tragic death of her father.

As the storm raged on, Melanie went to the kitchen, hoping to make coffee for the long night she knew she had ahead of her, but the storm had already knocked out the power.

"Great!" Melanie said, "Alone in the dark once more!"

The storm was raging outside; the wind was howling as though warning everyone of what was about to come. Melanie was trying to avoid the windows, but she could not resist looking outside.

As Melanie looked out into the blackened night, she saw trees bent back and forth submitting to the powerful force of the wind. Many branches and small trees lay on the ground, the less fortunate victims of the storm. Melanie watched and waited, hoping the storm would pass quickly, thereby alleviating the anxiety she could not find a way to overcome.

Neatly tucked away in a U-shaped alley, Les and Paul waited as Katrina began to bring her full strength

THE CITY BENEATH THE SEA

to bear. Their patrol car gently rocked as the occasional gust sneaked into the alley, discovering their hideout.

Of all the places Les and Paul could have chosen to ride out the storm, this particular location was not chosen by accident. Across the street, there was a convenience store, the focus of their attention.

The convenience store, like most of the other buildings, was being battered by the high winds. The steel bars covering the door and windows offered only a small measure of protection from flying debris, and virtually no protection from the wind.

"You owe me a hundred bucks," Paul said, lifting up from his reclined position just long enough to sneak a quick glance at the convenience store.

"It's not morning yet," Les countered, still hopeful their man would show.

"You're an optimist," Paul said, pulling his hat down over his eyes. "You want to try to make it back to the station?"

"No, we're safer here, besides my man will show."

The winds were picking up outside, and the storm's full fury began to unleash herself on the dome. The sound was deafening with the dome acting like a giant bell, intensifying the sounds as they bounced off wall after wall, drowning out the cries of the people inside.

LaToya had laid out clothes from her suitcase, making a mat for Jamal and Jameal to lay on, as they somehow slept through the chaos that was all around them.

The Superdome still had power up to this point, and the air conditioning had been able to keep the temperature inside the confined space in a range that was somewhat bearable. This, however, was about to quickly change as the lights, suddenly and without warning, went out, casting the dome into darkness, followed by the fearful screams of its occupants.

The winds pounded the dome's outer shell with gusts hammering against it like a hammer on an anvil, wanting desperately to crack its shell. Finally, the storm's evil hand was able to accomplish what it had sought to do.

No one immediately saw the roof of the dome tear away, but everyone knew something was wrong as the sound suddenly intensified, stirring even the soundest of sleepers. The storm had torn a one-foot wide, six-foot long section of the roof off, allowing rain to pour in; some people panicked not knowing if more of the roof would be ripped away, or if the roof would collapse all together. People began to crowd to the sides gathering their makeshift beds as they went.

LaToya reassured Jamal, who had awoken when the roof of the dome tore away. He was scared, and as LaToya reached for her boys, she felt them trembling. "It'll be alright!" she said, although not fully believing it herself.

Stan and Janelle were awoken by the loud crack of a large oak splintering, then the branch breaking away from the tree, barely missing their house as it slammed to the ground, shaking the house as it landed. Awoken by the fallen tree, Stan looked out the window at the raging storm he had been sleeping through only moments earlier.

It looks really bad. The street is starting to flood, Stan thought, seeing the water covering the street.

Janelle tried to turn on a lamp, but with no luck.

"The power's out," Janelle said, slipping out the bed and feeling around for her robe.

"Wow! This has become more than we expected. It looks like we got a direct hit! I never saw such flooding, not in this area," Stan said, as he looked out the window, again amazed by how much water had accumulated outside.

Gusts of wind shook the house, scaring an already frightened Janelle.

"Stan, I'm scared!" Janelle cried out from the darkness.

"It's ok baby," Stan said, picking up a flashlight from his dresser and turning it on. "I'm right here. Let's get in the center of the house, away from the windows. We'll be safer there."

Stan and Janelle moved to the hall in the center of the house. Stan got blankets and pillows to form a bed, he then lit a candle, extinguishing the flashlight to conserve its battery. Here in their makeshift bunker, Stan and Janelle waited for the storm to pass, feeling as safe as anyone would feel when a killer storm loomed over their head.

It was late when Donald returned home to his spacious New York apartment after having dinner with Susan. His thoughts were full of the day's events. He wondered if Ken Franklin, his DWI client, was out driving around. Would he be able to live with himself if Ken killed someone, knowing he was the one responsible for getting him back on the road? It's easy to say, "I was just doing my job!" But when a mother of a DWI victim looks down on her child's coffin, she couldn't care less about your job diligence.

Also troubling Donald was his forthcoming wedding and the fact that he had never told his parents about Susan. Maybe knowing they would not approve, he wanted to wait to the last possible minute. It wasn't that his parents were racist, far from it, but they did believe that races should marry within their own race. To some, this may seem racist, to others, just good practical advice. One thing was sure, he was going to have to break the news to them, and it would have to be sooner rather than later.

Trying to clear his head, knowing he would not be able to sleep right away, Donald plopped himself on the couch and turned on his big screen plasma TV. Fox News was on the air live, talking about Katrina.

"The expected turn in the path of Katrina away from the Big Easy appears not to have materialized. Katrina is now bearing down on the Big Easy. This cannot be good news for the population of New Orleans who wouldn't or couldn't evacuate. This is a bad one; a category three storm, which means catastrophic destruction in its path,." the newsman concluded.

Donald sat motionless, a surprised look on his face as he felt a sinking feeling coming over him. He knew his parents did not evacuate, they never did. Now somewhere, his parents were bracing themselves for the worst hurricane in decades, and he was powerless to help them. Donald knew about Katrina, it wasn't as though it was a surprise to him. What was a surprise, was the fact that it hadn't turned turn. All preliminary reports projected the storm would turn and make landfall around Alabama.

As Donald continued to watch the storm coverage, the explanation for the change in the projected landfall was the result of the storm's delayed turn. Katrina had turned just as expected, except the turn was several hours later than earlier thought. Thus putting landfall off the coast of Louisiana, rather than Alabama.

Donald picked up the phone and started to dial his parents. He knew it was unlikely he would get through, but he wanted to try. In the past, the combination of jammed switchboards and downed communications centers, made trying to place a call to New Orleans before, during, or after a storm to be a crapshoot. Never knowing if you would get through the first try, or would have to try several times, each time, the message, "I'm sorry, all circuits are busy," burning a spot in your memory.

As Donald waited, he once again got the familiar message he had come to both despise and dread.

"Shoot! The lines are down already!" Donald said, his tone agitated.

Donald picked up the phone and dialed again, but still no answer. He would do this for the next three hours, before finally giving in to the fact there was nothing he could do.

THE CITY BENEATH THE SEA

CHAPTER SIXTEEN

In the Lower Ninth ward, the storm brought to bear its fury, power lines snapped with a loud crack as sparks burst into the darkened night. Trees bent back and forth, each in its own personal battle that would test its resilience against the unseen force determined to bring it to the ground. The sound of the snaps and cracks, as tree after tree submitted to the force of the wind, muffled by the wind's howl.

Waves slapped violently against the moored barges in the industrial canal. They shifted back and forth, trying to adjust to the force of the wind. Their mooring lines pulled taut, testing the strength of each line, stretching them till they could be stretched no farther, and finally pulling apart, sling shooting themselves to the now free vessels.

Carried by the force of the incoming tidal surge, the massive barges drifted down the canal, their momentum slowly increasing, ready to destroy anything that was unfortunate to come in contact with them. Several tons of steel steered by wind and current were heading for the concrete levee, and the unsuspecting residents of the Lower Ninth ward.

Slamming into the concrete levee, which offered little resistance to the massive barges, the levee cracked, spilling tons of water into the Lower Ninth ward. It was slow at first, as the levee only appeared to have been breached, with the barges acting as a cork, helping to hold some of the water back. Then suddenly, without warning, total disaster played its final card, as the levee collapsed completely, pulling the barges through, as millions of gallons of salt water surged through the opening, ready to destroy anything in its path.

Only hours earlier, when Evan crawled into bed, the howling wind and the bending trees could not possibly be viewed as a precursor to what would happen that night.

Many residents of the Lower Ninth ward went to bed without giving a second thought to Katrina. She would be just like the other hurricanes that passed before her. Little did anyone know after that night, the word Katrina would become synonymous with disaster.

In the darkened bedroom, Evan was awoken by the howling wind, but there was something else that stirred his senses.

Something's not right! Evan thought, clearing his head as he tried to fully wake.

The sound of water slapping against the house sent a sudden sense of fear through him. Evan turned on a flashlight he kept on the nightstand, and found himself surrounded by water in his bedroom. Evan knew this amount of water could have only come from one place, and one cause. "The levees have broken!"

Crawling out of bed, Evan's feet landed in the chilly water, which had now risen to his knees and was continuing its rapid rise unabated.

"My goodness!" Evan said, trying to adjust to the sudden chill of the water and the circumstances he now found himself in.

Using his flashlight, Evan peered out the window. His new car was underwater, and the water was continuing to rise; a rapid stream of water flowing past, like rapids in a river, sweeping up everything in its path.

Breathing heavily as fear started to take hold of him, Evan sloshed through the water, for the hideaway stairs leading to the attic. This, he thought would be his only hope. If he were to try to risk going outside, he would surely be swept away in the powerful currents. His only hope, he reasoned, was to get as high as he could, hoping the water would not reach him, and wait for rescue.

THE CITY BENEATH THE SEA

Tucking his flashlight under his arm, Evan pulled down on the hanging string, to the hideaway stairs. Swinging it downward, Evan unfolded the stairs into the now waist-deep water. Trembling now as the chilly water began to lower his core temperature, he could feel his heart racing, fighting to control his fear and keep a cool head; Evan knew this would ultimately be the only way he could survive this ordeal.

As Evan began to ascend into the dark attic, he stopped as though remembering something. Heading back into his bedroom, the beam of the flashlight leading the way, he made for his dresser, retrieving his cell phone, knowing this could very well be his only link to the outside world. Holding it above his head, he headed for the high safety of his dry attic.

At the top of the stairs at the landing of his attic, Evan took a deep breath and tried to gain his composure. The noise of the hurricane blasting against the roof was deafening. Shining the light back into his home, he saw the water's rapid rise continuing to carry in its wake the personal possessions that had taken Evan a lifetime of hard work and sacrifice to obtain. Evan realized that the water would ultimately destroy everything. As the light shone down from the attic opening, he caught a glimpse of a photo of his deceased wife. Running down the stairs without giving it a second thought, he retrieved the photo off the wall, knowing it could never be replaced.

All his photos, all the memories of his life, the children's photos, marriage certificates, documents; everything would be lost. Realizing there was nothing else he could safely save, Evan settled for the picture of his wife, not wanting to risk his life over objects and property he probably could not save anyway.

Where is all the water coming from? Evan thought, but already knowing it could have only come from the levees.

THE CITY BENEATH THE SEA

Evan looked down the stairs, as the water reached a new high of just below the ceiling, thereby permanently sealing his fate.

Evan started to scurry about, he would have to break through the attic if the water got any higher. Shining the flashlight around the attic, he could find nothing that he could use to break through. Evan had hoped the water would find its level and stop rising, but this was not to be the case as the waters rose higher and higher. With water now at his ankles and continuing to rise, Evan opened his cell phone and dialed 911.

"911, what is your emergency?" the operator asked, her voice even, measured with no emotion.

"I'm about ready to drown. The water is rising so fast, I'm trapped in my attic. Can you send help?" Evan pleaded into the phone.

"What's your location?" the operator asked, trying to obtain as much pertinent information as possible.

"138 N. Galvez, Lower Ninth ward," Evan said, as he tried to balance himself on the rafters of the attic while holding onto a cell phone and a flashlight.

"Ok, sir, we'll try to get someone out there," the operator said, trying to reassure Evan.

"Please hurry!"

Inside the 911 office, it was a beehive of activity, phones were ringing off the wall. Latanya Jones, Evan's operator, began to hang her head and cry.

Latanya, a large African American female bordering on obese, had always had a heart equal to her size. Always compassionate and sensitive towards people, her personality was what had gotten her selected over so many other candidates for the job. On the job for only a week, she was getting baptized by the fire of Katrina.

THE CITY BENEATH THE SEA

Always slow to show too much emotion, the overwhelming suffering that was going on in the city was proving more than she could handle. Call after call had began to pour into the office, with each and every emergency call, lives hung in the balance.

With every call Latanya answered, it was as though she could feel their pain, their desperation, a sense of hopelessness that she could detect in their voices. She wanted so much to somehow reach out through the phone lines and rescue them, stop their screaming and pleas.

As Latanya struggled with the calls, she would have no way of knowing how this moment in time would affect her for the rest of her life. The sleepless nights, the voices of the victims forever etched in her memory. This one night would haunt Latanya for the rest of her life.

She would ultimately seek counseling and therapy, for the voices that she could never expel from her mind, but nothing would help. Unable to cope, Latanya's life would ultimately spiral downwards until it found the train wreck that would finally end her suffering. Overdosing on heroin, Latanya would finally silence the voices that had haunted her, and become yet another victim of Katrina. That would be much later, for now, Latanya had to wrestle with the present.

Latanya's supervisor came up behind her, putting his hand on her shoulder, trying to comfort her and give her support. Everybody was overwhelmed, both by the number of calls and the emotions they were fighting to control.

"Another Ninth Ward caller?" the supervisor asked, already knowing the answer.

Latanya nodded her head, as she tried to compose herself enough to talk.

"They're dying and I can't do anything for them!" Latanya burst out.

THE CITY BENEATH THE SEA

"The only thing we can do is answer as many calls as we can, and offer as much hope as you can," the supervisor said, explaining to Latanya their objective for the night.

"I've been answering calls for an hour, are we going to rescue any of them?" Latanya asked.

"No one's available, everyone is becoming rapidly overwhelmed. We're also getting reports of levee failure at the 17th Street canal. The levees are giving way and there's nothing we can do about it!" the supervisor said, starting to elevate his monotone voice with emotion, but then catching himself.

"So I'm giving them false hope!" Latanya asked, trying to make sense of what she was doing,

"You're giving them hope, and that might just give them enough strength to hang on. Hope is hope, there's nothing false about that," the supervisor concluded, then walked away to another operator.

Latanya regained her composure and answered a call, her voice even, clear, unemotional, giving no indication of what she had gone through only moments earlier.

The water had risen to Evan's chest, showing no signs of stopping. He franticly struck against the inside of his roof with both kicks and blows from his fists. The nails from the shingles that broke through the wood pierced his hands as he delivered blow after blow with both hands and feet at the walls, which were quickly forming the sides of his coffin.

No longer able to touch the floor joists, he used the rafters to help support himself. In desperation, he dialed 911 again. Amazingly enough, his phone still worked.

"911, what is your emergency, how can I help?" LaTanya once again received Evan's phone call, in the back of her mind wondering what the odds of that was, with several other operators taking calls.

"I'm trapped in my attic, the water is rising, I don't have much time left. You're not going to make it here in time!" Evan said, only now beginning to come to terms with what lay ahead. A sense of calm came over Evan as he looked at his wife's picture, realizing he would soon be with her.

"What's your name?" Evan asked, his voice calm.

"Latanya," her voice cracked as she said her name, and tried to fight back tears. Knowing her voice was the last voice the person she never met would ever hear.

"Are you a Christian, Latanya?" Evan asked, dropping his wife's photo as he struggled to keep his head above water.

"Yes, I am."

"Can I ask you one last favor, Latanya?" Evan asked, tears starting to form in his eyes as he accepted his fate.

"Yes, sir, what can I do?" Latanya asked, fighting every emotional urge in her body to keep herself from bursting into tears once again.

"Would you pray for me?" Evan asked, his voice starting to crack with a sense of sadness as he said the words.

Latanya finally lost it and started to cry, unable to put up a positive, hopeful façade any longer.

Pulling himself to the crown of the attic, the highest part that still trapped air, Evan knew he had little time left.

"It's ok, Latanya, I'm at peace with this. God is a great and powerful God, all this is happening for a reason. I've got to go, the water is too high," Evan said, pausing for a moment then remembering one last thing he forgot to tell her. "Latanya?"

"I'm here!"

THE CITY BENEATH THE SEA

"Thank you," Evan said, the last words Latanya would hear as the phone went dead.

Inside the attic, Evan struggled to stay above the water, releasing the cell phone as he tried desperately to cling to the rafters. As the water finally rose above his head, Evan struggled and fought, trying desperately to cling to life, but finally succumbed to his fate, and drowned in his attic as Katrina claimed another life.

THE CITY BENEATH THE SEA

CHAPTER SEVENTEEN

After a while, the worst of the storm had passed, leaving only the occasional wind gust behind.

Les looked over to Paul, who was sound asleep. "Amazing," Les thought. "This guy can sleep through anything.

Les was just about to give up on the convenience store stakeout, when from the shadows, an African American male appeared.

Seeing their man, Les reached over and nudged Paul. A groggy Paul awoke just as the young male removed a brick he had hidden in his hooded sweatshirt.

"Damn!" said Paul, seeing what was about to go down. "There goes my hundred bucks."

The young man threw the brick at the convenience store window, shattering the glass, then he quickly pulled the metal bars which had already been loosened by time and the storm. Squeezing between the bars and the door, he disappeared inside.

Les and Paul rushed to the convenience store with guns drawn. After a few moments, the burglar slowly emerged from the building with a six-pack of beer in his hands and a surprised look on his face.

Repeat, as he was known on the street, was cursed with a combination of stuttering and a habit of repeating what people asked him, thus earning him his nickname.

Only sixteen, Repeat's tall muscular stature often misled others into thinking he was much older. An alcoholic, and high school drop-out, Repeat had continuously found himself in and out of trouble with the law; in every case, the crime usually involved alcohol. Either he was trying to steal alcohol or he was intoxicated while committing a crime to get money for alcohol.

THE CITY BENEATH THE SEA

Having arrested Repeat several times before, Les and Paul were very aware of his tendency for an easy mark, and he was a creature of habit. During the last two voluntary evacuations of the city, Repeat had tried to take advantage of the opportunity. Knowing the shop owners would evacuate, he thought the convenience store would be easy to break into. Knowing there would be no cash on hand did not matter to Repeat. What would be on hand and what he prized was alcohol, and the convenience store housed plenty of it.

Through the years, having been broken into so many times, the owner had tried to deter criminals by increasing his security efforts, surveillance cameras, alarms systems, and finally, security bars. All these things deterred, as they were intended, but never stopped the break-ins. Taking reports from the store owners had become so routine for Les and Paul, they were able to start the paperwork before they had even arrived on location, knowing all the pertinent information by heart.

"Put your hands up!" Les ordered, his gun trained on the burglar.

"Put my hands up!" Repeat said, shocked that his carefully thought-out plan had gone array.

Les looked at Paul and smiled, "Here we go again."

"Put your hands up!" Paul yelled, his voice more gruff, more hostile, hoping it would make a difference.

"Put my hands up!" Repeat once again repeated the order.

"Yes!" Les yelled, his patience and professionalism being tested to the max.

"Ok, no problem, don't be going all Rodney King on me! I'm not resisting," Repeat said, then removing a beer from his six-pack, he quickly popped it open, and began to guzzle its contents.

THE CITY BENEATH THE SEA

"Can you believe this guy?" Les said, holstering his weapon. He and Paul rushed over to Repeat and grabbed him, bringing him to the ground.

"If I'm going to jail, can I at least finish my beer?" Repeat asked, not really believing the officers would go for it.

"If you can drink it with handcuffs!" Paul said, his tone a little perturbed.

"Can I try?"

As they escorted Repeat back to the car, Paul could not resist sharing his opinion with Repeat. "You must be the dumbest criminal in the world! Every time the city evacuates for a storm, you rob this store. You're an idiot and you cost me a hundred bucks!"

Les smiled as they placed Repeat in the back of the patrol car, fighting the urge to tell his partner, "I told you so!"

No sooner did they sit down in the patrol car, the radio began calling for them.

"Dispatch to Unit 23," the radio crackled, the reception distorted, probably from the storm knocking down a repeater.

Les picked up the mic, "This is Unit 23."

"Please respond to 17th Street canal, we have reports of a levee breaking," the dispatcher announced.

Les and Paul looked at each other in disbelief, not immediately knowing what to think of the dispatch.

After a couple more moments and more confused stares, Les finally answered. "10-4."

"The levees breaking?" Paul repeated what the dispatcher had shared with them.

"She must have meant they were toppling over."

"We'll know soon enough," Les said, putting the car in gear and heading toward the levee.

As they drove, the occasional shake of their patrol car reminded them of what the building had sheltered them from. The shelter of the buildings had given them the false impression that the storm was over, but on the open interstate, they could feel and see the wind gusts whipping away at awning, and lifting loose debris airborne, transforming their once mundane purpose into lethal projectiles.

Undeterred, Les continued towards the 17th Street canal.

THE CITY BENEATH THE SEA

CHAPTER EIGHTEEN

Les drove towards West End. As he came onto West End Boulevard, he immediately knew something was seriously wrong; the boulevard had begun to flood. In all his years on the force, he had never seen flooding like this.

"Unit 23 to dispatch," Les called into the radio, trying not to seem too panicked over what he had just found.

"Dispatch," the crackling reply came back.

"We've got a problem, West End is starting to flood, I don't know where all the water is coming from, it looks like more than toppling over," Les said, informing dispatch of the status of the area he was sent to respond to.

"Are you at the 17th Street canal levee?" the dispatch questioned.

"Not yet."

"We need eyes on that levee to see what the damage is," the dispatcher informed Les of their new mission.

"10-4 heading that way," Les said, returning the mic to its cradle.

"You ever see so much water before?" Paul asked, also taken back by the severity of the flooding.

"No, I haven't."

As Les drove down the street, the water was almost high enough to come inside the patrol car, but with specific orders, Les pressed on, creating a wake as he drove.

Turning down Cypress Street, Les headed towards the 17th Street canal levee. It wasn't long, however, before the water became deeper and faster, pushing its way around the car like a rushing stream would pass around a rock.

THE CITY BENEATH THE SEA

Switching his bright lights on, Les and Paul were able to see into the far distance. There up ahead, water was pouring out of a narrow gash in the levee. It appeared like two French doors had been partially opened as the surge of water flowed towards the patrol car.

Les's facial expression dropped, he knew the severity of the situation, if that wall gave way, everyone in this area would be underwater! Les picked up the mic and immediately called dispatch with the terrifying news.

"The levees didn't top over!" Les cried, "They're giving way!"

"Dispatch this is Unit 23!"

"Go ahead, Unit 23," the crackling voice came through, growing fainter and fainter with every transmission.

"The 17th Street canal levee is broken. I repeat, the 17th Street canal concrete levee has water rushing through it. It's only about a three-foot section, but it could give way anytime!" Les informed the dispatcher of the severity of the situation.

"Get out of there!" the dispatcher said. "Find some high ground!"

Les thought only a moment of the irony of the dispatcher's remarks. "High ground, in a City Beneath the Sea!"

As Les started to put it in reverse, he realized that the people in many of these houses were not aware of the imminent danger that had arisen in addition to the storm.

"We need to warn these people!" Les said, throwing the car back in park.

"You take the right side, I'll take the left, let them know what's going on. That's all we can do," Les said, as he flipped on his lights and sirens hoping the noise would awaken the area. "They'll have to save themselves if this thing goes!" Les said, climbing out of the car and into the water, followed by Paul.

Repeat looked out from the back of the patrol car, anxious that he was alone. He saw the two officers run towards the houses. He thought they would remember him in the car and come back for him, but they did not.

"Officers! Officers!" Repeat called, but there was no-one around to hear his pleas.

Looking out the front windshield of the patrol car, the bright lights were still on, shining on the distant break. Repeat pulled at his handcuffs, desperately trying to free himself, but to no avail. His fate, like so many others in the city this night, had also been sealed.

Les and Paul banged on door after door, remaining only long enough for lights to come on before heading to the next residence.

Suddenly, a loud noise was heard, almost like a roar as the levee gave way, sending thousands of gallons of water rushing through, removing any obstacle in its way.

Repeat looked out the front windshield of the patrol car, he saw the wall of water rushing towards him. He continued to struggle with his handcuffs. Flesh had been ripped away and he was bleeding profusely as he pulled away at the steel restraint.

The water slammed through the front windshield, and carried the patrol car down the street. Any hope of escape disappeared, as the disoriented Repeat gasped for air, but found only water.

Les only now realized that in the excitement and confusion, he had forgotten Repeat in the rear of the patrol car. He started to head back to the car, just as it went careering down the street.

The wall of water slammed into the patrol car lifting it and sending it sideways, then rolled it along its path of destruction. Les knew there was no way Repeat would be able to escape the patrol car, which had now become his tomb.

THE CITY BENEATH THE SEA

With the water rising rapidly to the front doors of the area's homes, the force of the water began to pull on Les, threatening to drag him away in its destructive fury. Looking across the street, Paul had already kicked in a door trying to escape the deadly torrents of water. Just as Les was about to follow suit, an older man opened the door, allowing the officer to escape inside and the waters begin to rush into the house. Les pushed hard on the door trying to secure it, to possibly buy themselves a little more time.

"Officer!" the old man said, seeing what was taking place outside his door for the first time.

"Quick, get your family up and get them up stairs!" Les ordered.

Les, out of sheer luck, was fortunate, enough to have found shelter in a two-storey house.

"Everyone's upstairs!" the old man informed Les, obviously shaken.

"Good, that's where we're going! After you!"

The old man quickly made his way up the stairs with Les close behind.

Sarah King was awoken, not by the wind or the raging storm. At her age, she had seen it all, and over the years, had become able to sleep through most things.

But what stirred Sarah was not the howl of the wind, but the the cries of people screaming and the shouts of loud voices.

Sitting up in her bed, Sarah looked out the window. A lightning flash illuminated the area for only a moment, but long enough to cause a chill to go up her spine.

Outside, where the lawn once was, water now covered every inch of the nursing home lawn, and judging from the height of the water, she could tell it had made its way inside. Looking down from her bed confirmed her suspicions as about two and a half feet of water was now in her room and rising quickly.

"Well, I know why people are screaming," Sarah reasoned, as she slid out of bed and into the chilly waters, searching for her walker.

Looking out the window, movement caught Sarah's eye, causing her to focus more intently on what she thought she had seen.

There fleeing for their lives were the facility nurses and orderlies, running out of the nursing home in a panic, fighting the surging water that was rushing in.

Reaching for her walker, Sarah tried to make it to her door, sliding her walker through the water as she went. Finally reaching the door, she tried the handle, but it would not turn. *My God! They've locked us in!* was Sarah's first thought, the sight of the nursing home personnel fleeing still fresh on her mind.

Not willing to give up, Sarah used both hands to turn the knob, using the doorknob to help stabilize her wobbling legs. Suddenly, and to Sarah's surprise , the door burst open followed by a surge of water, which quickly filled the room equal to the height of the water outside the window, knocking Sarah off her feet and throwing her against the distant wall.

Struggling to regain her footing, and gasping for air after having swallowed some water, Sarah was able to climb back to her feet with the help of her bed. In the darkness, she could hear screams for help coming from the hall. Some were screaming, others crying and begging for help that would not come.

The water continued to rise, moving towards the ceiling. Sarah struggled to keep her footing, but her legs were too weak; she would not give up easily, exhausting every ounce of her strength. Finally exhausted by the struggle, and unable to escape, Sarah slowly slipped below the rising water. Bubbles appeared for a few moments, then there were none.

THE CITY BENEATH THE SEA

Inside Stan's house, he and Janelle slept peacefully in the hall. Having only been able to get a little rest after the storm had begun to subside, Stan awoke first, rolling off his makeshift mattress in the hall, trying not to disturb Janelle.

The storm had passed, and the loud deafening sound along with it. Going to his living room window, Stan looked out onto his lawn. What was once a well-manicured lawn now had branches and broken limbs scattered upon it.

Going to the kitchen, Stan tried the light switch, hoping but knowing the power would probably be out; he was right, no power.

"Dodged another one," Stan thought as he sat down in his recliner.

The high-pitched sound of William's beeper going off stirred him to his feet. Quickly reading the message, he had been called up for duty. With the threat of civil unrest looming on the horizon, it was determined by the powers that be to have his unit ready for a rapid deployment to New Orleans if the need should arise.

"I've got to go," William told the man who he escorted from the bar last night, that now lay in his bed. "I've been called up."

"Time for you to go play soldier?" the man asked jokily.

"Something like that," William said, not cracking a smile. If there was one thing he took very serious, it was his job.

Seeing the man was slow to move, William pulled the covers off him, exposing his naked body. "Get up, get dressed, and get out!" William ordered. The man, seeing how serious he was, began to comply.

THE CITY BENEATH THE SEA

LaToya awoke the next morning as thousands of people began to stir around her. Looking up, LaToya could see the massive tear that the storm had ripped away during the night, sending scores of frightened evacuees running for cover. With the electricity still out, the only source of light to illuminate the entire dome came from the tear in the roof, which doubled as the only source of ventilation.

The foul odor that had began to be released during the night had grown stronger and stronger, the unmistakable smell of raw sewage now filled the air. Sometime during the night, the sewage had backed up, and began sending its foul odor into the unventilated heat of the Superdome, adding one more element to the unbearable conditions, which had been quickly deteriorating.

In the distance, LaToya could see the crowd moving to the exits, hopefully she thought they may be going home soon. But as the crowd began to pack up and then disperse, her hopes were quickly dashed. Her main focus now was giving the boys something to eat and drink; she would learn soon enough about the situation the storm had left the city in.

It was not until an older man came by that LaToya was able to get a little information on what was going on. Eavesdropping as he talked to some ladies farther down, she was able to find out at least a little of what was going on outside the dome. Not knowing it would not be the news she wanted to hear, her fears were once again renewed.

"The storm's passed," the old man informed the ladies camped out not far from LaToya. His voice was agitated and loud enough so she could hear without any trouble.

"But they're not letting anyone leave!" the old man continued. "The whole area is flooded, they say we're

THE CITY BENEATH THE SEA

safer here. They don't have food and water for us, but they won't let us leave. They say help is on the way."

Overhearing the man's message, she quickly inventoried the meager supplies she had brought. A bottle of water and some crackers was all she had.

I wonder how long it will truly be before help arrives, LaToya wondered.

Looking out among the thousands of faces, she knew the greater challenge may not be in making her meager supplies last, but in keeping them.

If help doesn't arrive soon, desperation along with a basic survival instinct will kick in. It could get bad, in here, LaToya reasoned, *very bad.*

THE CITY BENEATH THE SEA

CHAPTER NINETEEN

Les sat on the balcony of the two-storey house he had burst into the night before. The water had totally engulfed the first floor, bringing the balcony just above water level. Looking out at a sea of water, Les could only see rooftops as a visual reminder that houses were there under all the water.

Across the way, in another two-storey house, Paul also sat and waited. Trying to place a call on his cell phone, but the frustration in his look and mannerisms indicated he was not having much luck.

Hearing the sound of a small boat in the distance, Les focused his attention in the direction of the sound. A small boat moved towards him, though the boat operator had not spotted him at this point. Les grabbed a shirt he found inside the house, and returning to the balcony he began to wave it, trying to draw attention to himself.

"Officer, need a lift?" the boat operator asked as he pulled alongside the balcony.

"Please, and thank you," Les said, making sure to express his gratitude. "My partner is across the way. How many can you take?"

"You two for now," the boat owner informed Les. "I'll come back for more later."

"Ok," Les said, he then stuck his head inside the house, "I'm going to take this boat, you should be ok up here, another boat is on the way."

"Go!" the old man said, waving him on. "You're needed elsewhere!"

Les climbed into the boat and headed towards Paul, who climbed in without hesitation.

"Cell phone's down!" were the first words out of Paul's mouth as he took his seat in the boat. "Can't reach Gina!"

THE CITY BENEATH THE SEA

Turning to his rescuer, Paul inquired as to the extent of the damage, overlooking the obvious.

"How bad is it?" Paul asked.

"Pretty bad!" their rescuer began to bring them up to speed. "Several levees have broken, the city is underwater. Plaquemine Parish has been wiped out, along with Slidell."

"Slidell!" Paul burst out, wanting his rescuer to elaborate more.

"Slidell was hit really hard," their rescuer continued. "All those marinas, there are boats all over the place, houses destroyed, even some reports of bodies in the streets."

Paul looked at Les, it was apparent to Les what was on his mind.

"Gina!" Paul finally said, his emotions on the verge of breaking down.

"I'm sure she's ok," Les said, trying to make a feeble attempt at reassuring him. However, looking around to the devastation they passed as they headed for higher ground, he knew the daunting task they faced was bigger than just one person.

"I can't get in touch with her," Paul explained further, just as the boat came to what was once an overpass, and slid to a stop.

Jumping out, Les and Paul headed to a command center van that had been stationed nearby. Les recognized the officer in charge. William Steel, was a big white man, standing six feet three inches tall and every bit of three hundred pounds. His size alone would gain respect and attention. Les found Steel giving orders and directions as an orchestra leader would. Calmly yet forcefully, he was in his element, he shined in this type of crisis.

"What can we do?" Les said, reporting to Steel.

"Les! Paul! Glad to see you. A hell of a mess we've got here, communications down, people stranded all over the place. Coast Guard and National guards are on their way. We just need to hold on until they get here," Steel explained the status of their situation.

"Hold on!" Paul interjected after Steel had concluded. "I've got to get to Slidell!"

"That might be tough," Steel began to explain. "The storm took down the twin span, the Causeway is damaged, and we don't know the status of I-55."

"I'll go around to Baton Rouge if I have to!" Paul said, "I need to get to my fiancée!"

Steel looked hard at Paul, agitated he wanted to leave.

"What the hell are you talking about?" Steel barked, "Look around you, these people need our help! They have rescue workers in Slidell! They will help your fiancée! We need you here!"

"I'm sorry, I've got to go!" Paul said, then turned away, disappearing into the crowds that had already been rescued. Les started after him, but was stopped by Steel.

"Let him go," Steel said, "I don't need two of you deserting me."

Reluctantly Les stayed, he knew he was needed here, but a part of him wanted to run after his friend and knock some sense into him.

"Where do you need me?" Les said, committing to stay.

"The Superdome," Steel said, "the last text I got, they were being overwhelmed."

"Text?" Les repeated, confused by what Steel had just said.

"Yea," Steel said, then began to explain. "Damn cell phones are down, but the text messaging still works. It's the only way we have to communicate."

"I'll be darned!" Les said, wondering if Paul had tried this, or if he even knew about it.

"That rescue boat will take you as close as he can to the Superdome, good luck!" Steel said, shaking hands with Les as he left.

THE CITY BENEATH THE SEA

"Thanks," Les said, then headed for the waiting boat.

Quiana and her sister Kirra watched the events in New Orleans as they began to unfold. Live broadcasts by Fox News from on the scene brought the aftermath of Katrina into everyone's home. Visual images of people on roof tops, on overpasses, people looting, vandalizing, ripping the thin fabric of law and order to shreds.

Timmy walked in catching Quiana and her sister by surprise, as she hastily turned off the TV.

"What is it, baby?" Quiana asked, as she went to him.

"I'm thirsty."

"You go back to your room, I'll bring you some water," Quiana said, as Timmy nodded and returned to his room.

"I sure hope Les is Ok," Quiana said, only now sharing her fears with her sister.

"Superman?" Kirra replied sarcastically. "Please, the only thing that can stop him is kryptonite."

"I hope you're right," Quiana said, getting a glass of water and heading towards Timmy's room. "It looks pretty bad down there."

Inside Donald's apartment, it was very early morning. He was busy packing a couple of suitcases. Tossing clothes in the bags for what seemed to the casual observer to be an extended stay.

In his bedroom, the TV was on, covering the rapidly unfolding events of Hurricane Katrina live.

Katrina had made landfall, delivering a direct hit to the Big Easy. The city known for its historic sights and good times would forever be known as the site of the nation's worst natural disaster. Early reports were sketchy, but Katrina hit New Orleans with a one

THE CITY BENEATH THE SEA

hundred and seventy-five mile per hour, category five force. But it was not the wind damage that had the people most concerned. Would they be able to stand up to the massive storm surge that threatened to top the levees.

Donald turned off the TV, grabbed his bags and headed out the door.

Outside his apartment, the moon still shone into the night sky as Donald hailed a cab and climbed inside, placing his bags on the seat next to him.

"JFK please," Donald said, as the driver nodded.

"You got it!" The driver acknowledged in a middle eastern dialect.

As they headed for the airport, the radio played various songs from the sixties and seventies, all of which Donald found very interesting as a music of choice to someone with an obvious Middle Eastern heritage.

After a couple of songs, the news came on, the topic, Hurricane Katrina.

"Hurricane Katrina has wreaked havoc on the city of New Orleans," the newsman began. "Even after a mandatory evacuation, there are still thousands of people in the city. The potential for a catastrophic disaster the likes of which this country has never seen is beginning to unfold. Levees have failed and the city is beginning to fill with water."

Donald leaned back in his seat. Obviously stressed, he pulled out his cell phone and flipped it open, scanning the contacts until he found home, he pressing the button again, like he had so many times during the night. Deep down, he knew the result would be the same.

"We're sorry, all circuits are busy now, please try again later," the familiar voice came on the phone.

Pulling up to JFK, Donald paid the driver and exited the cab with his bags. As the cab pulled away, Donald wasted no time heading into the terminal; his pace quick, his demeanor that of a person in a hurry. Donald was a man on a mission.

Arriving at the ticket counter, a middle-aged woman with a big smile greeted him, ready to assist him.

"Hello, how can I help you?" the cheerful attendant asked, contrasting Donald's somber mood.

"I need to get to New Orleans," Donald said, very business-like, without a smile in sight.

"You're kidding right?" the cheerful attendant asked.

"No I'm not, next available please!" Donald said, his tone removing any possibility that this was a joke.

The attendant tapped away at the keyboard searching for all available flights, but finding none, she gave Donald the bad news.

"I'm sorry, all flights to New Orleans have been cancelled."

"When's the next flight?" Donald asked persistently.

"We don't have any scheduled. A hurricane just hit down there."

"I know, that's why I got to get there, my parents are in New Orleans. I need to get to them," Donald explained, only now making any sense to the attendant.

"I'm sorry, no flights to New Orleans, there's not a whole lot I can do."

"What's the closest you can get me?" Donald asked, thinking if he could get close enough he could rent a car and drive the rest of the way.

"I can get you to Houston via Chicago. But there's a layover in Chicago."

"I'll take it!" Donald said, jumping at the possibly of getting a little closer to Louisiana.

The attendant began to type the information in the computer, and printed out the tickets.

"Checking two bags?"

THE CITY BENEATH THE SEA

"Yes," Donald said, confirming the obvious as he placed the bags on the scales, the attendant placed a tag on them, then puts it on a conveyer belt.

"Just need to see some ID and you'll be all set," the attendant said, holding his tickets in her hand.

Producing a driver's license, Donald handed it to the attendant.

"Thank you Mr. King. Gate B-17."

"Thank you," Donald said, mustering his first smile of the night, and headed for security to begin the arduous security screening.

THE CITY BENEATH THE SEA

CHAPTER TWENTY

As Les's boat approached the dome, he was not prepared for what he saw. Thousands of people were around the walk-around apron, with more arriving every minute. Les knew the dome had been designated as a refuge of last resort, but far more people had arrived than anyone could have possibly expected.

Hopping out the boat as it neared the dome, Les waded through the knee-deep water with the newly arrived refugees, some coming with just the clothes on their backs, others carrying their belonging in garbage bags. Each one with a common goal in mind, to get to some place dry.

Heading up the ramp to the main entrance, Les looked for the Captain. The crowds did not make it any easier, as the disorganized chaos seemed to have no-one in charge at all. Finally, after looking for several minutes Les spotted the Captain on a military field phone.

As Les approached, he could see the Captain was not happy, as he screamed into the field phone.

"I don't care if he's the President of the United States! You don't let anyone commandeer your vehicle!" the Captain yelled, far more angry than Les had ever seen him before. Slamming the receiver in its holder, the Captain now turned his attention to Les.

"You all right, Captain?" Les asked, with a smile, more so to inquire about the conversation than his well-being.

"Damn State Representative had the balls to commandeer one of my trucks to take him to his house to get money out of his freezer! What kind of crooked bastard keeps money in his freezer?" the Captain shouted, getting upset all over again. "Anyway, glad to see you Les. Where's Paul?"

"It's a long story, what's the situation here?" Les

asked trying to change the subject, not wanting to explain Paul going awol, and not really knowing how.

"Desperate!" the Captain began to explain. "The dome now has thousands of people inside with no air-conditioning, no water, the sewage is backing up and there doesn't seem to be any relief in sight. I got old people, young, sick, and people dying, with more arriving every hour," the Captain finally concluded, trying not to show the frustration and helplessness he felt, but somehow it came through in his explanation.

"You have any good news?" Les asked, trying to bring a little levity to the situation.

"Yea," the Captain said. "Katrina left us one hell of a skylight."

"What do you want me to do?" Les asked, ready to jump in wherever he could help.

"Here, take this," the Captain said, handing Les a flashlight. "I want you to patrol the dome for now, I want people to see a police presence. As the days go on, people are going to be more and more on edge and desperate," the Captain explained, trying to prepare Les for the worst possible scenario.

"Days?" Les repeated, surprised by the Captain's comment. "How long are we going to be here?"

"Hopefully, the Guard will get here and begin to evacuate these people out of here. But we have thousands of people here that we are going to have to ferry through water. It's going to take some time," the Captain explained, then continued. "When they get here, maybe they'll free us up to address the needs of the city."

"What do you mean?" Les asked, not having been privy to news reports he was totally unaware of what was going on in the city.

"People are going crazy!" the Captain said, "Looting, vandalizing, murders, and rapes. There are reports of roving gangs terrorizing people. I've got some men deployed in the Quarter, hopefully that will help."

THE CITY BENEATH THE SEA

"Where's the rest of the police force?" Les asked, knowing the city had enough police to put down any disorder that may occur.

"That's the really sad part, I can't tell you how many officers have simply abandoned their posts and taken off!" the Captain said, visibly saddened by his men's unexpected departure.

Les was saddened also, but on a more personal note. He thought about his partner, a brave officer who had always performed his duty. Would he now be haunted by his impulsive act for the rest of his life?

"Ok Captain, I'll get started," Les said, heading into the dome.

No sooner did Les break the threshold's entrance, the odor of the building got his attention. The backed up sewage reeked, making it almost unbearable for him to continue; he wondered how so many people could endure the heat and the smell.

Continuing on, Les approached one of the restrooms that had backed up. It was a sight that he would reflect on over and over again, unable to get the sights and smells out of his mind.

Entering the restroom, shining the light as he went, Les saw toilet paper scattered about, mixed in with human waste, causing an overpowering smell which almost made Les physically sick. In the stall, Les tried to flush one of the toilets, but nothing happened. "No water!" Les discovered. Unable to alleviate the problem, Les left the restroom and continued his rounds.

Walking through the dome, the only light source were flashlights and the large gash in the dome's roof. Shining his light as he walked, Les could hear the cries and moans of suffering people. No training could possibly prepare him for such an overwhelming experience. The rock hard façade Les had perpetuated over the years began to crack, as the officer fought back tears. Never in his life had he experienced such a scene.

THE CITY BENEATH THE SEA

CHAPTER TWENTY-ONE

A sense of calm had momentarily settled around Melanie's house when she awoke. Exhausted from her all-night vigil, she had been able to dose off in a chair.

The early morning tranquility would not last, as a gang of black youths passed her house. Shouting loud obscenities, the gang of ten carried sticks and bats, ready to beat down anyone who would challenge them.

But what really alarmed Melanie, was the fact that a couple of the thugs were carrying guns!

Melanie checked her locks, and tried the phone, but it was dead. Going to the kitchen island, she retrieved her cell phone, but it too did not have a signal. A cold chill came over her as she realized just how alone she really was.

Inside his Algiers' office, Ferrell watched the live TV coverage of a city gone mad. Looters in New Orleans were breaking windows, prying open doors, all on the premise that they needed food and water.

With law and order in the city collapsing, partially because so many of the New Orleans police force had abandoned their posts, looters and thugs were free to reap whatever havoc they saw fit on the helpless city.

"Not here!" Ferrell yelled, his blood boiling, as he watched two looters carrying a big screen TV down the street. "Food and water, my ass!" Ferrell said, then headed to the Desk Sergeant's desk.

"I want you to put a patrol car on the bridge!" Ferrell ordered, obviously agitated. "Turn back anyone who tries to cross. Keep the rest of the force on patrol. If they see any looting, I want it dealt with in the harshest manner possible. They're not going to do to our city what they're doing to New Orleans!" Ferrell yelled, then stormed back to his office.

THE CITY BENEATH THE SEA

Listening to a portable radio, Stan and Janelle were shocked by what they were hearing, as the radio announcer brought the listeners up to speed with the aftermath of Katrina.

"Coast Guards and various government agencies continue their rescue operations," the newsman said. "Unconfirmed reports are in that the industrial canal levee has been breached, along with the entire Ninth Ward levees. Reports coming in, report the entire Ninth Ward is under water."

"Oh God! EVAN!" Janelle cried, visibly upset from the announcement.

Stan sat silent, but the look on his face said much more than words. He was saddened, as though he somehow knew his brother was dead.

"St. Bernard and all of Plaquemine Parish is under water," the news continued, as Stan and Janelle tried to comprehend what was happening to their city. "Communication to these areas are non-existent. The tidal surge has also wreaked havoc on the north shore. Early reports put the damage in the millions. Looting is also quickly becoming a problem, with so many people out of the city and with the police engaged in rescue operations, the streets have rapidly become the domain of many gangs. There are widespread reports of looting, rapes, and vandalism. The Mayor is asking everyone to stay indoors as night begins to fall on the city, it's going to be a long night."

Turning off the radio, Stan reached for the phone but it was still dead.

"The levees broke!" Stan said, "I can't believe it! The Lower Ninth is underwater, 17th Street canal broke. If they don't plug that up soon, we're all going to be underwater."

"You heard what he said about the roaming gangs?" Jarelle asked, obviously not sharing the same concerns as Stan. "I'm scared. The police are all tied up in rescue efforts, they can't help us."

"Don't worry, I'll dig out the shotgun from the closet, we'll be fine. It's not as bad as they're making it out to be. They do that for sensationalism."

Looking out the window, Stan for the first time was beginning to see the water on his lawn. He knew the water was rising and there was nothing they could do about it. He kept this information to himself, not wanting to alarm Janelle anymore than necessary, as they prepared themselves for the long night ahead.

THE CITY BENEATH THE SEA

CHAPTER TWENTY-TWO

Heading towards Metairie, Paul followed the crowds over the 17th Street canal overpass. Looking down onto the canal, he could get a much better view of the extent of the damage to the levee. Tons of water poured in through the levees, as helicopters flew overhead surveying the damage, trying to formulate a plan.

The blast of a horn from an emergency vehicle brought Paul's attention back to the mission at hand.

I've got to get to Gina! thought Paul, and he began to think of a way he could somehow commandeer a vehicle to Slidell. Then up ahead, as though an answer to his prayers, a used car dealership came into view.

Hurrying over to the dealership, Paul wasted little time selecting a vehicle, taking the first one he came to.

There shouldn't be a whole lot to this, Paul thought, having recovered many stolen vehicles, he was very aware as to how a car was hotwired.

Not looking or caring who was around, Paul smashed the driver's window and unlocked the door. Then reaching under the console, he pulled a group of wires out and began to hotwire the car. Within seconds, the vehicle roared to life, bringing a smile to Paul's face as he prepared to drive off.

Not even risking getting tied up with the Causeway, Paul rolled the dice hoping I-55 would not be damaged too much to make it impassable.

Luckily, his bet paid off, as he road down I-55 without incident, seeing up close the destructive force of the tidal surge on the camps just off the interstate.

In some cases, walls had been completely ripped away, where others only had the pilings as a landmark of where a camp once stood.

Paul had not seen another vehicle on the highway since he exited the off ramp from I-10 and he began to wonder if sections of the bridge had not been torn away. He wondered if the possibility existed of him just driving of the elevated bridge and plummeting the forty feet to the marsh or water below.

Proceeding with caution, Paul was driven by a more immediate overriding desire to reach Gina, as he threw caution to the wind and sped down the interstate.

It would not be until he reached the outskirts of Slidell that he would encounter his first roadblock.

Approaching the roadblock with a certain degree of apprehension, as an officer systematically turned car after car around. Paul was not sure how the officer would react to his obviously stolen car. Driving up, the officer saw the broken window, but was confused by Paul's uniform.

"New car?" the officer asked, seeing the broken window and the hanging wires on the console.

"Yep, just stole it!" Paul said, deciding to take the offensive. "Listen Officer, my girlfriend is trapped in Slidell. I don't know if she's dead or alive, but I've got to get to her," Paul began to explain. "New Orleans is flooded, our patrol cars are destroyed, taking this car was the only way I could get here."

"Let me see some ID," the officer requested, still keeping Paul in the dark to the approach he would ultimately take towards him.

Producing his badge and credentials, Paul waited, knowing his fate was in the hands of the officer.

The officer quickly examined Paul's credentials then handed them back to him as the traffic began to back up behind him.

"Go on, get out of here!" the officer said, "Good luck finding her."

"Thank you!" Paul said as he drove towards Slidell.

As Paul drove, bucket trucks and rescue vehicles swarmed the roads the closer he got to the city, finally exiting I-12 to I-10 and to what had become a massive parking lot.

Police and rescue workers struggled to try to establish order to the chaos which had ensued. The area looked as though a bomb had exploded, sending debris scattering throughout the surrounding area.

Realizing the futility of trying to drive any further, Paul abandoned his vehicle on the side of the road and began the rest of the journey on foot. Fighting fatigue and hunger, he knew he couldn't stop.

Heading towards the lake, Paul saw the spectrum of the storm's aftermath. Individuals who had obviously been looting were in handcuffs being hauled away. Body bags from some of the unfortunate victims and hordes of rescue workers facing the massive task of a house-to-house search.

But none of this concerned Paul, his only thoughts were of Gina. As he neared Oak Harbor, the true magnitude of the destruction could be seen. Boats of every size and description scattered about, like toys from an overturned toy box.

Some boats blocked the streets making passage difficult, if not impossible. Others sat inside or next to houses and townhouses. The devastation had touched everything, the buildings and structures displayed the brown watermarks, a visual reminder of how high the water had risen. Everything below that line projected a light brown, almost surreal landscape.

As Paul neared closer to Oak Harbor, the mud that covered the area became thicker, more difficult to traverse. What was once solid concrete was now covered with three or four inches of wet mud. Only the surface had begun to dry, forming a light crust you would easily step through as you walked.

A bobcat tractor worked feverishly trying to scrape the mud to the side of the road, facilitating a more rapid response for rescue workers and emergency vehicles to the apartments and houses that still lay ahead. Despite the operator's best efforts, the work was tedious and progress was slow.

It wasn't until a grader arrived that real progress was made. The large blade of the grader picked up and pushed the mud to the side of the street, making it possible for emergency vehicles and rescue workers to move closer with more equipment, and resources.

Oak Harbor was only a few hundred yards away, but unfortunately, the limited resources of the rescue teams were assigned to begin the systematic search and rescue of the nearby townhouses first. If Paul was to get to Gina, he would have to do it on his own.

Tracking trough the mud, Paul began to pass disaster victims trying to make it on their own to the distant lights of the rescue vehicles. Most carried nothing with them, content to escape their nightmare with only the clothes on their back.

Passing boat after boat, Paul reflected on the hundreds of thousands of dollars these boats were once worth, now destroyed, destined for some landfill.

In the distance, Paul could see Gina's apartment, one of the outer walls was ripped away, revealing what was once a bedroom they shared.

Fighting the sinking feeling which had begun to come over him, Paul pushed himself even harder determined to reach the apartment, though unprepared for what he might find.

Finally, after exerting much effort and energy, his relentless determination paid off as he arrived at the foot of the stairs leading to Gina's apartment. Rushing up the stairs, calling on strength he didn't know he had, weighed down by his mud-clad boots, he still pushed on, his resolve absolute.

Arriving at the apartment, that sinking feeling he had been able to suppress was once again rearing its ugly head as Paul discovered the door open and debris of what was once their possessions lay scattered about.

THE CITY BENEATH THE SEA

If the scene itself wasn't enough to be overwhelmed by, the discovery of trails of blood added yet another dimension to the mix, confirming Paul's worst fears.

Gina was hurt, if not dead! Paul thought, as he began to search for Gina. The crunch of broken glass could be heard underfoot, as Paul went from room to room, searching for his fiancée, but finding no-one.

Righting an overturned chair, Paul sat down for a moment to catch his breath and gather his thoughts. Putting his head in his hands he stared at the floor and the blood trails he had observed earlier.

But it was only now that Paul observed something he hadn't seen previously. The trail of blood led out the apartment!

Getting to his feet with renewed hope, Paul began to follow the trail as it led him down the short breezeway to another apartment on the opposite side of the complex, the side facing the marina. It was here Paul got his first good look at the devastated harbor.

The boats that had not made it out of the harbor and into the street now rested either inside the apartment complex sunk, or piled together in a massive bulk. Many were sunk, the only proof of their presence was the tall mast of the sailboats still sticking up.

Over two hundred boats lay pushed together, along with the fragmented remnants of a once-floating dock. It was as though the hand of God, with one mighty sweep had piled all the boats to one side, stacking some on top of others; turning the once serene peaceful harbor into an unrecognizable nightmare.

Following the blood trail right to the door of an apartment a couple doors down, Paul began banging on the door, calling out for Gina.

"Gina!" Paul yelled, as he banged on the door, determined to arouse anyone inside before kicking it in.

The door finally opened revealing an older man with an oxygen cannular in his nose. He was sweating and breathing hard, giving Paul the impression he would collapse at any moment as he pulled the door open wide for Paul to enter.

"Come on in!" the old man said. "She's in the back laying down. She had a pretty close call. I saw your place, a whole wall is gone."

Just then Gina walked in, her arm and head were bandaged.

"Gina!" Paul cried out, rushing over to her, taking her in his arms.

"Easy!" Gina said, trying to warn Paul of her condition.

"You alright?" Paul asked, ecstatic to finally have found her.

"Yes I'm fine, when the wall got torn away, I was in bed," Gina began to explain, "Flying glass cut me up, and I was bleeding. I made it down here and Mr. Bell was nice enough to let me in and bandage me up. What are you doing here, aren't you on duty or something?" Gina asked.

"I tried to get in touch with you, but couldn't. I got scared and came right over," Paul explained, not wanting to get into the circumstances that led to his departure from New Orleans.

"Well, get us out of here," Gina said. "Mr. Bell here is down to his last bottle of oxygen."

"Rescue workers are close behind me. We'll get you taken care of, Mr. Bell," Paul said, reassuring the elderly man help was on the way.

Mr. Bell nodded his head in understanding, then flopped himself into his recliner to wait for rescuers to arrive.

THE CITY BENEATH THE SEA

CHAPTER TWENTY-THREE

The amphibious military vehicle rolled down Canal Street as it began its tour. Having been called up, William and his team had been assigned a rather large area to both patrol, establish order, and collect bodies when discovered.

With plenty of room inside, and a fifty-caliber machine gun mounted above the cab, the vehicle was well prepared not only to fulfill its assigned task, but also prepared for any eventuality that might arise.

Inside the the walls of the vehicle, William's men eyed the large stack of body bags, and contemplated how many they would ultimately have to fill.

Turning down Decatur nearing the French Quarter, William began to get a sinking feeling in his stomach. It had been five years since he had been here, not since that fateful day when his life was turned upside down.

Five years earlier, William lived in the Quarter. He and his partner both fell in love with the city's culture, history and diversity. Planning to make New Orleans their home, William and Frank, his partner of three years, were out on the town when their lives and destiny would collide.

William and Frank had risked venturing outside of the parameters of the gay district and headed to the Moon Walk that overlooked the river. It was late, Frank carried a white rose William had just purchased for him from a street vendor. The night was cool, the air still, Jazz playing in the distance, a beautiful night in New Orleans.

They probably should have known better than to put themselves in such a vulnerable position, but whether it was the alcohol or the spontaneity of the moment, William and Frank found themselves alone on the Moon Walk.

THE CITY BENEATH THE SEA

A gay couple in New Orleans was not by any means an unusual sight, and the city as a whole seemed to have a certain amount of tolerance for the growing community of gays that had began to slowly migrate to the city. They even had parades such as the Decadence Parade, where thousands of heterosexuals, came to enjoy the parades and festivities. For the most part, the acceptance of gays in New Orleans was beginning to be more and more commonplace.

There were however, those with no acceptance and no tolerance for an alternative lifestyle. It was when these people's paths crossed, the results were usually tragic.

On this night, it was just such a night. Whether it was the alignment of the planets, or sheer fate, something had put William and his partner Frank on the Moon Walk that night, and one life would end, while another would be changed forever.

From the shadows, a man emerged who would be destined to destroy one life, while putting the other on a fanatic crusade for gun control.

"Give me your wallet and jewelry!" the masked man ordered, brandishing a gun.

"No problem," William said, starting to comply, while his partner showed some reluctance.

"Take your rings off!" the man ordered Frank, beginning to show his agitation with him.

"Take everything else!" Frank pleaded, "Please don't take my ring!" Frank cried, the sentimental value of William giving him the ring overriding his own personal safety.

"It's ok, Frank, give him the ring," William said, trying to reassure his partner. "Just give him the rings."

The gunman's patience waning, he reached for Frank's rings, as Frank pulled away at the same time, flinging his wallet at him.

The gunman fired his gun, more out of surprise than intentionally, but there was no retrieving the lead projectile as it tore into Frank's chest, throwing him backwards.

William grabbed for Frank as he fell to the ground, but could not catch him. All he could do was follow him to the ground and kneel down beside him.

Holding his dying partner in his arms, William cried out. "WHY!" The question almost everyone screamed at one time or another in a city where senseless violence knew no bounds. Frank died in his arms still holding the now bloody rose,

Since that day, William had been an advocate of gun control. Marching, writing letters, perpetuating the removal of guns from the citizens. He knew it was a policy that could work.

While in Iraq, he and his men embarked on a campaign to remove guns from the area they patrolled. Through search and seizures, they were able to confiscate thousands of weapons, and the amount of violence in the townships they patrolled was practically eliminated.

A closely-knit group, his soldiers looked up to William, never questioning, never wanting to know why. When William gave an order to his men, it was as though God himself had spoken.

William knew if the citizenship could be disarmed, violent crimes could be reduced if not eliminated. It worked in Iraq, unfortunately, he had never had an opportunity to test his theory in the United States.

Passing Café DuMon, William could not bring himself to look in the direction of the Moon Walk, the memory was just too painful.

THE CITY BENEATH THE SEA

CHAPTER TWENTY-FOUR

Impatiently sitting in the Chicago airport, Donald passed the time watching the events of the aftermath of Katrina unfold, as night closed in on the city.

Live reports from New Orleans were broadcast, showing Coast Guard helicopters retrieving stranded people off rooftops in the lower Ninth Ward.

Another shot was taken of the levees as water poured through unabated, raising the water level in the already flooded city even higher.

Flipping open his cell phone, Donald repeated what he had done over the past few hours more out of habit than a realistic expectation that anyone would answer. He tried to place a call to his parents, but the frustrated look on his face made it clear it was yet another unsuccessful attempt.

Overlooking the sights and sounds of New York, Susan stared into the night sky, sipping a glass of wine, as the ringing of her phone disturbed the tranquility of the moment.

"Hello. Hi, Mommy," Susan said, rolling her eyes as though not looking forward to the conversation.

"How's my baby doing?" Honey asked.

"I'm fine," Susan said with a heavy sigh.

"Have you heard from Donald?"

"No I haven't. It's so unlike him just to pick up and leave like that," Susan said, still puzzled by Donald's sudden departure.

"Your father is none too happy, Donald left him in a bind with his clients. Very irresponsible of the boy."

"I know," Susan said. "But you can best believe he will be doing a lot of apologizing to Daddy when he comes back."

THE CITY BENEATH THE SEA

"After all your father's done for Donald, I think it shows a certain degree of ingratitude."

"I know, Mommy, he should be more thankful."

"Yes," Honey agreed. "He should."

"Well, he'll either be back soon or I'll hire someone to find him," Susan said, "One way or another, I will bring him back to the plantation."

"Now, Susan!" Honey said, pretending she was shocked by her remarks. "You know that's not politically correct, you sound like a slave master."

"I know," Susan said, "but it's accurate; if he's going to develop a mind of his own, I don't know if I have much use for him. Right now, he's a runaway, but between me and Daddy, we should be able to get his head right."

"I'll trust you with it, baby," Honey said, "I'll talk to you later."

"Bye, Mommy," Susan said, hanging up the phone, returning to her stargazing, and wine sipping.

"Ok, Mr. Donald King, I think it's time to bring you back in line," Susan said, showing a side of her true personality not seen until now.

Night had fallen on the city as Sweet and his gang sat around candles inside his housing project crib, smoking a joint. Surrounded by ten other members of his gang, Sweet knew each gangster was street hardened and tested, with little reservation of violence, or with not complying with the laws that govern most of society.

Birdie, though relatively new to the gang, sat next to Sweet, hanging on his every word, viewing Sweet as a mentor.

"Y'all know this Katrina was a gift from heaven," Sweet said, passing the joint to Birdie. "The police are overwhelmed. This city could be ours with just a little effort," Sweet explained to his receptive audience.

THE CITY BENEATH THE SEA

"What you got in mind, Sweet?" Birdie asked, wanting to be the first to show his enthusiasm for any plan Sweet would come up with.

"First we each need a piece." Sweet began to lay out his plan. "Then we take whatever we want!"

"Yea!" one of the gang members yelled out, showing his enthusiasm for the plan, even though it had not been fully explained.

"What they gonna do?" Sweet says, "They can't call no-one, the phones are down. The police can't respond even if they wanted to. Plus with all the gun restrictions, very few people have guns. It's a perfect situation for us."

"Well, where are we going to get guns?" Birdie questioned, careful to keep his enthusiasm apparent.

"There's a pawn shop down the street," Sweet explained, "I know he don't have a safe, just a good alarm system and that's not working now," Sweet explained, pausing for only a moment to let the gang absorb what he had just said. "You guys in? You ready to put this city on its head?"

"Yea!" the gang yelled, jumping to their feet.

"Then let's shake it!" Sweet said, leading the way out of the housing project apartment, heading for the pawnshop.

THE CITY BENEATH THE SEA

CHAPTER TWENTY-FIVE

Exiting the plane in Houston, Donald looked tired, disheveled, and well traveled as he walked down the concourse. Flipping his phone open, he searched the directory for Susan's number.

"Hello," a familiar voice answered the phone.

"Hey, baby."

"Donald? Where are you?" Susan asked.

"I'm in Houston."

"Texas?" Susan asked, knowing the answer but not believing it.

"Yes, Texas."

"What are you doing there?"

"Trying to get home," Donald said, knowing it would take a great deal more of an explanation to make clear how he ended up in Houston.

"Donald, your home is here," Susan said, correcting his suggestion that his home was anywhere other than with her, and puzzled by his impulsive departure.

"You know what I mean, I can't get in touch with my parents. I'm worried about them," Donald explained.

"How long are you going to be gone?" Susan asked, still a little peeved that Donald would make such a hasty departure without even calling her to let her know first.

"Not sure, I'll call you, got to go," Donald said, hanging up the phone and leaving Susan in limbo.

"Donald – " Susan said, trying to make one last attempt to keep him on the line, but was unsuccessful as the phone went dead.

Heading for the baggage claim, the carousel had already begun when he arrived. Bag after bag was pulled from the belt, but Donald's bags never appeared. Patiently he waited, until he was the only passenger from the plane still waiting. Finally, the belt stopped, Donald knew this could not be good.

"I can't believe this!" Donald said, growing more and more frustrated as he walked to the baggage claim office. A young lady, who couldn't have been more than nineteen sat behind the counter, doing her nails and reading a magazine.

"I just got off a plane from Chicago and my bags are missing," Donald explained to the uninterested attendant.

"I'm so sorry, Sir. If you fill out this form, we will notify you when we find them," the attendant said, never once looking up as she handed Donald the form.

"And what do I do in the mean time?" Donald asked, growing more frustrated by the attendant's obvious nonchalant attitude.

"Sorry, Sir, I can't answer that."

"I'll put my cell phone number on there, please call when you find it," Donald asked, trying to contain his frustration and growing anger.

"I said we would," the lady came back with attitude.

It was at this point Donald knew it was time to leave before he went off on this woman.

Outside the terminal, Donald flagged down a cab and climbed in.

"Take me to the nearest hotel," Donald said, as he leaned his head back on the seat, trying to calm down from the frustrating ordeal he had just experienced.

"No problem. I noticed you don't have luggage," the cabbie asked.

Donald could not help but smile at the cabbie's question.

"I had some," Donald began to explain, trying to find the humor in the situation. "But the airline liked it more than I did."

"Oh, I hate it when that happens."

THE CITY BENEATH THE SEA

The two-minute cab ride was soon over as the cab pulled up to the entrance lobby of the Best Western Hotel.

Donald started to hand the cabbie a five, but he waved him off.

"It's ok, mister, it's on me. You deserve a break."

"Thanks!" Donald said with a big smile, "I appreciate that."

Entering the Best Western Hotel, Donald headed for the check-in desk. A young, attractive lady soon emerged from an office behind the counter to greet him.

"Hello, can I help you?" she asked in a pleasant voice, a sharp contrast to what Donald had experienced earlier at the baggage counter.

"I need a room," Donald said, removing his wallet and credit card.

"I'm sorry we're all booked up, with the hurricane evacuees and all," the clerk explained.

Donald exhaled heavily, just another frustration in a day that had been filled with them.

"You don't have anything?" Donald asked, as though somehow she would change her mind.

"Nothing, I'm sorry."

"You mean to tell me if the President of the United States walked in and requested a room, you would not give him one?" Donald posed the question to the clerk.

Of course! I would have to give a room to the President," she replied, somewhat surprised by the question.

"Well, he's not coming, can I have his room?" Donald asked with a big smile, causing the very professional clerk to smile too.

"Look." Donald began to make one last argument for a room. "I know you guys keep a couple of rooms for emergency, messed up rooms, etc. It's late, the chances of you needing one of the extra rooms are slim. Can you help me out? I'm tired, worried, and aggravated, and on top of everything else, the airline's lost my luggage."

THE CITY BENEATH THE SEA

"Having a rough night, huh?" the clerk said, hearing the frustration in his voice.

"You could say that."

"Ok, I got a room," the clerk finally admitted, as she began the paperwork.

"Thank you!" Donald said, handing the clerk his credit card.

Within a few minutes, the clerk was handing Donald the key.

"Ok, you're in Room 222, straight down this aisle, second floor," she said, pointing in the direction of the room.

"Thank you," Donald once again thanked the clerk. "Thank you so much." Donald headed down the hall and to a room which only moments earlier did not exist.

Flipping on the light as he entered the room, Donald emptied his pockets on the dresser, then turned on the T.V. Fox News was on live from New Orleans.

"Rescue efforts continued into the night," the newsman explained. "Hundreds of people are still trapped on rooftops. Helicopters have been flying non-stop most of the day. The Superdome, which had been characterized as a refuge of last resort, has swelled to thousands of refugees. The conditions inside the dome is said to be deplorable, with no running water or electricity. The folks inside are spending another agonizing night waiting to be rescued.

"Still no good news for New Orleans," Donald said then turned off the TV and fell on the bed, instantly falling asleep, not even taking the time to get out of his clothes.

THE CITY BENEATH THE SEA

CHAPTER TWENTY-SIX

Night had settled in on the city and the Superdome, with still no sign of rescue; only more and more refugees poured into the already crowded dome, increasing its capacity in each passing hour.

In total darkness, the sounds became magnified, more intense. Cries and pleas overlaid each other, creating an even more intensified sound. Without air conditioning, the temperature in the dome had risen to a sweltering one hundred degrees, making the already unbearable conditions even worse.

Then in the darkness, LaToya heard a different type of plea. "Don't take my water!" the woman's voice cried out from the darkness.

"Shut up or I'll kill you," the gruff voice of a man ordered, demanding her to comply.

"No," she pleaded, hoping the commotion she was making would be enough to deter the robber. But as the sound of a fist making contact with the woman's face was heard through the crying and moaning, it quickly became apparent that the robber would not be deterred. Blow after blow could be heard, being delivered to the helpless victim, as her cries were slowly transformed into moans, then finally even the moans stopped, and no more sound could be heard at all coming from the woman.

Fear shot through LaToya, wondering if the woman was dead, wondering if she would be next! Sliding close to the wall, each footstep, each sound she heard near her, brought renewed fear. Finally bringing her to tears she began to pray for God to get her through this night.

Awoken by the sound of breaking glass, Melanie slowly slid out of bed to investigate. As she peered around the corner, her worst fears were realized as someone was attempting to break into her house.

Holding a flashlight and sticking his hand through the broken window, the burglar attempted to unlock the door.

Moving as quietly as she could, Melanie retreated to the spare bedroom. Opening her closet, she slipped inside, pulling suitcases and clothes on top of her.

In the living room, she heard the sound of glass being shattered. Things were being thrown about. Looters were inside her house, and there was nothing she could do. All she could do at this point was to try and ensure her own safety.

Hearing footsteps, Melanie's heart skipped a beat as they grew closer and closer to her location. The intruder went to the nightstand first, pulling drawers out and throwing them to the ground. Finding nothing, he moved to the dresser, only to be thwarted once again.

Finally, the closet doors were opened and a light shone inside.

Melanie, motionless and holding her breath, waited to be discovered. After a few horrifying moments of scanning the contents of the closet with the light, the intruder left, leaving a terrified, but thankful Melanie behind.

Listing intently for every sound, Melanie could hear a door slam as the intruder left.

Still too terrified to leave her hiding place until morning, she remained in the closet and started to cry. Finally, she was able to vent her fear.

Stirred by voices outside his window, which was open to help cool the house, Stan eased himself out of bed, picking up his shotgun on the way. It was loaded, ready to go, but deep down, Stan hoped he would not have to use it.

THE CITY BENEATH THE SEA

Stepping into the hall, he moved towards the front door, then suddenly stopped when he saw the reflection of flashlights moving about and the sound of inaudible voices approaching his door.

Suddenly, and unexpectedly, Stan's door was kicked open, a young thug with a pistol stood in the threshold and began to scan his new surroundings.

Surprised to see Stan, he fired at him, but the shot missed, burying itself harmlessly in the wall. Stan returned fire, with an aim truer than the intruder's as the blast of hot lead made contact with the intruder, catapulting him backwards, onto the porch.

As Stan reloaded the single shot shotgun with trembling hands, Janelle ran up to him, fearful some harm may have come to him.

"Stan! You all right?" Janelle asked, frightened and shaken.

"Yea, I'm all right! Someone tried to break in!" Stan said, closing the shotgun, readying it to fire again. "Get the flashlight!"

Heading back into the bedroom, Janelle soon returned with a flashlight, which she handed to Stan.

Tucking his shotgun under one arm, Stan scanned the outside through the windows onto the porch, trying to detect any other would-be intruders who might still want to enter his home. Slowly, with a great deal of caution, Stan moved towards his front door. The frame was splintered and shattered from where the intruder had kicked it in, and the blast of the shotgun had splintered the frame.

Walking onto the porch, Stan shone the light where the intruder had fallen, but found no body. Just a blood trail leading off the porch.

Suddenly, the porch was filled with light as though someone had flipped a light switch. A loud voice soon followed on a PA.

"Drop your weapon!" William demanded, catching Stan totally by surprise.

THE CITY BENEATH THE SEA

Slowly, not wanting to make any quick moves, Stan lay the shotgun on the porch and raised, his hands above his head, as Janelle watched from the doorway.

Hearing the sloshing of water, Stan knew men were approaching, even though the light had rendered him all but blind to the surrounding area.

Soon, William and one of his team mounted the porch, each armed with automatic weapons.

William retrieved Stan's shotgun, while the other entered the house, gun on his shoulder, using the rifle mounted light to search the area.

"I'm glad to see you fellas, I just had someone break in," Stan tried to explain.

"We heard shots, was that you?" William asked, keeping his rifle trained on Stan.

"Yea, someone kicked my door in, then he shot at me. He missed, I shot back. By the looks of it, I hit him," Stan concluded, pointing to the blood on the porch.

"We'll never be able to track him in all this water," William informed Stan, lowering his weapon.

Not noticing it earlier in all the excitement, Stan looked out towards his front yard and into a sea of water, which now surrounded his house and was threatening to enter.

"The water is still rising?" Stan questioned with surprise.

"The levees broke, we can't stop the water," William informed Stan, who had been unaware of the extent to which the levees had been damaged.

Just then, the second guardsman returned from inside the house, holding a pistol in his hand.

"Found this one in the closet," he said, showing the weapon to William.

"That's my pistol!" Stan began to protest. "What you doing going through my closet?"

THE CITY BENEATH THE SEA

"We have orders to confiscate as many weapons as possible. Since you were involved in a shooting, we have to confiscate your weapons," William explained an order that didn't exist to a still confused Stan.

"Ok, take the shotgun, that's the one that I used. Don't take my pistol!" Stan pleaded, but to no avail, as William and his men started back down the steps. "What if they come back?" Stan asked. "You gonna leave someone here with us?"

"Sorry, Sir, we have no-one available and we have a rather big area to patrol." William explained.

Stepping down into the water, Stan continued to call after the guardsman.

"How are we supposed to protect ourselves?" Stan yelled, angered and shocked by the recent events.

"Get to the Convention Center, there's security, food, and water," William called out as a powerful diesel engine started, a door slammed and the spotlight went out.

It was only now that Stan was able to see the type of vehicle that had transported the guardsmen to his house through so much water. An amphibious vehicle, designed to maneuver in both water and land, pulled away, leaving Stan standing in his front yard in waist-deep water, shocked in disbelief over what had just happened to him.

"Stan! What are we going to do?" Janelle asked, coming onto the porch, just as Stan was walking back on it.

"We wait till morning," Stan said, "and walk to the Convention Center. We can't stay here, not now."

Located next to a construction site in an older part of the city, the pawnshop, was located on one of the many main drags around the city.

THE CITY BENEATH THE SEA

Though heavily barred to deter theft, it would ultimately prove to be only a nuisance to the determined band of thieves.

Sweet and his gang pried away at the security bars, popping them off with only a minimal effort.

"We're in!" Sweet said, as the steel bars fell to the ground.

Entering the pawnshop, several of the gang members had the forethought to bring a flashlight, those who hadn't were forced to team up with those who did.

"Look for guns and ammo!" Sweet ordered. "Spread out!"

The gang began to search the area, finding only guitars and empty cases where guns and jewelry were once displayed. Then from the back room, a voice called out.

"In here!" the voice called, directing the rest of the gang into the back room. There, to their shock and disbelief, a six-foot by four-foot steel combination safe door stood securely attached to the concrete wall, which protected the most valuable objects the pawnshop had to offer.

"I thought you said he didn't have a safe?" Birdie asked, only to be rebutted by Sweet's hard stare. A stare so cold, it could send almost anyone into a full retreat.

Looking at the safe in frustration, Sweet closely examined the entire length of the safe, trying to formulate yet another plan.

His gang would not have to wait long; shortly after, Sweet yelled, "Everybody out!"

The gang did not ask questions and immediately complied with Sweet's orders and piled out the door they had pried open earlier.

Outside, Sweet grabbed Mouse by the shoulders. Mouse was one of Sweet's most reliable gang members.

THE CITY BENEATH THE SEA

Small in stature and not too bright, Mouse had quickly proved himself as a natural born follower.

"Mouse, I need you to hotwire that bulldozer and put a hole in this cinderblock wall right about here." Sweet said, pointing to a spot on the wall.

Without hesitation, Mouse nodded his head and hurried over to the bulldozer. Climbing into the cab, Mouse began pulling wires from under the console. The tangled web of multicolored wires held significance to only the most informed as to the purpose each served.

But to someone who had made a career out of stealing cars and knowing how to hotwire, Mouse's talents would often come in handy.

Within minutes, the large diesel bulldozer was moving forward towards the rest of the gang. Little Mouse was dwarfed in the large cab, barely able to see out over the console, as he headed to the pawnshop wall at full speed.

The blade of the bulldozer crumbled the wall, pushing bricks inside the building. The force of the contact threw Mouse from the seat and into the controls, causing the tractor to want to turn, once it had broken through.

Putting the bulldozer in reverse, Mouse backed the bulldozer out, allowing easy access for the gang. With beams of light leading the way, the gang poured into the safe, ready to steal anything of value they came across.

Inside the safe, the gang found the guns they were looking for, along with other items of value, such as gold and diamonds, which proved to be an added bonus.

"Load up, boys, take all you can carry!" Sweet said, happy to see his plan come together.

With great haste, Sweet's gang quickly stuffed their pockets and picked up as many guns as they could carry, along with the ammunition, leaving behind an empty safe, with an enormous hole in it.

THE CITY BENEATH THE SEA

"What do you think, Birdie?" Sweet asked, "We ought to be able to keep some cops at bay with this," Sweet said, holding up a rifle.

"Absolutely!" Birdie said, agreeing with Sweet.

"This is our city now, Birdie and I don't want to give it back. At least not until I've stripped everything of value out of it," Sweet said, with a menacing look on his face as he turned to Birdie.

"You with me?" Sweet asked Birdie.

"You know I am!"

THE CITY BENEATH THE SEA

CHAPTER TWENTY-SEVEN

As morning dawned, LaToya awoke to the sound of a woman screaming once again. Her cries were deeply intense. Looking in the direction of the sound, LaToya saw two medical workers tending to a pregnant woman, obviously in the process of giving birth. Beyond that, LaToya once again saw people moving towards the exits.

This time, she was not going to wait. If there was anyway possible, she was not going to spend another night in the dome. If there was a way out, LaToya was determined to find it.

Waking her two boys, LaToya quickly packed up her few possessions in her suitcase, observing the crowds moving towards the northeast corner of the dome.

LaToya knew there would be no way for her and her two small boys to fight such a crowd and come out the other side unharmed. LaToya knew her only hope was to be smarter; to find a way around the bottleneck, and possibly position herself in an advantageous position outside.

Then, suddenly it came to her. She would not risk fighting the surge towards the door, instead she would literally go around it. While everyone was trying to push their way through the bottleneck at the one exit, she would take another, using the walk around that circled the dome to get ahead of the masses. That was her idea, whether or not it would work was another story all together.

Gathering up her two boys, she headed for the distant exit, passing the woman in labor, her screams of pain had subsided and been replaced with the cry of her newborn child, which she held in her arms. The first Superdome baby, one of five that would ultimately be delivered in a facility in which childbirth must have been the farthest thing in the minds' of the designers.

"Watch your step, boys," LaToya cautioned her boys as they walked, urging them not to step in the human faeces and urine that had been scattered about in the total darkness of the dome, adding to the unbearable stench that could bring tears to the eyes of even the most tolerant.

Serpentining her way to the distant exit, LaToya, through her patience and perseverance, was able to negotiate the crowded floor as people lay about, some sick and dying, some in wheelchairs, some just laid out. Each in their own personal hell, pleading for help, though no one knew when it would arrive.

Climbing a flight of stairs, cautious to keep her boys in tow, LaToya was finally able to ascend to the wrap-around walkway which encircled the dome, and hopefully lead her to the other side.

As she exited the dome, the cool fresh air was such a welcome relief after having spent two days in the foul stench of the dome. She inhaled deeply as though trying to purge all the air from the dome that may have been trapped in her lungs.

Hugging the wall, LaToya moved north around the dome. As she went, she noticed several people had set up camp outside in the fresh air. This, LaToya thought, would be where she would stay if by chance, she was unable to escape the dome. One thing was sure, after once again smelling and breathing fresh air, there was no way she was going back inside.

Looking over the guardrail, LaToya was able to see for the first time the devastation Katrina had done to the city; torn roof tops, some roofs caved in, as far as the eye could see was devastation, and water! Water was everywhere, totally encircling the dome, making it an island, trapping everyone inside.

As LaToya reached the North East corner, the crowd began to thicken. People pushed and shoved, trying desperately to assure themselves a little better position in the crowd, with others equally determined to maintain their hard-fought position.

Moving closer to the guardrail, LaToya was able to see for the first time the objects of the people's anxiety. Several buses had arrived to begin to ferry people out of the dome. But with so few buses, and so many people, the reality was it would probably take days to accomplish the task.

Suddenly, without warning, a fight broke out near LaToya. Two rather large men had reached their boiling point and were taking it out on each other. As the two titans swung wildly at each other, landing blow after blow and in some cases striking innocent bystanders, the crowd surged backwards catching LaToya and her boys in a sudden stampede. Acting quickly, LaToya pushed her boys against the concrete rail, but did not have time to secure her own safety as she was thrown to the ground in the tussle.

Feet stepped on her hands and back, each time she tried to get up she was knocked down again. LaToya could not breathe, her beaten, battered body was about ready to give up.

Then out of nowhere, as though being rescued by her guardian angel, a powerful hand pulled her to her feet, giving her a second chance at life.

Regaining her footing, she came face to face with a white NOPD officer, not far away, several more officers had broken up the fight that had almost cost her life and secured its combatants in cuffs.

"My children!" LaToya screamed. looking around, then finally seeing them right where she had left them. Rushing over to them, she hugged them and began to cry.

"Are you all right?" the officer asked as LaToya composed herself, looking at the crowd that had once again began to surge towards the buses.

THE CITY BENEATH THE SEA

"Yes," LaToya said, hesitating only long enough to read the officer's nametag. "Officer Moore, thank you, I think you saved my life," the grateful LaToya said. "I couldn't have lasted very much longer down there."

"You're welcome," Les said, then he noticed her two sons next to her. "Two fine looking young men you have there, I have one of my own about his age," Les said, pointing to Jamal.

"We were trying to get to the buses. So many people, are there more buses on the way?" LaToya asked.

"Yes," Les said, "but it's going to take time. You and your boys better not risk fighting that crowd again," Les said, trying to warn LaToya of the danger. "Next time, you might not be so lucky."

"We don't have a lot of choice, I can't go back in the dome, I just can't!" LaToya cried, a tear slipping from her eye as she held her boys.

"Don't cry, Mommy," Jamal said, "I'll protect you."

Les, moved by the expression of love and sacrifice, decided to come to LaToya's aide somehow.

He remembered the story that was once told to him about a man walking along the beach. During the night, the tide had beached hundreds of starfish destined to die in the heat of the morning sun. As the man walked, he was observed bending over to pick up a starfish and casting it back to the safety of the sea. This scene was repeated over and over again, until finally the man who had been observing him approached in amazement and disbelief.

"There are hundreds of starfish on the beach," the man began. "There is no way you can save them all, it won't make a difference."

The man who had been tossing the starfish into the sea simply reached down, picked up a starfish, and cast it into the sea. "I made a difference to that one," he said as he continued down the beach.

LaToya would be Les' starfish.

THE CITY BENEATH THE SEA

"Come with me," Les said, directing LaToya to follow him, leading her away from the crowd.

Taking a ramp guarded by a National Guard, he led LaToya to the ground floor and into three feet of water.

"Come on boys," Les said, reaching down and picking up each of them, placing them on his hips. While LaToya struggled with her the suitcase, wading through the water as she followed Les.

Up ahead, there was a military transport with guardsmen inside, along with some medical personnel.

"I need these people transported out," Les said. "Can you help us?"

The sergeant obviously in charge of the transport was less than sympathetic.

"There're buses up front to transport civilians!" he said, informing Les of something he already knew.

"Sergeant, this lady almost got killed, crushed in a stampede upstairs. She's got two small boys. I would look upon it as a professional courtesy towards me if you could find it in your heart to help," Les pleaded on behalf of LaToya.

The hard-nosed sergeant softened his position as he eyed LaToya and the boys. Seeing her scarred face, he knew she probably hadn't had too many breaks in her life.

"Alright get in, but get towards the front. I don't want everyone and his brother knowing I'm using this transport to move civilians. I'll be overrun," the sergeant said, as he consented to LaToya's transport.

"Thank you, Sergeant," Les said, as he lifted the boys into the arms of one of the nurses, then helped LaToya in the transport.

"Why are you helping us?" LaToya questioned, finding it hard to believe a white man would go to so much trouble for her.

"I told you," Les said, "your boy reminded me of mine. Good luck!"

THE CITY BENEATH THE SEA

Les left as the transport began to pull out, creating a small wake as it went.

THE CITY BENEATH THE SEA

CHAPTER TWENTY-EIGHT

Awakened by the sound of helicopters overhead, Melinda wondered if they were coming to save her. Still hiding in the closet, she peeped out to see if it was safe to come out, still terrorized from last night's break in. As she emerged from the closet, she began to see what she had only heard last night. The destruction the intruder had committed to her home was senseless. If he didn't have a use for it, he tried to destroy it. Pictures, her china, her TV, everything.

"Where in the world do people like this come from?" she questioned, as she began to cry. The house was a shambles. As Melinda went from room to room, the scene was repeated.

Trying to compose herself, Melinda returned to the closet to retrieve one of the bags that had hidden her, and probably saved her life during the night.

Packing only a few changes of clothes, Melinda tried to be as practical in her selection as possible, as she went through her wardrobe. Sliding garment after garment to the side, she realized that the clothes and many of the other possession she had worked so long and so hard for would probably not be here when she returned. There was little doubt in her mind that the looters would come back again and again, until finally there would be nothing left.

Returning to the living room with her bag, Melinda began to search for her purse.

"My purse!" Melinda said, only now realizing it had been one of the prizes taken by the thief. "Damn it!" she said, trying to vent some of her anxiety and frustration.

Grabbing her bag, she headed out the door, knowing it would not be safe for her to risk another night in her own home.

THE CITY BENEATH THE SEA

Nudging Janelle, Stan tried to get her moving as early as possible. It was light outside, they had somehow managed to make it through the night. Perhaps the thugs that broke into the house probably thought he still had a weapon, and did not want to risk a repeat of what had happened to their friend. If there was one thing Stan knew it was that his luck could not hold out for very long.

"Come on, baby," Stan said, trying to stir Janelle who had never been a morning person. "We're going to have to go."

Stan slid his feet over the side of the bed and into water.

"Oh no! Baby, the water's still rising!" Stan cried, having thought it had reached its highest point during the night.

"What we gonna do!" Janelle asked, now wide-awake on hearing the news of water in her house.

Not waiting for an answer, Janelle got out of the bed and began trying to pick up various things on the floor, drying them off with a towel she retrieved from the bathroom.

Stan just watched for a moment, knowing the futility of the situation, then finally walked over to Janelle, giving her a hug.

"Baby, we're not going to be able to save everything," Stan tried to state the obvious.

"We need to try!" Jarelle said, not willing to give up on so many of the possessions that had taken her so long to obtain.

"Listen to me!" Stan said, grabbing her by the shoulders, giving her a little shake to get her attention. "We can't stay another night here! It's not safe!"

Janelle began to cry, as she looked around her home, knowing what would be lost if the water kept rising.

THE CITY BENEATH THE SEA

"Everything we've worked for!" Janelle cried through her tears.

"I know," Stan agreed. "But now we need to focus on saving our lives. If last night was any indication, we're on our own."

Conceding the loss of her property, Janelle nodded her head in understanding.

"Let's try to save as many pictures as we can, I'll put them in the attic," Stan offered, trying to give Janelle a little time to save at least some of what she thought was dearest to her. "Gather up what you can, but hurry, the water is still rising."

Janelle busied herself trying to gather as much as she could, while Stan pulled down the attic ladder.

Walking out on his porch, Stan was able to see in the daylight the true magnitude of what the night had concealed. As far as he could see in any direction, there was water! Water was everywhere!

As Stan stood on his porch trying to comprehend what he was witnessing, something caught his eye. In the street, something was floating, then the realization of what he saw came to him. It was a body!

Jumping into the waist-deep water, Stan waded out towards the body; reaching the body, he rolled it over, initially thinking it was just another tragic victim of the storm, but what he saw quickly eliminated that possibility.

The man was shot in the head! Recognizing the man as his neighbor Mark from a couple of doors down, Stan wondered how many others of his friends and neighbors might have met the same fate.

Stan pushed the body away. A disturbed look on his face, knowing if it had not been for his shotgun, he could be the one floating face down in the water.

As Stan turned to walk back to the porch, he saw Janelle standing there.

"Is it anyone we know?" she asked, as the body slowly drifted away.

THE CITY BENEATH THE SEA

"It's Mark, from two doors down," Stan said, as he walked back towards her.

"How did he drown? The water never-"

"He was shot!" Stan said, interrupting her.

"Oh my God!" Janelle cried, turning pale with fear.

"Let's hurry," Stan said, trying to keep their focus on the task at hand.

Going to the attic, they began placing their few possessions they were able to save onto the attic flooring. Unless the water rose another eight feet, it should be safe, at least from the water.

"Pack a bag with a couple of changes of clothes," Stan instructed his wife. "The Red Cross should be here somewhere, maybe at the Convention Center, like the police said last night."

Janelle threw together clothes in a canvas backpack, stuffing it full, she then started on a suitcase.

"I'm done!" Janelle called as she closed the suitcase.

"Good!" Stan said, coming to the room to pick up the suitcase. "It's time to go."

Stepping out onto the porch, Stan and Janelle pulled the wooden door, which had represented a form of security to them for so many years, into the splintered frame, then stepped off the porch into cold, waist-deep water.

Taking Janelle's hand, Stan offered her one more caution, only after they had entered the water.

"Baby, I don't want to scare you, but keep an eye out for snakes," Stan said, as he led the way through the lake which was once his front yard.

"Snakes!" Janelle cried, "Just when I thought it couldn't get any worse!"

THE CITY BENEATH THE SEA

As Donald prepared a pot of hotel coffee, the TV was tuned to Fox News, and the live coverage of hurricane Katrina.

Standing framed with the backdrop of road traffic backed up as far as the eye could see, the newsman began his report.

"This is the scene in Baton Rouge," the newsman said as the camera panned to the miles of stagnant traffic which had transformed the normally rapid flowing interstate into a parking lot. "Traffic is at a virtual standstill. Even though Katrina is gone, police are not allowing anyone to return. Many motorists are simply being turned around when they get to La Place, creating a circular nightmare of traffic."

Donald turned off the TV and opened his laptop. "Does the nightmare ever end!" he said as he began to type. After a few moments of scanning the internet, Donald reached for his phone, punching in a pre-programmed number.

"Harrington and Associates, Mr. King's office," the familiar pleasant voice on the other end of the phone said.

"Celena, this is Donald."

"Boss!" Where you at?" Celena asked, not having been notified that Donald would be leaving town, she had been bombarded with questions she could not answer.

"I'm in Houston," Donald informed his secretary.

"Texas!" Celena replied, surprised he would be so far away.

"What is it with you women?" Donald said, Susan's similar reply still fresh in his memory. "Is there another Houston I don't know about?" Donald asked, tongue in cheek.

"Sorry, boss. What you doing there?"

"It's a long story, and I'll share it with you, but not today," Donald said, wanting to get on the road as soon as possible. "I emailed you some information. I need you to purchase the list of items and a boat."

"A boat!"

"Yes, a boat, I emailed you the type and the dealer in Baton Rouge. Have the boat delivered to the dock next to the USS Kidd in front of the Centraplex," Donald explained, knowing Celena's curiosity was absolutely killing her.

"I just pulled up your email. This is a big list," Celena said, as she scanned the email list.

"I've got to go, but I'm counting on you, Celena," Donald said, knowing once he gave her the assignment she would move heaven and earth not to disappoint him. "I should be in Baton Rouge some time this afternoon. Make sure the boat is there."

"Ok, boss, it'll be there, you can count on me."

"I know I can," Donald said, acknowledging the trust he put in her. "Thanks, Celena. You're the best."

"Remember that next time I ask for raise," Celena said, with a laugh, then became very serious again. "And boss, be careful, New Orleans is pretty crazy right now."

"Don't worry, I'll be fine."

Hanging up the phone, Donald began to pack up his few possessions in his bag. Still having not heard anything about his luggage, he had all but given up on it.

Returning once again to his cell phone, Donald punched in a series of numbers.

"What city?" the electronic operator asked.

"Houston."

"What listing?"

"Enterprise car rental."

" The number is –" the electronic operator called out the number, but Donald did not want to waste the time dialing so he punched a number which would connect him automatically to the business he had requested.

THE CITY BENEATH THE SEA

"Enterprise, we'll pick you up," the male voice on the other end of the phone said.

"Yes, I need a car delivered. I'll be using it for a few days," Donald said, informing the salesman of his intent.

THE CITY BENEATH THE SEA

CHAPTER TWENTY-NINE

Leaving her house for the first time in two days, Melanie stepped off her porch and into waist-deep water. Helicopters continued to buzz overhead, but not knowing the current state of the city, she had no way of knowing what was going on with the rescue effort.

After her close call last night, Melanie had adopted the approach that she would no longer wait for someone to rescue her. She was going to take matters into her own hands.

As Melanie started down her flooded street, other evacuees could be seen struggling to escape the rising tide of the floodwaters.

Some were carrying suitcases, some carrying nothing at all. Tugging along with her suitcase in hand, Melinda walked, and as she walked, the progression of people behind her began to grow.

Twenty or thirty people were following her within a short time. Some old, some young, all with one thing in common. They all sought dry land.

A sound of a loud splash caught Melanie's attention, she turned and, she saw an old woman, who had tripped, go under the water.

Rushing to her, Melanie grabbed the woman by the arm and helped her to regain her footing.

"Thank you!" the old woman said, through her coughing, obviously having taken in a little water when she went under.

"It's ok," Melanie said, "let me help you. Take my arm."

The old woman leaned on Melanie as they continued their trek. No one, including Melanie knew when or where they would ultimately find high ground and rescue, but the group followed Melanie like she somehow knew where she was going.

THE CITY BENEATH THE SEA

As the group emerged onto a boulevard, Melanie noticed a city bus just sitting there on the neutral ground. The water was half way up the tires, but it looked like it might not have gotten to the engine.

"Maybe that bus is our ticket out of here," Melanie said, "that is if we can start it."

Moving towards the bus with the group close behind splashing through the water, Melanie knew that they would not be able to go on too much further. Trekking through waist-deep or knee-deep water can quickly take its toll on a body. Not to mention the fact that many in the group were old. This bus for some, would be their only hope.

Reaching the bus, Melanie pushed the door open, resistant at first, she had to persuade it with a kick, which finally caused the door to fly open.

Climbing in behind the wheel, while the group waited outside, she checked for the key, which by chance or luck was found to be in the ignition. Turning the key, the engine whined at first, as though trying to state its objection, but eventually the engine came to life, sending a cloud of black smoke behind it as it did.

The crowd cheered when the engine started, knowing their walk had finally come to an end. From now on, it would be smooth sailing.

"Get in!" Melanie said, trying to hasten the celebrating people on board.

Quickly complying to Melanie's request, the group piled aboard, quickly finding a seat on the bus.

"Is that everybody?" Melanie asked, as she prepared to close the door.

"Not quite!" the harsh voice of Sweet was heard as he climbed the steps his pistol drawn; behind him the rest of his gang.

"Alright folks, this is a robbery," Sweet yelled, terrifying everyone on board as he brandished his pistol about. "My boys will be coming down the aisle picking up any valuables you may have. If you co-operate, no one will get hurt."

The gang piled on the bus, as Birdie climbed aboard Melanie met his eyes. Melanie almost started to say something, but she saw Birdie shake his head as though warning her off.

The gang went through the bus, pulling rings and earrings off its passengers, having little regard for the old or the young.

One man tried to assist a young woman who was being assaulted, but as a shot from the front of the bus rang out, he was sent in full retreat by Sweet.

"I'll kill all of you if I have to!" Sweet yelled. "You resist, you will die!"

Having taken everything of value off the passengers, the gang began going through some of the luggage the passengers had brought on board, dumping their contents on the floor, scattering them about.

Some of the gang were more interested in the women. One started fondling one of the more attractive ones, then slapped her hard sending her backwards on the seat when she resisted.

She fell back in tears as the gangster pulled her legs up and lay her on the seat.

As he started to undo his belt, he was slapped from behind by Sweet.

"No one wants to see your naked ass! If you want that, take her in one of these abandoned houses," Sweet ordered.

"Ok, Sweet!" the gangster said, more than willing to comply.

Grabbing the woman by her hair, the gangster pulled her off the bus screaming, but nothing could save her at this point.

Having gotten the idea from the previous gangster, two more women were dragged off the bus and into nearby houses.

THE CITY BENEATH THE SEA

The remaining gangsters were content to leave with just the loot, leaving the remaining passengers and Sweet alone on the bus.

Returning to the front of the bus, Sweet's eye caught a good look at Melanie legs that were slid into the aisle.

"Nice legs," Sweet said, as he approached Melanie. "Maybe you should come with me."

Sweet tucked his gun into his pants then leaned over to grab Melanie. As he did, Melanie leaned back lifting her legs as she went.

Placing both feet on Sweet's chest, she pushed as hard as she could, catapulting Sweet out of the bus and into the water.

Slamming the door closed, Melanie threw the bus in gear, a grinding sound was heard as she franticly tried to find the gears.

Seconds ticked by like minutes, each one possibly being the deciding factor of whether they lived or died.

Finally finding the gear, the bus pulled away, leaving Sweet trying to regain his footing, as his gang rushed up to him.

"What happened?" the first gang member to reach Sweet asked.

Sweet reached for his gun, but it had been lost when he landed in the water.

"Don't just stand there!" Sweet yelled. "Shoot!"

The gang hesitated, at first, either not understanding or reluctant to fire, until Sweet grabbed a pistol from one of them and began to fire at the bus. He was quickly joined by the rest of the gang as everyone unloaded their weapons on the fleeing bus, but to the disappointment of everyone, it failed to stop it.

Slamming the accelerator to the floor, Melanie drove through the water-soaked street, not having a real direction, only aiming to get as far away from the gang as quickly as she possibly could.

THE CITY BENEATH THE SEA

Only after she had driven a safe distance away did she stop to pick up the occasional person wading through the water.

Driving down the boulevard, Melanie slammed on the brakes as Stan appeared in front of the bus out of nowhere, narrowly avoiding being run over.

Walking to the door of the bus, Stan tapped on the door, trying to get Melanie's attention, her head was on the steering wheel trying to slow her heart down.

"You crazy!" Melanie yelled as she opened the door. "I could have killed you!"

"Well, I'm glad you didn't," Stan said with a broad smile, totally unaffected by the close call. "To survive Katrina, only to be run over by a bus wouldn't look good on my headstone."

"Get in!"

Stan and Janelle got on the bus, taking a seat behind Melanie.

"My name is Stan, this is my wife Janelle," Stan said, introducing himself while Melanie drove.

"My name is Melanie."

"Where are we heading?" Stan asked, not really caring, just anywhere safe.

"I was thinking of the Superdome," Melanie said, as the bus bounced down the street.

"The National Guard were at the house last night, they told us to go to the Convention Center," Stan said, sharing with her only a portion of the previous night's events.

"Well let's head for the river and we'll see where we go from there," Melanie said, knowing the French Quarter was the highest ground in the city.

As Melanie rolled down the street, a group of young men tried to flag her down. They carried sticks and clubs, and didn't appear to be up to any good.

Melanie slammed the accelerator to the floor, as one of the young men stood in the street, thinking he could make it stop for him.

THE CITY BENEATH THE SEA

"What are you doing?" Stan yelled, surprised by Melanie's actions and not knowing what had transpired earlier.

"Just had a run in with a gang earlier," Melanie began to explain. "They dragged some people off, it's not going to happen again."

As the bus bore down on the teen in the street, he waited till the last possible moment, not so much believing that Melanie wouldn't stop, but more trying to save face with the rest of the gang.

"Hang on!" Melanie yelled. "This is going get bumpy."

As she neared the gang member, he dived safely to the side, as the bus leapt up and down hitting high and low spots in the road, throwing the passengers around a bit, but luckily everyone recovered without incident.

"Where'd you learn to drive like that?" Stan asked, impressed with Melanie's driving skills.

"Bumper cars, Ponchatrain beach," she said with a smile.

"Well you go, girl! Keep on, keeping on!" Stan said, leaning back in his seat.

THE CITY BENEATH THE SEA

CHAPTER THIRTY

Stuck in traffic it was bumper-to-bumper for hours, Donald's progress could only be measured in inches rather than miles. Motivated by the Baton Rouge Mississippi river bridge in the distance, Donald knew that once he was over that bridge, he would not be stuck in this traffic any longer. A song on the radio ended and the latest update on the aftermath of Katrina began.

"Rescue efforts continue in the Big Easy, as both military and Coast Guard helicopters continue removing residents from their rooftops," the announcer reported as traffic began to move, bringing a smile to Donald's face.

"The Superdome continues to present concern at this time. Thousands of people remain trapped with no food or water, and no electricity. Conditions inside the Superdome continue to deteriorate," the announcer reported what Donald had heard over and over again since he left Houston. "Other news is the road conditions as residents attempt to return to their homes. Officials are asking residents not to return at this time. If you're somewhere safe, stay there. The roads are being blocked off to the city and no one is being allowed in except police and medical workers. I have been informed that additional units of the National Guard have been called up as civil order inside the city has collapsed."

Donald shook his head at the news. "All right, enough already!"

On top of the bridge now, Donald looked down towards the USS Kidd. There at a dock next to the Kidd, a boat was moored, waiting for his arrival.

"There she is," Donald said, "I knew Celena could make it happen."

THE CITY BENEATH THE SEA

Taking an off ramp, Donald headed towards the dock and his waiting boat.

"Reports continue to flow in about the condition inside the city," the newsman stated. "There have been reports of roaming gangs prowling the streets, looting, beating, raping and in some cases, killing anyone who crosses their path. With the few police who still remain in the city involved with rescue efforts, these gangs remain unchecked."

Under the bridge now, Donald pulled off the road and parked near the levee. Cars were everywhere, the Centraplex being the largest and closest of the shelters had obviously become overwhelmed by the number of people being transferred from New Orleans to the shelter.

Approaching the Center on foot, Donald was able to observe bus after bus lined up outside, but instead of taking people off, they were putting people on.

Seeing a police officer approach, Donald stopped him to ask why.

"Excuse me, sir, why are they putting people on the Bus? I thought this was the evacuation center."

"Don't have room for them all, some are being bussed to Houston," the officer explained, then continued on his way, leaving Donald just as confused as before.

Moving towards the front entrance through the crowd, Donald worked his way into the registration desk. "Wouldn't it be ironic," Donald thought, "if I drive all the way from Houston, only to have my parents transferred to Houston."

Before going all the way to New Orleans, Donald wanted to make sure his parents had not been brought to this particular shelter.

Finally, after much shoving and squeezing, Donald arrived at a desk where a disheveled woman sat. She looked exhausted, there was no way of knowing how long she had been working at the desk, but by the looks of it, it was quite a while.

"Hello, Sally," Donald said, reading her nametag. "I'm trying to find my parents, could you tell me if they're here?"

"Are you kidding me?" Sally said, "We started out trying to keep track of who was coming in, but we were quickly overwhelmed. We're trying to get a count and names now, but the biggest priority right now is getting everybody settled with food and water. I'm sorry."

"Well, can you tell me what area your evacuees are coming from?" Donald asked, "Do you have anyone here from the Superdome or the Convention Center?"

"No!" Sally informed Donald. "Those evacuees are being directed to the Astro Dome in Houston.

A smile came across his face as he almost asked, "Texas?" remembering his conversations with Susan and Celena.

"This shelter has been shut down, no new evacuees are being sent here. If they are, they're being sent on to Houston."

"Thank you, you saved me a lot of time," Donald said. "I just have to find out if and where they evacuated to and I can narrow my search down from there."

Leaving the Civic Center, Donald headed for the pier, where he saw a young white male in his early twenties, nervously pacing back and forth.

"You Donald?" the young man asked as he approached.

"Yes I am."

"Carl Youngman," he said, introducing himself and extending his hand to shake. "I guess this boat's for you."

"Sure is, is it ready to go?" Donald asked, wanting to verify it had been fueled and the supplies were inside.

THE CITY BENEATH THE SEA

"Yes sir, it is fueled and ready to go," Youngman confirmed with a certain amount of pride. "Provisions and the rest of the items you requested are on board."

"Good, thank you," Donald said, as he began to get aboard.

"One more thing, if you would," Youngman said, blocking Donald from boarding the boat. "Everything was paid and ordered by a Miss Celena," Youngman said, referring to his clipboard.

"She's my secretary," Donald said, then attempted to board once again, but Youngman hadn't shifted his position any.

"Is there anything else?" Donald asked, starting to become frustrated with the young man.

"She requested I.D. verification," Youngman said, "I'm sorry."

Donald smiled at the additional precaution. "That's Celena," Donald said and produced identification for Youngman.

The young man examined it closely and handed it back to Donald along with a set of keys.

"She's all yours, just sign right here."

Quickly signing the invoice, Youngman left, clearing the way to his boat.

The dock in front of the Centraplex is one often used to accommodate riverboats and the occasional ship. With an initial straight runway, it spirals at the end to allow access regardless of the height of the river, which could vary quite a bit. The USS Kidd was proof of this; when the river was low, the battleship sat in a special cradle, when the river was high, the ship actually floated, kept moored in place by steel piers.

Spiraling downward to the boat moored at the bottom, Donald climbed aboard the thirty-foot speedboat, then unlocking the door to the galley, he disappeared inside.

THE CITY BENEATH THE SEA

The once spacious galley was now full of bags and boxes, some continued food and water, while others clothes.

Pulling a black T-shirt out of one of the bags, Donald changed his shirt then donned a pair of black pants, socks and shoes to match.

Returning to the helm, Donald powered up the powerful engines, then tossing the mooring lines to the dock, he pushed the throttle forward causing the powerful vessel to surge forward in response, pushing Donald against the seat as it did.

Leaving Baton Rouge, Donald knew he had a couple of hours of daylight left, but was uncertain if he could make it to New Orleans before nightfall, which had been his original intent. But regardless if it was day or night, Donald would somehow make it home and either find his parents, or hopefully find a clue indicating where they had gone.

Speeding towards New Orleans, Donald passed just about every type of vessel imaginable. From small fishing boats, to massive oil tankers and everything in between.

Refineries, ferries, kids swimming, the Sunshine Bridge, and plantation homes were just some of the many sights Donald enjoyed as he sped toward the devastated city, the seriousness of his mission dampening any true pleasure, which would have ordinarily be received from such a trip. But now his thoughts were on one thing, his family.

THE CITY BENEATH THE SEA

CHAPTER THIRTY-ONE

Bouncing along the narrow streets of the city, Melanie finally reached the boulevard of Elysian Fields. It was here where the bus which had brought so many people so far, spluttered to a stop.

"What's wrong?" Stan asked, as the bus rolled to a stop.

"I don't know."

As the bus stopped, Melanie opened the door and headed out, followed close behind by Stan.

Walking to the back of the bus, smoke was billowing from the engine compartment.

"You said you had a run in with a gang?" Donald asked, as he put his finger in one of several bullet holes in the engine shroud.

"What do we now?" Melanie asked, seemingly all out of ideas.

"We walk," Stan said, picking up the leadership mantle for the time being. "Get everybody out of the bus, tell them to take only what they can carry."

"That's all they've got," Melanie said, disappearing inside the bus then returning with everyone from inside a short time later.

"Folks, we're at the end of Elysian Fields, we need to get to the Convention Center. It's a good walk, but we're on pretty high ground from here out, so the walk should be easy. If someone falls behind, call out. We're all going to get there together," Stan said. "We're not leaving anyone behind."

Following Esplanade street to the levee, the group walked several long blocks, but finally arrived at Decatur, then entered the heart of the French Quarter.

As they walked, they noticed none of the shops seemed to have been vandalized, not realizing why until they walked a little further down the street where a police presence was clearly visible.

THE CITY BENEATH THE SEA

In the distance, Melanie saw a police officer and ran towards him.

"Officer! Officer!" Melanie cried trying to get the officer's attention.

"Yes, ma'am," the officer said, stopping to address her concerns.

"I was on a bus and a group of thugs robbed us and took some of the people off,." Melanie explained to the officer. "Can you help me go back and find them, Officer?"

"No, ma'am, I'm sorry," the officer said, refusing her request for help. "I've got strict orders to protect the Quarter against looters. I can't venture outside."

"They may kill them!" Melanie pleaded.

"I'm sorry I can't help," the officer said, reiterating his original position.

Melanie stood there in shock as the officer walked away. The symbol of law and order, refusing to help her. Turning back to her group, she rejoined them, as they continued to walk towards the Convention Center.

"Y'all keep going," Stan said, breaking away from the group to talk to a different police officer. "Officer, could you tell me if the Red Cross is set up at the Convention Center?" Stan asked, trying to verify their presence.

"Probably so, they've got a lot of people down there," the officer said, "I heard they were bringing some ambulance transports, but haven't heard anything else."

"Thank you, Officer."

"No problem."

The group continued down Decatur, bound for the Convention Center. Up ahead, two police cars were parked in front of a liquor store. But what had appeared to be the officers protecting the establishment proved to be just the opposite.

The doors of the patrol car were open as well as the trunk. One officer stood guard with a shotgun, ready to repel anyone who tried to deter their criminal activity. Coming from inside the liquor store, three other officers were filling the patrol cars with booze.

The crowd stared as they passed, but said nothing as they walked by, the looks of disbelief and contempt they showed the officers said what words could not.

After a another three-block walk, the group passed Harrah's casino, then after another shot walk, finally arrived under the greater New Orleans bridge where they were met by another crowd heading in the opposite direction.

"Where you guys going?" Stan asked, talking to the man in the lead.

"Mayor Nagin said to cross the Bridge, they've got buses on the other side, to take us to shelters," the man explained their purpose for leaving the Convention Center.

Turning to his group who had overheard what the man said, Stan asked them for their decision. "Do we follow them?" Stan asked, "They've got buses waiting for us on the other side of the river."

Without a formal vote, most people just nodded their heads in agreement. Most just wanted the nightmare to be over with and really didn't care how. Stan's group merged into the other group, Stan positioning himself towards the front of a large mass of people, with Melanie and Janelle close behind.

Some of the group were on crutches, some in wheelchairs. Some were carrying suitcases and garbage bags. Some pushed shopping carts full to spilling over.

Leading the ascent up the ramp which led to the bridge, the two groups merged on their way up, then emerged onto the bridge just as the sun was setting on the darkened city.

THE CITY BENEATH THE SEA

On the Greater New Orleans bridge, a patrol car sat, turning back the occasional black migrant attempting to leave the beleaguered city. The easy job was about to take a rapid turn for the worst. At the foot of the bridge, one of the observant officers noticed a massive crowd forming and heading their way.

Getting on the radio, the officer called for backup. "Dispatch! Dispatch! Come in, Dispatch! This is unit 12!" the excited officer called into the radio.

"This is dispatch, go head, unit twelve."

"I need backup! We have hundreds of blacks heading our way! They're going to try to cross the bridge!"

"10-4 unit twelve, hold your position, help is on the way."

As night began to fall over the bridge and the massive crowd grew closer, a large amount of men and personnel, responding to the officer's request for backup, converged on the bridge. On arriving at the location, they wasted no time as they quickly deployed across the span of the bridge.

Ferrell, in the back of a jeep, yelled out to his officers. "No one gets across!" Ferrell ordered to the deployed officers. The lights on every patrol car on the bridge were flashing, along with every spotlight trained on the bridge, ready for the inevitable showdown.

As the crowd neared, Ferrell picked up the PA, mentally preparing himself for what was about to come. He knew the decision would be his to repel any attempt to cross the bridge. He knew his loyal officers would follow his commands. This was the showdown he always knew would come. The line in the sand was now stretched across the bridge. Ferrell knew only two possible outcomes would come out of this.

Either the crowd would disperse and return to New Orleans, or violence on the scale this city had never seen was about to take place.

THE CITY BENEATH THE SEA

One thing was sure, the bridge would not be crossed if Ferrell had anything to say about it.

THE CITY BENEATH THE SEA

CHAPTER THIRTY-TWO

As the crowd emerged off the narrow ramp, they began to spread out across the four-lane bridge, allowing more and more people to exit the ramp.

But the upward ascent, with the promise of rescue on the other side of the bridge, still proved too much for some, as they began to fall off to the side, unable to continue.

Most continued on, determined to find the bus that would take them away from all the destruction and heartache.

Soon, before even realizing it, Stan found himself shoulder to shoulder with the group leader who organized the march.

Nearing the top of the bridge, the group saw the unmistakable red and blue lights of police vehicles, ready at least in the minds of most, to provide assistance and escort them to the buses.

"Looks like we've made it," Stan said, breathing a sigh of relief for the first time today. Reaching back, Stan took his wife's hand. "We made it, Janelle! We're safe now!"

Suddenly, the blast from a shotgun shattered the serenity of the moment, as the crowd stopped dead in their tracks. The loud blast was soon followed by a stern, harsh voice on a PA.

"That's far enough!" the voice screamed out over the P.A. "You need to turn around and go back!" the unseen voice commanded, just as several police officers dressed in riot gear marched out, forming a line across the bridge.

The group leader who organized the march tried to approach one of the officers who was dressed in riot gear, to try to explain to him what was going on.

THE CITY BENEATH THE SEA

"Officer, the mayor said they had buses over here," the group leader informed the officer why they were there.

But instead of the verbal response, the man had expected, two of the officers charged forward, pushing the man to the ground.

"Get back!" they ordered. "You won't get a second warning!"

"What are you doing!" Stan yelled, rushing over to help the man to his feet. But instead of the man standing shoulder to shoulder with Stan, he ran into the crowd, not wanting anything more to do with the officers.

"Turn around and go back before someone gets hurt!" the voice ordered the crowd.

"Go back to what?" Stan yelled, "In case you haven't heard, the city's underwater!"

"If you don't go back, we'll be forced to send you back," Ferrell warned. "You're not going to do to our city what you did to yours."

Stan held his ground, continuing to yell and challenge this unseen person, who didn't even have the courage to face him, face-to-face.

"So that's what this is about! You're afraid we're going to loot your city!" Stan said, with a laugh. "Look around, we've got old people, children, people in wheelchairs. We just want food and water, a safe place to rest. Now please let us through."

As Stan stepped forward, the sound of shotguns loading rounds into their chambers could be heard.

"Y'all would shoot us to keep us out!" Stan yelled, not believing what he was experiencing. "This is America! Who are you people?"

Janelle stepped up and tried to pull Stan back. As Stan turned, he saw some of the crowd starting to turn around and go back. To what he didn't know.

"This isn't right, baby!" Stan said, trying to reassure his wife that he knew what he was doing.

THE CITY BENEATH THE SEA

"I know Stan, but you can't win this!" Janelle cautioned him about taking a stand against such overwhelming odds.

"Melanie, look after my wife," Stan said, then turned back towards the officers.

Melanie stepped forward, pulling Janelle back.

"Stan! No Stan!" Janelle yelled.

"Baby, I've lost everything!" Stan yelled back, as tears began to form in his eyes. "I'm not going to lose my self-respect! If they want that, they're going to have to take it."

The riot police stepped forward, just as Melanie pulled Janelle back.

With batons in hand they swung at Stan, striking him several times on the back and head, sending him to the ground in a dazed, confused state.

"Stop!" Melanie yelled, running forwards throwing herself on Stan.

The riot police stopped, returning to formation, allowing Melanie and Janelle time to help Stan to his feet and carry him away.

"He's an old man!" Melanie yelled, as she helped Janelle carry Stan away.

Bleeding from his head and mouth, Stan was confused and disoriented, but was still able to walk as Janelle and Melanie lead him back down the bridge.

"Has he always been like this?" Melanie asked Janelle as they walked.

"As long as I've known him, the David never afraid to stand up to Goliath."

Arriving at the foot of the bridge, everyone was ecstatic to find trucks and buses had arrived to transport the group to shelters.

Merging into the crowd, Melanie, Stan and Janelle patiently waited to be transported. Melanie used a handkerchief she had in her pocket to help stop the bleeding on Stan's head wound.

THE CITY BENEATH THE SEA

As they waited, he remained silent, though conscious, he leaned his head on Janelle's shoulder. It seemed as though he had somehow been defeated. Dehumanized by the same people who had taken an oath to protect him. Reflecting back on his beating , not a single blow he received was delivered by an African American police officer. Every man on that bridge was white. Each relished the opportunity to beat him with impunity.

"Have we not learned anything as a society?" Stan wondered, "Why is the over-riding factor of a man still the color of his skin?"

Finally, after a long wait, Stan, Janelle and Melanie were loaded onto transport, leaving behind everything but the memory of the bridge behind them.

"Where you taking us?" Melanie asked one of the guardsman.

"Not sure, someplace safe," the guardsman said, "A mandatory evacuation is underway, there won't be anyone left in the city."

Leaning back in her seat, she leaned over to Janelle. "The entire city's being evacuated, it must be a lot worse than we thought," Melanie said, sharing with Janelle the information she had just obtained.

THE CITY BENEATH THE SEA

CHAPTER THIRTY-THREE

Speeding down the river, with the throttle pushed to the max, the powerful speedboat had made good time. Just passing under the Huey P. Long bridge, Donald set his sights on the distant Greater New Orleans bridge. As he approached the bridge, his attention was drawn to the flashing lights and the crowd of people moving towards them.

"What the –" Donald's thought were interrupted by a shotgun blast from the bridge.

Pulling back on the throttle, then putting the boat in neutral, Donald began to watch the historic event play out right before his eyes.

The crowd stopped when the shotgun blast got their attention. Donald knew someone was giving instructions on a PA, but he was just too far to understand what he was saying.

Sometime went by and the crowd began to move back the way they came, obviously deterred by the police presence, not to mention the shotgun blast.

With the show over, Donald pushed down on the throttle once more, heading for the French Quarter.

Within minutes, he had arrived at the Moon Walk, named for a former mayor of New Orleans, Moon Landreu, he often remembered spending hours a day on the boardwalk pondering what direction he wanted his life to go in. Now it would be armed National Guards who were about to determine the direction he would be going in.

"Hello," Donald said, as he guided up to the two guardsman posted on the boardwalk.

The guardsmen nodded, not really sure what to make of Donald at this point.

"I've come to find my parents, is it ok if I dock here?" Donald asked politely.

THE CITY BENEATH THE SEA

"Sorry, sir, the city is in lock down. Everyone has been ordered to evacuate, and no one is being allowed back in," the guardsman informed Donald of the latest news.

"Ok," Donald said, knowing he would not be able to change their mind, he didn't want to bring any more attention to himself than he had to. "Just thought I'd ask, they're probably in a shelter by now anyway," Donald said as he put the boat in reverse and slowly headed downriver.

The guardsmen watched as he left the area. The sun had set by now, and the once bright city and well-lit bridges, were hidden under a blanket of darkness. The only lights in the city were from the few vehicles that now patrolled the streets.

Maneuvering his boat next to the warehouse wharf some distance down river, well away from the curious eyes of the guardsmen, Donald slipped the vessel between the pilings, and virtually under the high wharf, out of sight.

Securing the boat, Donald then disappeared below the deck, only to emerge moments later resembling a ninja ready for combat. Dressed all in black, Donald carried with him a black backpack, which held the few necessities he might need along the way. Other than that, Donald carried nothing else.

Using the wharf's crossbeams, Donald maneuvered his way to the inclined embankment under the pier. Then, jumping over crossbeam after crossbeam, he made his way to the end of the wharf and freedom.

Peering out into the darkened city, Donald orientated himself and embarked on his journey towards his home.

Heading down Elysian Fields, Donald stayed close to the side of the street to avoid detection. A lot of things had been going on in the city and plenty of it had not been good. Many of the houses he passed looked like they had survived the hurricane, but could not survive the vandalism which followed.

Doors had been kicked in and widows shattered. With the amount of senseless damage that had been dealt to the city, Donald was surprised no one had set any fires. That would have really delivered a knockout blow to the city. With no water pressure and few fireman to battle the fires, the city would have gone up in flames with nothing to stop it.

In the distance, Donald saw movement. Heading to the side of one of the houses, he watched from around the corner.

About five men were heading his way. From this distance, he couldn't tell who they were, or what their intentions were, so he erred on the side of caution and hid.

As they neared, he realized they were one of the many roving gangs moving about the city looting and destroying property. The five African American males were armed with guns. Donald slid under the house as they neared. He watched as they passed by. He wanted to avoid any confrontation if possible, especially with people who carried guns. After they were gone, Donald emerged from his hiding place, then continued down the road to his house. As he walked, Donald noticed the water was beginning to rise. Soon, he found himself treading through waist-deep water as he pushed forward toward his house.

After a long tiring journey through water and avoiding roving gangs, Donald had finally arrived at his parents' house. Just ahead of him now, Donald headed for the front door, which was open. Luckily, the water had only come a few inches into the house.

Removing a light from his backpack, he shone it inside. Examining the doorframe, he could see it had been kicked in, and on the door had what appeared to be a shotgun blast and blood.

THE CITY BENEATH THE SEA

Entering the house, Donald could immediately tell it had been ransacked, the broken scattered possessions of his parents', was in sharp contrast to his mother's meticulous housekeeping.

It was not until Donald entered the kitchen, did he discover what he had come for. There on the kitchen counter was a note, written by his mother.

"Gone to Convention Center."

Donald took the note, tucked it away in his pocket, and headed out the door and onto the porch.

As he exited the house, bright lights pierced what was once darkness.

"Don't move a muscle or I'll put a hole in you!" Sweet ordered, as Donald raised his hands.

Several flashlights shone in Donald's face, but he couldn't see who was holding them, just the silhouette of the forms as they began to move around the water.

"Birdie, search him," Sweet ordered.

Birdie headed for the porch, splashing through the water as he went. Birdie never would reach Donald, for as he neared, a floodlight engulfed the area transforming the darkened landscape into virtual daylight.

"This is the Louisiana National Guard. Do not move," the strong powerful voice of William ordered over the PA.

Not willing to go quietly, Sweet fired a shot in the direction of the light, taking it out in the first shot. Under the cover of darkness once again, Sweet and his gang made their escape, with automatic weapon fire hot on their heels.

As soon as Donald heard the first volley of gunfire, he immediately hit the deck of the porch, tying to avoid any stray round finding him in the darkness. Birdie, who had managed to get on the porch before the guard showed up, ran without hesitation to the end of the porch, clearing the handrail without even touching it, then disappearing into the night.

THE CITY BENEATH THE SEA

After what seemed like an eternity to anyone who had just had live rounds fired over their heads, the gun fire stopped, but Donald remained motionless on the porch not wanting to trigger happy guardsman mistaking him for one of the gangsters.

Donald could hear men coming in his direction. He could see the lights. Their intentions at this point were still unclear.

"I got one here, sir!" one of the guardsman called out, indicating a body he had discovered in the water, the only casualty of the recent shootout.

"Bag him and put him on the porch," a guardsman ordered, obviously in charge.

Then suddenly, out of nowhere, a light shone in Donald's face.

"Let me see your hands!" the man yelled.

Raising his hands as far as he could, while still being on his stomach, Donald tried to comply with the man's orders.

"I'm not armed!" Donald yelled, as several guardsman climbed the porch, with guns drawn, to bring Donald to his feet.

"What are you doing here?" William asked.

"This is my parents' house, I'm looking for them," Donald explained.

"Why did you and your gang fire on us?" William asked, not immediately believing Donald's story.

"They weren't with me! They were about to rob me when you showed up. I'm an attorney from New York," Donald said, trying to make sure he was not characterized with the group of thugs that had just had a shootout with the guardsman.

"You got ID?" William asked, as he walked up.

Removing his wallet, Donald presented his identification to the guardsman.

"You know the city's locked down. How did you get in?" William inquired, curious as to where the break in their system security net was.

THE CITY BENEATH THE SEA

"I've got a boat at the river."

"Smart! We couldn't block that, now could we. I guess you didn't find your parents?" William said, already knowing the answer, not seeing anyone else around.

"No, they weren't here."

"You're lucky we came along when we did. They have a lot of gangs going around looting and killing. Come on, we'll get you back to your boat. You can't do anything else here," the guardsman said, leading the way off the porch to his waiting vehicle.

"They left me a note," Donald said, not quite wanting to leave without confirmation they weren't still in the city somewhere. "They said they were at the Convention Center."

"The Convention Center! Well, I can save you some time, my friend, because we personally evacuated everyone from the Convention Center, and I have men posted there just in case any stragglers arrive, they too will be immediately evacuated," the guardsman assured Donald.

"Where did they take them?"

"Houston."

In the distance, gunfire could be heard.

"You got to get out of here, it's not safe for you here."

William and another guardsman escorted Donald back to their waiting vehicle.

Climbing aboard, they headed back to the river. Donald noticed as he boarded the vehicle several body bags on the floor, and they weren't empty. Luckily, within no time at all, Donald was right back where he started.

"Thank you, guys," Donald said, jumping out of the vehicle.

"No problem, I hope you find your parents," the guardsman said, then headed back to where they had heard the gunfire earlier.

THE CITY BENEATH THE SEA

As the vehicle pulled away, Donald disappeared under the wharf. A few minutes later, his boat was rocketing up the river back to Baton Rouge.

Passing the Sunshine bridge sometime later, the bright lights of the Convent refinery illuminated the area, casting huge shadows from objects that dared try to block its path.

The throttle still pushed to the limit as the boat roared past the refinery, completing yet another milestone to his return journey to Baton Rouge.

A short time later, Donald pulled up to the dock he had departed from only a few hours earlier.

Mooring the boat, he headed towards the Centraplex, where the crowds had not diminished, possibly only getting larger.

People were everywhere, many in uniform, many were National Guards, trying to maintain some sense of order in a catastrophe that had overwhelmed so many areas of public assistance. From firefighters, police officers, doctors and volunteers, everyone was feeling the aftermath of Katrina.

Bypassing the Centraplex, relying on information he had obtained from the guardsman in New Orleans, Donald headed to his car on the levee.

Finding it right where he left it, Donald fired it up and headed for the bridge, and Houston. Hoping his parents were there.

THE CITY BENEATH THE SEA

CHAPTER THIRTY-FOUR

Melanie walked down the aisle of the moving bus, it was late and the bus was dark, with only a few individuals passing the time by reading, their overhead lights offering Melanie her only light as she negotiated the aisle. For the most part, everyone was asleep, exhausted both physically and emotionally over the unbelievable nightmare they had experienced first-hand.

Reaching Stan and Janelle, she sat across from them, preparing to share with them what she had just learned from the bus driver.

"How's your head?" Melanie asked, reminded of Stan's wound by the bandage on his head.

"Fine, thanks to you," Stan replied, with gratitude, knowing if it hadn't been for her help, he might have been injured far worst.

"Where are they taking us?" Janelle asked, having been forced on the bus. She, like everyone else, did not even know their destination.

"They're bringing us to a shelter, we're going to have to be there a while," Melanie said, sharing with her friends what she had learned from the bus driver. "New Orleans is shut down, they're only allowing emergency personnel inside."

"We're heading for Baton Rouge?" Stan asked, wondering what shelter they would ultimately end up at.

"Baton Rouge is full, we're going to the Astro Dome in Houston," Melanie said, leaning back in her seat. "Try to get some rest, it's going to be a while."

Hours later, another of a long line of buses pulled up to the front of the Astro Dome. A scene that had been repeated over and over, during the course of the night.

THE CITY BENEATH THE SEA

With plenty of people moving about, some police, some military, the atmosphere seemed to have a sense of order about it, which once anyone had experienced a breakdown in order, they quickly longed for its return.

The doors to the Greyhound bus opened up and people begin filing out, some holding trash bags, others with just the clothes on their backs.

Stan and Janelle emerged from the bus, with Melanie close behind, helping to support a wobbly Stan, still having trouble with his equilibrium.

They followed the crowd as it was being directed to the processing area of the dome. As they entered the large opening, more military were on hand, ready to respond to any unexpected eventuality. One of the guardsman was shouting instructions, but from their distance, the orders were just muddled. It was not until they got closer that they were able to understand what he was saying.

"Women to the right, men to the left," the guardsman ordered, using his hands to gesture, reinforcing his instructions.

The evacuees were being separated by sex. In the distance, tables and curtains were set up where everyone was being searched. First their bags, then their person.

Female military personnel undertook the task of searching the women, while the men were being searched across the room.

To Melanie, it was necessary, though the insensitive nature of the task, brought still another grim comparison to the process the Germans used when they processed thousands of Jews a day. Families were separated and searched; could this really be happening in America?

Most people relinquished the last remaining bit of pride and self-respect they had without incident. Some, however, had had enough! Being transported and treated only a little better than cattle, they had reached their breaking point.

"No, you're not going to put your hands on me!" the angry African American evacuee screamed his objection to being searched by the white guardsman.

"Sir, it's for the safety of everyone that we search evacuees before they enter," the guardsman tried to calmly explain to the irate individual, who was old enough to be his father.

"You know, son," the evacuee began. "I just lost everything I spent my whole life working for. All I got left is my name and you can't even refer to me by that. Even when you got my I.D. y'all are treating us like animals," the evacuee screamed for extra emphasis. "Tearing through the few possessions we were able to save, and if that's not enough, you want to put your hands on us."

"I'm sorry, sir, we have our orders," the guardsman explained, still remaining calm.

"Just give me some food and water and I'll leave," the evacuee said, offering what he thought was a reasonable compromise.

"The food and water is inside; after you're processed, you can have all you want," the guardsman said.

"You're not going to process me!"

About this time, another white guardsman walked up, it was quickly apparent this one had far more attitude and much less patience.

"What's the problem!" the guardsman asked, hearing the commotion from across the room.

"This gentleman won't be processed," the guardsman began to explain. "And he's making demands."

"Demands!" the evacuee yelled. "I just want some food and water."

"Sir, we have to process all evacuees," the newly arrived guardsman stated bluntly. "No exceptions!"

THE CITY BENEATH THE SEA

"My name is James!" the evacuee stated, no longer wanting to be referred to as just another number in a long list of numbers, or the generic 'Sir'.

"Whatever!" the second guardsman said, not willing to accommodate his request. "Come over here so I can search you, then we'll let you in."

"I don't think so!" James refused.

The guardsman began to take a defensive posture towards the evacuee.

"Is there a reason you refuse to be searched?" the guardsman asked, putting his hand on his baton.

The evacuee did not respond, to the guardsman's question, choosing to remain silent.

"I thought so," the guardsman grabbed James by the arm, but he pulled away and tried to leave. Before he could get too far, he was tackled by the guardsman, who pinned him to the floor and cuffed him.

"You had to do it the hard way!" the guardsman said, standing James up and hauling him off.

At a distance, Stan watched as the scene unfolded, then finally concluded, he then turned to Melanie and Janelle.

"What is wrong with these people? Where's their compassion, first the bridge, now here," Stan said. "I can't help wonder if the room was full of white people, would they be treated the same way."

"Let's just do what they say, we'll be all right," Melanie said, worried that Stan could not survive another beating. "Janelle and I will meet you on the other side. Just do what they say!"

Stan nodded in agreement as they were separated by gender to be processed.

To Melanie, a student of history, the last few hours brought to the forefront the events of Katrina and how they seemed to parallel the holocost. Some of the similarities were shocking, even though she was hesitant to make the comparisons, but even to the most casual observer, the similarities were so obvious.

THE CITY BENEATH THE SEA

The club-wheeling police officers on the bridge suffered from the same mental disorder, or brainwashing that thousands of Nazis must have experienced during the war. They were led to believe what they were doing was the right thing. They were protecting their community from the infectious hordes that threatened it. Much like the propaganda the Nazis spread about the Jews during World War Two. It is in this climate of disorder and chaos that normally decent human beings were able to do what, under normal conditions, they would not dream of. Who among the officers on the bridge would ever have dreamed of using batons on a defenseless old man, whose only crime was seeking safety for himself and his family. But the similarities did not stop there.

When the refugees were loaded onto buses, much like the Jews on boxcars, both experienced the uncertainty of not knowing where they were going or when they would arrive.

Then, upon finally arriving at their destination, the evacuees, like the Jews, were herded, culled and processed, by gender. Their possessions and person searched in a rapid insensitive manner, but they were helpless to object.

Anyone not submitting to the mandatory search was dealt with quickly and harshly, sending a clear message to the others that followed.

Someone once said, "Those who do not know their history, are destined to repeat it." The events that had unfolded within the last few days had made Melanie realize how thin the fabric of civilized society really was, and how easily decent people with the best of intentions, could become so cruel.

Lights from oncoming traffic shone inside the car. Itwas late and Donald's eyes started to close, exhausted from the nonstop roller coaster he had been on.

THE CITY BENEATH THE SEA

But despite his best efforts, Donald nodded off. The car sped wildly out of control, but finally came to rest harmlessly in the middle of the medium.

Wide-awake now, with his heart pounding so hard it threatened to leave his chest. Regaining his composure, Donald restarted the vehicle and put it back on the highway.

Up ahead, a crowded rest stop would offer the closest thing to a hotel he was going to find. Exiting the interstate, Donald headed towards it.

THE CITY BENEATH THE SEA

CHAPTER THIRTY-FIVE

Outside the courthouse, Susan was punching a series of numbers into her cell phone as she ran into a man, causing her to look up.

The tall distinguished Caucasian male, with a full head of hair, but graying temples looked down upon Susan with a smile.

"Daddy!" Susan said, "What are you doing here?"

"Thought I'd take my girl to lunch."

"Is everything ok?" Susan asked, wary of her dad's true motivation for asking her to lunch.

"Of course, why shouldn't it be?"

"Uh, I don't know, probably because you never took me out to lunch before."

"Really?" Harrington replied with a smile. "Well I guess I'm overdue then," he said, as he escorted his daughter down the steps.

Inside a busy restaurant, Harrington and Susan were engaged in random conversation while eating their lunch.

"Have you heard from Donald?" Harrington finally asked, revealing the true purpose of the lunch.

"So that's why you brought me to lunch," Susan said, with a smile.

"Don't be ridiculous, we're just talking here," Harrington said in his defense.

"No I haven't. I tried to call and text message a few times, but I haven't heard back," Susan explained.

Almost all communications are out down there," Harrington said, "They pretty much got thrown back to the stone age overnight. For a while, the only messages that were getting out was from Ham radio operators. I hope everything is ok."

"I've been watching the news, it looks really bad down there," Susan stated, sharing with her concerns with her father.

THE CITY BENEATH THE SEA

"Yea, my heart goes out to them. I hear most of them are being relocated to Baton Rouge and Houston."

"That's what I understand," Susan said, agreeing with her father.

"I guess those cities better brace themselves for a spike in crime," Harrington said, surprising his daughter with his comments.

"What do you mean?" Susan asked, making sure she fully understood her father's meaning.

"I mean, when that inner city trash hits Houston, they won't be the only victims," Harrington said, expounding on his insensitive comments.

"Daddy!" Susan said, objecting to her father's remarks, looking around to see if anyone else had heard them.

"I'm sorry, baby, but it's true. The liberal experiment of the south has long since failed," Harrington said, beginning to articulate his position. "The only reason politicians keep pouring billions into that city in social programs is not to improve the life of those people, all they want to do is secure their voting block. All we ever got out of our efforts in New Orleans was more and more people on welfare; second and third generations, it's become a way of life for some. Then we got the murder rate! Highest in the nation. Black men killing other black men, for the most part most incidents involved drugs. How can we help people who won't help themselves. Donald is a fine person, but he's an anomaly. He has been able to rise above the turmoil and chaos that was once his home. Since I've taken him under my wing, I've transformed him into a gentleman."

"You need to get this all out of your system before Donald gets back," Susan said, cautioning her father on his views.

"You know I would never do anything to hurt Donald, but I bet deep down he believes it himself."

Susan stared into her wine glass pondering her father's words.

THE CITY BENEATH THE SEA

Donald parked his car in the distance, away from the massive Houston Astro Dome; the only available spot he could find in the crowded parking lot.

Helicopters flew overhead, as Donald began to make his way towards the Astro Dome, serpentining himself between cars and people.

Finally, he arrived at the entrance of the Astro Dome, Donald saw an information sign a short distance away, where several people having the same idea as him were waiting in line.

After what seemed like forever, Donald finally reached the make-shift desk and came face to face with someone he hoped could help him locate his parents.

"Hi," Donald said, "I'm looking for my parents Stan and Janelle King."

The attendant typed the names into the laptop and it only took a second.

"They're here," the attendant said, sharing the good news with Donald. "Can't tell you exactly where, but they're somewhere inside."

"How do I get in?"

"Go in that line over there," the attendant said, pointing to a line not far away. "They will search you, then you can go in."

Moving immediately to the line the attendant indicated, Donald once again waited his turn.

After being scanned and searched, Donald entered the interior of the massive sports arena.

The sight was depressing: almost every inch of floor space had been taken up with cots and most of them had someone in them.

Descending the steps to the floor, Donald scanned the faces of the refugees, looking for his parents.

The faces were full of despair, and the lack of hope was undeniable on every face he saw. Each bearing the emotional scars of the worst natural disaster in the country's history.

After searching row after row of cots, for what seemed like hours, his efforts were finally rewarded when he saw his parents in the distance. They were sitting on a cot talking to a woman he had never seen before.

"Mom!" Donald called as he hurried towards them.

"Donald!" Janelle cried, "I knew you would come," She said, throwing her arms around her son.

Donald looked to his dad, a bandage on his head. "What happened to you?" he asked.

"I felt I could cross the bridge to the west bank," Stan explained vaguely.

"And?"

"The police thought I couldn't. I guess they were right."

"Almost got himself killed, the old fool, if it hadn't been for Melanie," Janelle stopped, in the excitement of seeing her son, she had forgotten to introduce him to Melanie. "I'm sorry I didn't introduce you. Donald, this is Melanie. Melanie, this is my son, Donald."

Donald and Melanie's eyes met. They both gave a big smile, it was as though at that moment lightning had somehow struck.

"Thank you for watching out for my dad, he's hard-headed sometimes," Donald said, smiling broadly at Melanie.

"Hello!" Stan objected. "I'm right here, if you're gong to talk about me, at least do it behind my back."

"It was nothing," Melanie said, oblivious to anyone other than Donald.

"I'm gong to be taking my parents back with me to New York. Is there anything we can do for you?" Donald asked. "You have family here? Somewhere to go?"

THE CITY BENEATH THE SEA

"Yes, ah, absolutely. In fact, they're on their way now," Melanie said, able to lie with a straight face.

"Ok. It was nice meeting you," Donald said, extending his hand to shake Melanie's.

"Same here."

"Ok Mom, Dad, get your things, I'm going to take you back with me until you can get back into your house," Donald said. "From the Big Easy, to the Big Apple."

"You know we can't stay long," Stan said, making it clear to his son he wanted to get back home.

"I know, Dad, just till you can get back to your house."

"Ok, Son."

Donald helped gather his parents' things and after Stan and Janelle exchanged hugs with Melanie, they headed out of the Astro Dome.

Melanie waved goodbye, then sat back down on the cot, a little saddened her friends were gone.

Sherry Henry sashayed up as the Kings left. A heavy set African American woman with short cropped hair, pleasant personality, and an infectious smile, Sherry was one of the ladies Melanie had rescued on the bus, and had earned Sherry's admiration and respect ever since.

"Couldn't help overhearing. Why you told that fine looking brother, that you have family on the way?" Sherry said, repeating the words she overheard her say to Donald. "You told me you don't have anyone."

"He is cute, isn't he?" Melanie said with a smile, then continued. "So I told a little lie, I think they have enough trouble without listening to my problems."

"I tell you what, if the brother wants to listen to my problems, I be more than happy to give him an ear full, and whatever else he ask for," Sherry said, with a smile.

Melanie gently slapped her friend on the arm.

"Girl, you so bad!"

THE CITY BENEATH THE SEA

Sherry struck a pose and snapped her fingers.
"The three B's, baby! Bad, bold and beautiful!"
The two woman laughed as Sherry left Melanie to ponder her thoughts alone.

THE CITY BENEATH THE SEA

CHAPTER THIRTY-SIX

Entering his apartment, carrying his parents' bags Donald was soon followed by his mother and father.

"This is it, Mom, Dad, make yourselves at home," Donald said, inviting his parents to his apartment for the first time.

"You have a beautiful place here, Donald," Janelle said as she walked around the spacious apartment.

Noticing a small table with photographs, Janelle was drawn towards it.

On the small table, there were several pictures depicting Donald in various settings and locations with a white woman. Pictures of them skiing, skydiving, on an island with a drink in hand.

"Donald, who is this woman in the picture?" Janelle asked, not having seen or heard of her before.

"That's a surprise I've been waiting to tell you about," Donald replied sheepishly, like a cat trying to convince its owner he did not really swallow the canary. "That's Susan," Donald continued, beginning to put all his cards on the table for everyone to see. "She's my fiancé."

The look on Donald's parents' faces was of shock and disbelief.

"A white girl? You marrying a white girl!" Stan said in disbelief.

Janelle heard the disapproval in Stan's voice and tried to calm him by taking his arm.

"You never mentioned her," Janelle said, trying to interrupt Stan's roll, but to no avail.

"He didn't mention her because she's a white girl," Stan said, more in a mumble as he walked to the window.

"I know, I should have told you about her. I'm sorry about that, everything's been going so fast,"

Donald said, trying to find an excuse for the inexcusable.

"Well, son, we're happy for you," Janelle said with a smile.

"You are?" Donald said, surprised by her sudden acceptance. "I mean, thank you."

Stan stayed in the background by the window, not speaking, still shocked by the revelation.

Donald looked to his father by the window.

"I wish you could speak for everyone," Donald said, sensing his father's obvious disapproval.

"You know your dad," Janelle said, "it takes him a little while to get used to new things. He'll come around. It's been a long day, I think I'll unpack and turn in for the night."

Janelle left the living room and headed for the guest bedroom, closing the door behind her. Donald walked up next to his dad, they both stared out over the lights of the city that never sleeps.

"This is a big city," Stan said, never breaking his stare.

"Yes it is," Donald said, finding something he could agree with his dad on.

"You happy here, son?" Stan asked.

"Yea, I think so."

"I always thought you would one day come home," Stan said, his tone soft and distant.

"What's the rest of it, Dad?" Donald asked, wanting to resolve any tension that may have arisen with the revelation of Susan. "You always thought I'd come home and marry a black woman?"

Stan just looked at Donald for a moment, trying to measure his response.

"You don't need to take that tone with me," Stan said, taking objection to the harsh manner Donald had spoken to him in.

"I'm sorry, Dad, I didn't mean to upset you," Donald said, apologizing for his tone, but not the words.

"She a lawyer too?" Stan asked, starting to move away from shock and into acceptance.

"She's an assistant DA."

"How did you meet her?"

"Through her dad," Donald explained. "I'm a partner in the firm."

"Really? I guess her dad got the whole package, a partner and a son-in-law." Stan paused for a moment as an eerie silence came over both of them, as though neither one of them could find any other words to continue the conversation.

"It's late, son," Stan finally broke the stalemate, "I think I'll turn in."

"Ok, Dad, I'll see you in the morning."

Stan nodded his head, then disappeared into the guest room, leaving Donald alone, as he stared out over the city.

Then as though on cue, the phone rang.

"Hello," Donald said, never breaking his stare at the city lights.

"Hey, stranger, you got your parents situated yet?" Susan's familiar voice was heard on the other end.

"Not really, we just got here."

"When do I get to meet them?" Susan asked, in her characteristic bubbly voice.

"Soon."

"My parents are planning a welcome to New York party for your folks. Isn't that sweet of them?"

"Oh, they really shouldn't," Donald said, trying to head off a potentially embarrassing situation. "My parents really aren't the party type."

"Don't be silly, who doesn't like parties?" Susan responded, casting aside Donald's objections. "Gotta go, see you tomorrow."

Donald set the phone down on the desk, his face anguished over the conversation.

THE CITY BENEATH THE SEA

Walking into the room, Stan found Janelle crying on the bed.

"What's the matter, baby?" Stan asked, not knowing what brought her to tears.

"You know what the matter is!" Janelle said. "He's marrying a white girl! My God, what will our grand-kids look like?"

"You seemed ok with it a moment ago," Stan said, confused by her sudden about face.

"What am I supposed to do, tell him how I feel? That won't accomplish anything other than driving him farther away from us," Janelle explained her reason for not showing her disapproval to her son.

"I know, I know," Stan said, tying to express his understanding. "But it's his choice, like it or not."

"I know," Janelle admitted, "but it hurts. You noticed the living room?"

"No, why?"

"Not a single picture of us anywhere. Yet there's pictures of her parents. I think our son is ashamed of us."

"Don't be ridiculous."

"You know what I feel," Janelle said, "you feel it too."

Stan did not speak, he just nodded then changed the subject.

"Tomorrow I'll try to get in touch with Kisha," Stan said, "See if she's heard from her dad, and find out where they moved Mom to."

"It probably won't be easy, everybody is scattered everywhere."

"I know," Stan acknowledged, "but we need to try."

"I know."

"Get some rest," said Stan, as he began to get undressed. "It's going to be a big day tomorrow."

THE CITY BENEATH THE SEA

CHAPTER THIRTY-SEVEN

Kisha King-Jones, walked down the aisle of the temporary morgue set up for Katrina victims, her task grim. Before today, Kisha never knew Carville, Louisiana had ever existed. After today, she would never forget it.

Standing in a large room, a wall of stainless steel doors before her, she thought she had prepared herself for this moment, but as it neared, the butterflies in her stomach once again began to shake her resolve.

The attendant went to one of the doors and opened it, the sound reverberated against the walls, creating an uneasy tension as the attendant pulled out the sheet-covered body on the sliding tray. As Kisha neared, he slowly pulled back the sheet.

"Is this your father?" the man asked in a soft voice.

Kisha looked at her pale, colorless father, swollen and partially decomposed from the days in the attic. He was almost unrecognizable, but still retained enough characteristics to identify him.

"Yes, that's him," Kisha said, as the tears began to flow.

The attendant replaced the sheet and slid the drawer back in.

"I've got to notify his mother, but haven't been able to locate her," Kisha said. "You wouldn't have access to some kind of database that shows where nursing home resident were evacuated to, do you?" Kisha asked, trying to find anyone who could help her.

"Nursing home?" the coroner asked, his curiosity peaked. "Which nursing home?"

"St. Nita's," Kisha said, "You know where they went?"

"You don't know?"

THE CITY BENEATH THE SEA

"Know what?" Kisha asked, puzzled by the coroner's remarks.

"They're here."

"What do you mean, they're here?" Kisha questioned, getting more and more confused and getting frustrated by the coroner.

"Only the workers escaped, the residents all died."

"What! They left them!" Kisha yelled, becoming quickly overwhelmed by the revelation of her grandmother's death.

"'Fraid so, would you like to try to ID her?"

"Yes," Kisha said, shaken, but willing to do what she had to.

"Give me a description of her so we can narrow down the search," the coroner requested, knowing there were hundreds of unidentified bodies to sort through.

"Mid-seventies, black, a scar over her right eye," Kisha said, giving a brief description of her grandmother.

The coroner's expression changed, as though the very limited description was enough for him to know where to find her.

Walking a short distance, he pulled a drawer out. Pulling the sheet back, he revealed Kisha's grandmother.

"That's her," Kisha said, thinking she could cry no more, but as her body released the tears, she realized she had plenty more to come. "I thought they evacuated!" Kisha cried. "How could they just leave them!"

"That's what a lot of people want to know," the coroner said, he too not understanding how it could happen.

Kisha left, emotionally drained, having been delivered a double blow with the discovery of her grandmother.

THE CITY BENEATH THE SEA

In Donald's New York City apartment, Stan and Janelle sat on the couch watching Fox News coverage and the aftermath of Katrina. The newsman was standing in front of the gaping hole of the 17th Street canal levee.

Having been unable to stop the flow of water from this location, engineers had to drive sheet piling where the canal entered the lake, thereby isolating the canal from the lake. As the newsman talked, the camera panned the area, giving you a view of the devastation.

"With the levee now secure and the city well on its way to being dried out, the long rebuilding efforts will now begin," the newsman began. "Roving gangs continue to pose a problem in the city, but with more National Guards being called up, Mayor Nagin has vowed to return order to the city by whatever means are at his disposal. If you remember some of our earlier reports, rival gangs have broken into pawnshops and have armed themselves. They now pose a significant threat not only to civilians, but to police officers and guardsman who try to once again restore order to this embattled city."

"It's going to be open season on blacks in New Orleans," Stan said, shaking his head. "The only thing they didn't set is a limit."

"They've got to restore order, Stan," Janelle said, not understanding his comment.

"It's how they're going to do it!" Stan stated emphatically. "This is probably the happiest day in the lives of some racist officers. Remember the bridge? How would you like to see those officers turned loose on the city? They will shoot anyone who fits the profile, and ask questions later! And the profile, in case you don't know is anyone who is black."

Just then, the phone rang, Janelle answered it.

"Donald King's residence," Janelle said and was greeted by a familiar voice on the other end.

"Aunt Janelle," Kisha said.

THE CITY BENEATH THE SEA

"Kisha, how are you?" Janelle asked. "Is everyone alright?"

"That's why I'm calling, Aunt Janelle," her voice somber. Janelle immediately knew bad news was close behind. "Is Uncle Stan there?"

"He's right here," Janelle said, handing the phone to Stan.

"Hello Kisha."

"Uncle Stan," Kisha said, hesitating for a moment. "I have some bad news."

"It's Evan, isn't it?" Stan said, already having suspected his brother's death since the storm.

"Yes, he's dead."

Stan began to tear up, but regained his composure quickly.

"Does your grandmother know? Were you able to locate the nursing home they have your grandmother in?" Stan asked.

"Uncle Stan, she's gone also."

"What do you mean?" Stan said, puzzled by the latest revelation.

"The bastards never evacuated her. They left her to die!" Kisha cried, breaking down with emotion as she informed her uncle of the news.

"What!" Stan said in disbelief.

"Yea, she never left the nursing home, she drowned there when the levees broke," Kisha explained to her shocked uncle. "I've got to go start making some arrangements. When are you going to be coming down?"

"We'll be down as soon as possible, your grandmother's arrangements are all ready made, we just need to notify the funeral home. She arranged everything in advance," Stan said. "Do you need my help with Evan's arrangements?"

"No, I think I got it, I was thinking about having one service, would that be alright with you?" Kisha asked through her tears.

THE CITY BENEATH THE SEA

"Yes, baby, whatever you feel's best. We'll be back soon," Stan said, then hung up the phone, the anguish evident on his face.

"Evan's dead?" Janelle asked, as Stan hung up the phone.

"So is my mother."

"My God!" Janelle said, shocked by the news. "I thought they evacuated them!"

Stan sat down on the edge of the sofa, trying to absorb so much bad news, delivered so quickly.

"So did I!" Stan said, then began to cry for the first time as Janelle tried to console him.

THE CITY BENEATH THE SEA

CHAPTER THIRTY-EIGHT

At Donald's office, his desk was stacked with files, the result of him missing just a couple of days of work.

Through a gap in the mountains of files, Donald was able to see Susan walk in.

"If Mohammad won't come to the mountain," Susan said with a smile. "The mountain will come to Mohammad."

"Hey, baby," Donald said, coming from behind his desk to greet her.

"I get a feeling you've been trying to ignore me?" Susan said, as Donald kissed her on the cheek.

"No, not at all, I've been trying to catch up," Donald tried to explain his not seeing her for a while.

"How are your parents? They see much of the city yet?"

"No, not really, in fact they haven't left the apartment."

"Well, that's all going to change tonight," Susan said, her voice gleeful.

"What do you mean?"

"Donald!" Susan said, her agitation with him showing. "I told you my parents were having a party in your parents' honor!"

"I didn't think it was tonight!"

"I told you!" Susan whined. "Please don't tell me you can't make it! I'm going to look foolish." A saddened look came over her. "Besides, Daddy has a surprise."

"Ok! I'll see what I can do," Donald said, trying to conceal his frustration with her. "What time?"

"About seven, daddy's going to send a limo for you and your parents."

"Ok, I guess I'll see you tonight."

Susan left the office as Donald once again started to return to his daunting task of catch up. He looked over his stack of files and thought about Susan's party, knowing he would have to take his parents shopping. Being pulled in so many directions, Donald just shook his head in frustration.

Grabbing his jacket, Donald headed out the office, stopping off at Celena's desk on the way out.

"Celena, I've got to take the rest of the day off," Donald said as he slipped his coat on.

"You caught up already?" Celena asked, as a puzzled look came over her.

"Are you kidding, I've just scraped the surface. I have to take my parents shopping, there's a party tonight. I just found out about it."

"Sounds fun," Celena said with a smile, knowing how much her boss hated social gatherings.

"You need to work on disguising your sarcasm a little better," Donald said, smiling at how well his secretary knew him.

"You got a final bill from the boat?" Donald asked, wondering how much money he would ultimately lose from the purchase and the quick resale of the boat he had taken to New Orleans.

"I got good news and I got bad news," Celena began. "The good news is the dealer was willing to buy the boat back, the bad news is they charged you a ten thousand dollar restocking fee."

"How do you restock a boat?" Donald asked, smiling at the irony of the remark. "Whatever you have to do to get rid of it will be fine." With those final instructions, Donald left his office.

As Donald entered his apartment, a sense of something wrong was apparent. The depressed, somber look on his parents' face, was a quick indicator to him that something bad had happened.

"What's wrong?" Donald asked, as he closed the door. "You look as though someone died."

THE CITY BENEATH THE SEA

"Your Uncle Evan has passed away, son, along with your grandmother," Stan said, breaking the news to his son.

"I knew Uncle Evan stayed behind, but I thought they had evacuated Grandma?" Donald said, reiterating what had been everyone's assumption.

"So did I, but according to your cousin, they left your grandmother to die," Stan said, trying to keep his anger and emotions under control. "They left her to drown like an animal!"

"Wow!" Donald said in disbelief. "How could this have happened?"

"I don't know," Stan said, "but I want to find out!"

Donald sat down on the couch next to his mom, trying to absorb everything that was said.

"When are we going back down?" Donald asked.

"Your mother and I are going back as soon as we can," Stan said. "They opened up the city, it's time for us to go home and try to pick up the pieces. I know how busy you are with everything up here, we'll let you know when the arrangements are in place."

"You said they opened the city back up?" Donald questioned, having seen the devastation first-hand, he was surprised it was opening up so soon.

"Yes, it's open; they're hauling in Fema trailers for the residents to stay in while they repair their homes," Stan began to update his son on the latest news from New Orleans. "I'm not sure we're going to need one or not."

"Probably not, the water didn't get that high in the house," Donald said, then paused, hesitating to even bring up the party, but knowing how much it meant to Susan, he decided to throw it out there.

"I know the timing couldn't be worse," Donald began, "but Susan and her dad are giving a party in your honor tonight."

"I don't feel much like partying," Stan said, stating his feelings up front and rather quickly.

THE CITY BENEATH THE SEA

"I know," Donald said, understanding how his parents must have felt with the bad news they had just received. "But this is important to Susan, so it's important to me."

"Ok," Janelle said, coming to her son's rescue without too much persuading on his part. "We'll come, I guess we'll finally get to meet Susan."

Stan looked at Janelle for a moment, giving her a disapproving look. "Come on Stan. It'll help take your mind off everything.,

"What are we supposed to wear?" Stan asked, the question coming from the least fashion conscience person in the room.

"Stan's right, we don't have anything to wear," Janelle said, only coming to the realization after her husband's remarks.

"I know, that's why we're going shopping," Donald said. "Come on, I won't take no for an answer."

In front of Donald's apartment, several people were waiting for cabs staggered short distances from each other as though to represent the party they were with and the number. One cab after another stopped to pick up the white passengers, leaving Donald and his parents, the only African Americans there, to wait on the curb.

It was so obvious to Stan what was going on; as the cabs pulled up next to the whites, some arriving well after them, but having no qualms about jumping in a cab before them. As Stan observed his son's reaction to this, he was surprised at how oblivious he was to such a blatant act of discrimination, but said nothing. Stan wanted to observe how his son conducted himself in his own city, and if this was any indication, he was not impressed.

Finally, after everyone else had been picked up and they were the only ones left, a cab pulled up and stopped to pick them up.

THE CITY BENEATH THE SEA

"Is it always this hard to get a cab?" Stan asked, as they drove down the street, making a subtle observation he hoped his son might have also observed.

"Sometimes," Donald said, "So many people and so few cabs."

Stan could hardly believe his ears. Not only was his son totally blind to the discrimination which was apparently perpetrated on him on a daily basis, he was actually defending it!

After a short drive, the cab pulled over to the curb in front of Pacy's department store. Paying the driver, they exited the cab and disappeared inside the largest department store in New York.

Following Donald as he led the way, they walked through the crowded department store, finally arriving at a section of ladies' dresses.

"Mom, why don't you look around to find something you like. I'll take Dad to get a suit."

"Ok, Donald," Janelle said, as she began to look through the clothes.

Not far away, Stan and Donald found the men's department, where the walls and racks were filled with every style and size of suit imaginable.

"You like a gray or black, Dad?" Donald asked as they arrived.

"I guess a black, I'm going to be going to a lot of funerals," Stan said, bringing to the forefront what they faced in the near future.

Donald looked at his dad and thought about his comment, and how much his parents had gone through already, and the realization of how much more they would have to go through before their life, once again found some sense of normalcy

"Here we are," Donald said, arriving at a large rack of black suits.

Stan took one off the rack and looked at the pants. "None of these have got hems in them, son."

THE CITY BENEATH THE SEA

"You'll have to be measured and they'll fit a suit to you," Donald explained.

"How long will that take?" Stan asked, knowing he would need it for tonight.

"An hour or so."

"That's fast!" Stan said, surprised at the quick service.

As Donald and Stan looked through the rack of suits, a clerk parted the curtains, separating the back room from the showroom. He was a relatively young man in his early twenties with an air of sophistication and superiority about him as he approached.

"How can I assist you gentlemen?" the clerk asked, his tone somewhat uppity, Stan noticed, while Donald was oblivious to the man's mannerisms.

"My father needs to be measured for a suit," Donald said, motioning to his father.

The clerk nodded and walked to a small platform about six inches high.

"Would you stand on the platform please?" the clerk asked, as he pulled a measuring tape from his pocket.

Stan stood on the platform and the clerk went right to work measuring Stan's chest, arms, and inseams, making a quick notation after every measurement.

In the women's department, Janelle had not been fortunate enough to have anyone assist her, even though several white clerks monitored her every move. Janelle saw them watching her, but tried to ignore them. She had experienced this type of treatment her entire life, New York was no different, just a different city. In their twisted minds, they had formulated a stereotype that every African American is a thief, they and waited for their perceptions to be reinforced.

THE CITY BENEATH THE SEA

Continuing to ignore the female clerks, Janelle found a dress she liked and brought it to the dressing room, walking up to one of the white clerks.

"May I try this on?" Janelle asked politely, while the clerk eyed her shabby appearance. Wearing clothes she had gotten from piles of clothes that had been donated and brought to the Astro Dome, Janelle was not projecting her best appearance.

The clerk did not say a word as she walked to the dressing room door and unlocked it, then returned back to her counter.

Janelle felt the chill in the attitude of the clerk, but said nothing as she entered the dressing room.

"What color would the gentleman prefer?" the clerk asked, having completed his measurements.

"Black," Stan said without hesitation.

"Does the gentleman like these?" the clerk asked walking over to a wall of suits, which were displayed on the wall.

Stan walked over to one of the suits and picked up a sleeve, looking for the price.

"How much are they?" Stan asked, not being able to find a price.

"Which one, sir?"

Stan pointed to one of the numerous suits on display.

"Eight hundred dollars."

Stan's jaw dropped, as the clerk informed him of the price, but he remained silent.

"That one will be fine," Donald interjected accepting the suit for his father, as he handed the clerk his Platinum Visa card.

Taking the card, the clerk headed to his counter to conclude the transaction.

"Son, that's a lot of money for a suit," Stan said, objecting to his son's quick purchase.

"You're worth it, Dad," Donald said with a smile.

THE CITY BENEATH THE SEA

The clerk returned with a slip for Donald to sign.

"When can we pick it up?" Donald asked, as he handed the slip back to the clerk.

"It'll be ready in an hour."

"Thank you," Donald said as he began to lead his father back to the ladies' department. "Let's see how Mom's doing."

Inside the dressing room, Janelle looked at herself in the mirror. The dress looked great, far prettier than anything she had ever owned before. Seeing the tag as it dangled, she looked at the price for the first time and her facial expression changed.

Donald and Stan arrived at the ladies' department and began searching for Janelle, but not immediately finding her.

"I wonder where she is." Donald said, as he and his dad looked around.

"Wonder where she is?" Stan said, "This place is so big, I wonder where I am."

Janelle exited the dressing room and headed for Donald and Stan.

"There she is," Donald said, spotting her first.

Seeing the dress his mother held as she approached, Donald commented on it.

"That's a pretty dress," Donald said, "how does it fit?"

"It fits, but it's a little pricey for my blood," Janelle said, as she started to return the dress to the rack.

"I'm buying it, Mom, my treat," Donald said, taking the dress back off the rack.

"But Donald!" Janelle began to voice her objections.

"No buts," Donald said. "After all, I'm the one making you go to this party."

Donald took the dress to the counter to pay for it, leaving Stan and Janelle behind.

THE CITY BENEATH THE SEA

"He did the same thing with my suit," Stan said, sharing with Janelle the cost of his suit.

"I wonder what kind of fancy party we're going to." Janelle wondered, for the first time beginning to feel a little apprehensive about the whole situation.

"I guess we'll find out in a few hours," Stan said, not helping to alleviate any of her anxiety.

THE CITY BENEATH THE SEA

CHAPTER THIRTY-NINE

Charles Cunningham threw an African American male on the hood of his patrol car as he began to handcuff him. Securing the cuffs, Cunningham looked round to see if anyone was looking before slamming his fist into the kidneys of the cuffed man, causing him to collapse in pain.

"And that's for making me chase you!" Cunningham said, as the man rolled on the ground in pain.

The policeman's rough handling of the man did not go unobserved as Sweet watched the police officer from across the street.

In an abandoned four-storey building, Sweet and his gang lay around their most recent hideout. Having played a cat and mouse game with the police for several days while they pillaged at will, lately their activities had been severely curtailed by an increased presence of police and guardsman.

As Sweet watched the arrest of the man, his blood began to boil. Remembering one of his many arrests when he was handled so roughly by police.

"Looks like they're rounding up the bad actors in the hood," Sweet said, as he lifted a rifle to his shoulder. "They'll be here soon. I don't know about you, but I'm ready to bust a cap on their ass."

"We're with you, Sweet! We're going to bleed them!" one of the gang yelled.

"Alright! Spread out! Wait to shoot until I unload first, then give it all to them," Sweet said. "Let them know this is our hood!"

"Damn right!" one of the gang yelled.

The gang fanned out looking for a strategic spot to fire upon the police officers.

Sweet took aim and fired first, giving the signal to unleash an arsenal of gunfire.

THE CITY BENEATH THE SEA

Cunningham heard the shot and felt the bullet tear into his shoulder at almost the same time, giving him no time to react.

Hitting the ground, he rolled and crawled for cover as bullets flew past his head. His handcuffed prisoner ran down the street, fleeing both arrest and bullets.

Opening the passenger door of the patrol car, Cunningham reached for the radio and began his frantic plea for backup.

"Officer down! Officer down!"

A young officer ran up to a patrol car parked under the Superdome and flung opens the door.

"Sergeant Moore!" the officer asked, almost out of breath.

"Yes," a voice from within the car said.

"The captain wants to see you ASAP!" the young officer said.

A groggy, sleepy Les emerged from the car. His unshaven face and wrinkled clothes, indicating he had not showered in several days. He stretched, then turned to the rookie officer.

"Well, lead the way."

The young officer took off with Les close behind. Soon, they came face-to-face with the Captain.

"I have an officer call," the Captain said, "I need you to respond, you're all I have left.

"You make me feel so special," Les said, under his breath.

"He's on the third block of Canal, hurry up!"

"We're on it, Captain!" Les said, as he turned to run, the rookie close behind. When they reached the patrol car, Les took the passenger side.

"You drive!" Les instructed, as the rookie headed to the driver's side.

THE CITY BENEATH THE SEA

Burning rubber, the rookie sped away, throwing Les against the seat.

"Easy rookie! Or we're the ones who are going to need help."

Les turned up the radio in time to hear a panicked officer screaming into the mic.

"Shots fired! Officer down!"

"Shit!" Les said, "Step on it!"

The rookie floored the powerful vehicle, catapulting it forward.

As they approached the scene, a patrol car was up ahead and was taking fire. An officer lay behind it, trying to find cover from the barrage of gunfire that was being rained down upon him.

"There he is!" Les said, as he prepared to jump out, waiting for the rookie to position the car next to the other patrol car.

The rookie brought the car to a halt, screeching the tires as he braked. A fatal error in judgment on his part, but before Les could stop him, the rookie jumped out and began to return fire. Instead of pulling alongside the patrol car that was under fire, the officer stopped behind it, putting himself in the line of fire with no place to fall back to.

The inexperienced officer was only able to get off a couple of shots before several bullets ripped through his chest, sending him to the ground dead, as his life's blood began to slowly pool around him.

With bullets hitting the patrol car with rapid succession, Les slid out his door, using the car as cover. Then staying low, utilizing as much of the vehicle as possible for cover, Les quickly crawled to the wounded officer.

"How bad are you hit?" Les asked as he reached him.

"Don't know, took it in the shoulder," Cunningham said, fighting to remain conscious.

THE CITY BENEATH THE SEA

Quickly evaluating his wound, Les was encouraged. "You'll live, if we get out of this," Les reassured him, "but you won't be bowling for a while."

Another barrage of bullets pelted the car, as Les opened the door and grabbed the radio.

"Officers down! Officers down. Pinned down by sniper fire from nearby building."

"Hang on!" the Captain's familiar voice came back. "The guard is on the way, stay put!"

Another barrage of bullets hit the car, shattering what was left of the glass.

"Stay put! Easy for him to say!"

Les did not have to wait long; as he looked down the wide boulevard, an armored amphibious vehicle neared with a fifty-caliber mounted on top.

"They're almost here!" Les told Cunningham, wanting him to remain conscious.

Sweet looked out the window, one officer lay dead as a result of a failed rescue attempt, the other scurried behind the first patrol car. As the gang fired randomly at the patrol car, Sweet was far more selective as he stared down the scope of his hunting rifle.

In the distance, Sweet saw a National Guard vehicle approach with a fifty-caliber machine gun mounted on top. He knows the amount of firepower just one of these weapons could unleash, and the penetrating power each round had could easily penetrate the walls they now sought cover behind.

As the armored vehicle neared, Les shifted his position from his bottom to his knees, not realizing the shift had elevated himself in the crossfire of the sniper.

Looking through the scope once more, Sweet knew he didn't have much time. Then through the window of the car, one of the officers came into view, giving Sweet only a narrow opportunity at a shot.

THE CITY BENEATH THE SEA

Taking the shot, Sweet immediately began to retreat, grabbing Birdie as he went.

Without warning, Les was struck in the head. He fell backwards landing on his back, his hands out to his sides, his eyes still open, a pool of blood formed around his head as the sound of a fifty-caliber machine gun fire began to unleash its fury on the gunmen.

"Let's get out of here!" Sweet told Birdie, who followed without question.

No sooner than it reached the stairwell, the fifty-caliber bullets tore through the brick walls as though they were not even there.

"What about the others?" Birdie yelled as he looked over his shoulder, and saw no one following.

"No time!" Sweet yelled as he continued to run down the stairs. "They're on their own!"

Reaching the ground floor, Sweet and Birdie burst through the exit and into an alley.

Using the alley as cover for their escape, Birdie and Sweet did not stop until they reached the next block, listening to see if anyone had followed them. An eerie silence fell over the area, the gunfire had stopped. Looking down the alley, no other gang member had followed, either they were all killed or gave up waiting capture.

"Shit!" Sweet said, "these guardsman don't play!"

"You think anyone else made it out?" Birdie asked, breathing heavily from their run.

"If they did, they'll make it back to the crib," Sweet said getting to his feet. "In fact, that's where we should head right now, let's get out of here!"

THE CITY BENEATH THE SEA

CHAPTER FORTY

Dressed in his new suit, Stan came into the living room where his son was sitting on the couch.

"Look at you!" Donald said, "Sharp as a tack!"

"I gotta say, son, I've never had anything this expensive on my back before," Stan said, bringing a smile to his son's face.

"Mom almost ready?"

"Yea, she'll be out in a sec."

Almost on cue, Janelle exited her room.

"Whoo! Whoo!" Donald said, "Look at you, you're going to be the prettiest one there."

"You're right about that!" Stan said, "You're going to represent us well!"

"You two stop!" Janelle said, "You're going to give me a big head."

"Well if ya ready, the limo is waiting."

"Limo!" Janelle said with surprise, "Wow, I do feel special."

"Never been in a limo before," Stan said, "New suit, limo, I could get used to this."

Donald opened the apartment door for his parents then closed it behind him.

The night air was cool as Donald and his parents exited the building, not far away the limo driver waited.

As they approached, he opened the door. Once safely inside, the driver closed the door and headed to the driver's seat, already knowing the destination.

In the back of the limo as they were driven to the city, Donald, Stan and Janelle relaxed as they took the short drive to the Harringtons'.

"This is really nice," Janelle said, looking at the lights of the city.

"I can see how the rich folks get used to this," Stan said with a smile, as he played with the many gadgets in the limo, raising and lowering windows, just like a kid experiencing something new for the first time.

"How far away is this party?" Stan asked.

"Not far," Donald said, "We should be there soon."

Before long, the limo pulled up to a rather large house with a curved drive leading up to it.

"Here we are," Donald said, as the limo came to a stop.

"This is your boss' house?" Stan asked, looking at the size of the house.

"When you're a partner, you don't really have a boss; we refer to each other as associates," Donald explained to his father.

As they exited the limo, Stan stared at the massive multi-storey house.

"Well, son, if this is your partner," Stan said, "you'd better check the books. I think he's doing a little better than you."

Donald smiled at his dad's naiveté.

Walking up to the front door, Donald pressed the doorbell. In a few moments, the butler answered the door.

"Evening," the middle-aged man dressed in a tux said as he answered the door.

"Donald, Stan and Janelle King," Donald said, as the man nodded.

"This way, sir, I'll announce you."

The butler closed the door then led the group to the main hall, a larger room in the house where large gatherings were held. As they turned the corner, a large group of people were milling about, most engaged in conversation. The butler stopped at the entrance as he announced the newly arrived guests.

"Introducing Mr. Donald King, Mr. and Mrs. Stan King," the butler said in a loud strong voice, then retreated to his post.

The crowd stopped and turned their attention to the Kings. Donald slowly stepped into the room cautiously followed by Stan and Janelle. Susan was the first to greet them, walking up to Donald and giving him a big hug.

"Susan, I'd like to introduce my parents, Stan and Janelle."

"It is such a pleasure to finally meet you," Susan said with a big smile, extending her hand to shake theirs.

"These are my parents," Susan said just as they walked up. "Honey and Kevin Harrington."

Stan extended his hand first, and was met by Kevin's firm shake

"It's a terrible thing what that hurricane did to your city," Harrington said, initiating a conversation with Stan.

"It wasn't the hurricane, it was the levees." Stan said, correcting Harrington's assertion.

"Yes, that's what I understand, the levees gave way because of the hurricane."

Susan's father sounded a little annoyed at being corrected, but kept his composure.

Not wanting to get into an argument, Stan just smiled and shook his head.

"Donald, can I borrow your mom?" Susan asked, taking Janelle by the arm. "I have some people who are dying to meet her."

"Sure, you guys have fun," Donald said as Susan, Honey, and his mom walked away.

"I'll get us something to drink," Donald told his dad as he left to find them a drink.

"You must be pretty proud of the boy," Harrington said as Donald walked away.

Though Harrington thought his remark harmless, Stan took exception to his choice of words.

"He's hardly a boy," Stan said. "He's all grown up, but yes, I've always been proud of my son."

Sensing the tension starting to build between them, Harrington tried to head it off.

THE CITY BENEATH THE SEA

"We're off to a bad start, aren't we?" Harrington said, acknowledging the tension.

Stan smiled, neither confirming or denying Harrington's suspicions.

"Where are my manners?" Harrington said, "Let me introduce you to some of our guests."

As Donald returned with drinks, he saw Harrington leading his father away. He kept a close eye on his dad, not to rescue him, because over the years Donald had learned that his dad could take care of himself. However, he did want to be in a position to rescue whoever was unfortunate enough to tangle with him.

"Is this a beautiful party or what?" Susan's familiar voice said as she walked up behind him.

"Very nice," Donald said with a smile, giving Susan the reassurance she was obviously looking for.

"You think your parents like it?"

"They're pretty simple people, they don't get real excited about stuff like this," Donald tried to explain.

"Well, I'm excited that they came, besides my dad has a surprise."

"What's with this surprise?" Donald asked, still curious from earlier that day when she had first mentioned it.

"Can you keep a secret?" Susan asked, leaning over and whispering in his ear.

"Yes."

"So can I," Susan said, with a giggle and a smile.

"Since when did you start keeping secrets?" Donald asked, not seeing the humor.

"That's not nice! I can keep a secret."

Donald smiled, not wanting to disagree with her and have to deal with the argument that would inevitably ensue, instead, he just smiled and remained silent.

"I'm going to have to leave for a while. I'm going to be taking my parents back to New Orleans," Donald said, informing Susan for the first time of his intentions.

"What are you talking about?" Susan objected, "You just got back."

"My uncle and grandmother passed away," Donald explained, not taking immediate exception to her tone, since she didn't know the circumstances. "Now that residents are being allowed back in, my parents want to go back home. I'm going to try to help them get situated."

"I know you need to go for the funerals, but getting your parents back in their house?" Susan questioned, her lack of sensitivity starting to show. "Can't you pay someone to do that? How long are you going to be gone?"

"I don't know; until they're settled back in," Donald explained, his patience starting to wear thin.

"A week, a month?" Susan pressed for an answer.

"I'll be back when I'm back," Donald said, his tone beginning to get a little more stern.

"Does Daddy know?"

"He's your daddy, not mine," Donald said, his politeness starting to wane. "I was going to tell him tonight, it came up pretty quickly."

"He's not going to be happy. You have responsibilities here," Susan said, her tone harsh and abrasive. "The last time you left, you didn't tell anyone and you put Daddy in an awkward position trying to find someone to fill your court calendar."

Donald looked at her hard, restraining himself from just blowing up at her.

"Excuse me!" Donald said, his words and tone forceful. "I have a responsibility to my parents!"

Just then, Harrington got everyone's attention by tapping a spoon on his Champagne glass. The crowd stopped their conversations and turned their attentions to Mr. Harrington.

THE CITY BENEATH THE SEA

"May I have your attention," Harrington asked, as he stood before his guests. "I would like to propose a toast to Stan and Janelle King, our very own hurricane Katrina survivors."

Stan looked on in disbelief and turned to his son, who could see his father's displeasure with the choice of Harrington's words. But the worst was still to come.

"And I have a special gift from everyone here to help you rebuild the hood," Harrington said, removing a check from his pocket, as the crowd applauded.

It was unclear if Harrington was trying to be funny, or if it was the alcohol clouding his judgment. One thing was for sure, by his display of insensitivity, the cat was out of the bag, and everyone would have to hold on for a rough ride.

"Stan, would you come up here," Harrington asked, as he held out the check.

Looking at his son first, as though he wanted him to stop him, Stan reluctantly approached Harrington, as the crowd parted and applauded.

The look on his father's face should have given Donald a clue as to what was about to come; maybe he just didn't see it, or more likely, a little voice inside of him had said ENOUGH! So he unleashed his father to do what he did not have the courage to do.

Stan walked up to Harrington and shook his hand as he was handed a check for ten thousand dollars.

Harrington put his arm around Stan, as a photographer took a photo, as another round of applause ensued.

The look on Stan's face said it all, he was humiliated, but he still found the strength the crowd.

"You know, ten thousand dollars to most of the people in this room represents little more than lunch money. To an out-of-work janitor like me, it's a lot of money. You know, I never really had the opportunity to get any education, but I swore, along with my wife

THE CITY BENEATH THE SEA

Janelle, that we would try to give our son every opportunity, the rest would be up to him and he never once disappointed us. He's got a better life than we ever had. But he had to work for it. He had plenty of obstacles along the way, but through his hard work, he overcame them. Like me, he worked for everything he has been able to achieve, and he does not have to apologize to anyone. You know, many people like the ones in this room have been trying to help the less fortunate with handouts for the last forty years. It may make you feel good, but it ultimately destroys the will, the initiative, and desires of the people you're trying to help.

"Look at New Orleans, you have minorities, my people! They have been so institutionalized to government cheese, and handouts, you have second and third generations that have known nothing else. The highlight of their existence is to go to the mailbox at the end of the month to get their government check. There's going to be a ton of money pouring into New Orleans to help us poor people. The reality is that very little will actually get to the people who need it. And when it does, it will be in the form of handouts.

"We don't need more handouts, we need a hand up. We need families; fathers and mothers who work to raise their children to keep them off the streets and off drugs. Parents who instill the importance of education, and impress on them they can achieve whatever they desire. Even the best intentions can sometimes prove to have the cruelest consequences. What we need most is not new money, but a new direction. It is not my intent to insult anyone, but your intentions, though well meaning, have been hurtful. No one ever gave me anything. I've had to work for everything I have. I have no need to start now."

Stan tore up the check as the crowd gasped in disbelief. Stan walked over to Janelle and took her hand. Then he turned to address Donald.

THE CITY BENEATH THE SEA

"Son, it's time for us to leave," Stan said, looking to his son, who was almost in tears.

The truth of his father's words and the way he articulated them touched had Donald, and somehow changed him, as he felt such an enormous amount of pride in his father for standing up for his principles in such an intimidating gathering.

"I couldn't agree more," Donald said, bursting with pride. "I'll take you home, Dad."

Donald looked over to Susan and her dad, who by the looks of it were not very happy.

As Donald turned to follow his parents out the door, Susan approached him, pulling him by the arm to one side.

"Donald, I think you need to apologize to Daddy," Susan said, visibly upset.

"I don't think so," Donald said emphatically. "Your dad should be the one apologizing to my dad."

"You don't understand, you must go and apologize to my father right now!"

"Or what?

"Or it's over!" Susan demanded.

"Just like that?" Donald questioned.

"Just like that!"

"That's not going to happen," Donald said, surprising Susan with his answer.

"Donald! You can't just walk away from me!"

"Susan, I saw something tonight, something I hadn't seen in a long time," Donald said, to a teary-eyed Susan.

"What's that?"

"A proud black man, and I realized I wanted to be like him," Donald explained. "Not like your dad, have a good life, Susan."

Donald left, following his parents out the door, as the crowd whispered in the background.

"Donald!" Susan called after him, but he didn't acknowledge her pleas.

THE CITY BENEATH THE SEA

CHAPTER FORTY-ONE

The sound of the doorbell ringing sent Kirra to the front door. Opening the door, she was not prepared for what she saw. There standing outside her door she found two NOPD police officers, with a solemn look on their faces. Whatever they were there for, Kirra knew it could not be good, as she braced herself for some really bad news.

"Quiana Moore?" one of the officers asked.

"No, I'm her sister."

Just then, Quiana came to the door.

"Kirra who is it?" Quiana asked, pulling open the partially closed door.

Quiana saw the officers and immediately knew the meaning of their presence, as her facial expression dropped.

"Quiana Moore?" the officer asked, but already knew it was her.

"Yes," the trembling Quiana said, fighting to hold back her tears.

"I'm sorry to inform you, your husband has been shot and killed in the line of duty," the officer informed her. "I'm so sorry."

"No! No! It's a mistake!" Quiana yelled.

"Again, I'm sorry," the office said, as though confirming that there was no mistake.

Quiana, crushed, leaned on her sister as the two officers left. Crying uncontrollably, she was stunned by the devastating news.

Inside the Astro Dome, LaToya straightened Jamal's cot, not far away he and his brother played with other children who, along with their parents, found themselves stranded in Houston with no place to go.

THE CITY BENEATH THE SEA

Having been transported to Houston after leaving the Superdome, she had initially feared being thrown into another facility similar to the Superdome. The nightmarish hell of the Superdome had scarred her emotionally, and if at all possible, she did not want to trade one hell for another. But when you're poor, your choices are limited.

In the days that followed the evacuation, LaToya had tried to make the best of the situation for her two boys, who had adapted quickly and even made a few friends. But like everyone in the shelter, she longed to go home.

"Hey baby!" a familiar voice from behind her said, LaToya turned around to see Big Mama standing in front of her.

"Big Mama!" LaToya said, giving her neighbor and friend a big hug.

"I didn't think you were going to leave," LaToya said, remembering Big Mama's words before she left; proclaiming the only way she was leaving her home was in a box.

"I wasn't until a National Guardsman kicked my door in at gunpoint and escorted me out. I been bouncing around from one shelter to another. You ain't heard, girl?"

"Heard what?"

"The whole city has been evacuated, the only thing left in there are police, guardsmen, and criminals."

"No, I didn't know."

"The city went to hell in a handbag. Young brothers looting, robbing, and raping. The guards are trying to restore order, but the brothers aren't going easy. The governor herself issued an order to shoot to kill. I tell you, it's open season on brothers in the city," Big Mama said, bringing LaToya up to date with the latest news from the city.

THE CITY BENEATH THE SEA

"Well, at least you're safe, have a seat," LaToya motioned to the cot.

"Girl, you silly, I sit on that, they be taking splinters out my butt for a week. They're getting me a special metal one. Where your boys?" Big Mama asked.

"They're over there, talking to their new friend, Melanie," LaToya said, pointing to her boys and Melanie. "She works at the Community Center."

"I don't recognize her," Big Mama said, "but then again I don't get out much."

"Jamal, Jameal," LaToya called to her sons. "Look who's here."

Jamal and his brother come running when they saw Big Mama.

"Big Mama!" Jamal cried, as he threw his arms around her.

"How're my babies?" Big Mama asked, as she gave each boy a big hug. "You safe and sound, I see."

"They came through the ordeal pretty good," LaToya said, "I had a close call though."

"Really, what happened?" Big Mama asked, wanting to know more.

"We were at the dome, were trying to get to the buses and a fight broke out," LaToya explained. "The crowd stampeded and I fell to the ground, would have been crushed if it hadn't been for this white policeman."

"Lucky he was there," Big Mama said.

"He was the one that got us on a transport and to safety. It's been bothering me ever since," LaToya said, solemn in her explanation.

"What's been bothering you, baby?" Big Mama asked.

"That was the first time anybody white ever did anything for me. As long as I can remember, I've grown to hate white people, it was easy," LaToya explained, "I don't have any white friends, and in the projects, you don't see many white folks. So hating whites was not a problem, I was able to put all white folks in one neat, evil category."

"Until the white officer risked his life to rescue you, and shattered your perfect order of the way you thought things were?" Big Mama asked.

"Yea, that's right."

"Baby, there's good and bad in all of us," Big Mama explained, "it just depends on how hard you want to look."

"I guess so, he may never know how much he opened my eyes."

"Maybe one day, you can tell him," Big Mama suggested.

"I thought of that, I still have his name burned in my memory. Les Moore."

" Les Moore!" Big Mama repeated the name, a stunned look on her face.

"Big Mama," LaToya said noticing the change in Big Mama. "You know him?"

"Les Moore was shot in the city while trying to rescue a fellow police officer," Big Mama said, informing her friend of the news. "It was big news before I left. Baby, Les Moore is dead."

Tears began to stream down from LaToya's face realizing she would never be able to tell the officer how he changed her.

LaToya sat on the bed and cried for a man she only met once, but who she owed her life to.

"Mama, what's wrong?" Jamal asked, as he went to his mother's side.

"Your mama's just sad is all. You boys come walk with Big Mama and give your mama a few minutes," Big Mama said, taking the boys with her. "I'll show you my big metal cot."

THE CITY BENEATH THE SEA

Sitting on the edge of her cot, Melanie folded and sorted various items of clothing into a suitcase as she prepared to finally leave the Astro Dome.

Sherry Henry walked up carrying her bags. Since their stay at the Astro Dome, Melanie and Sherry had become close friends. A friendship they intended to bring with them back to New Orleans.

"Thank you so much for offering me a ride back to New Orleans," Sherry said. "Being so congested for all these days, the last thing I wanted was to be on a crowded bus for six hours."

"You're welcome," Melanie said, "you'll be the first person to ride in my new car."

"I'm honored," Sherry said, with a broad smile.

"Funny, we lived less than a block from each other and we never knew it," Melanie commented.

"Don't feel bad," Sherry said, "there was a lot of that going on. Maybe this storm, as tragic as it was, will bring people together again."

"People were afraid to venture out," Melanie added. "With crime as bad as it was, hopefully that may change."

"Speaking of which, you think they ever caught those thugs that came on our bus that day?" Sherry questioned, "I'd love to testify against them!"

"If the officer I reported it to is any indication, I don't hold out a lot of hope," Melanie said, remembering the heartbreak she felt when the officer in the quarter refused to help her.

"I hope they brought them gangs under control," Sherry said, "I don't ever want to experience what we did, ever again."

They have a strong police presence in the city now, maybe that will do it," Melanie said, trying to stay optimistic.

"Yea, they're basically cowards preying on the weak," Sherry said, "when they're confronted with anyone who can fight back, they cower like the spineless animals they are."

"You're right about that," Melanie agreed with her friend.

"Well, when I get home if there's anything left, and they didn't find Little Bertha," Sherry said, "I'll give them more than they can handle if they come around again!"

"Little Bertha?"

"Yea, that's the name of my pistol," Sherry explained, "and I'll bust a cap in the ass of the first gangster I see."

"You go, girl!" Melanie said through her laughter. "You're too much!"

Outside a distribution center Fema had set up downtown to assist returning residents, a rather long line had already formed to receive water and food.

In line waiting their turn under the watchful eye of guardsmen, Sweet and Birdie waited. Their dirty clothes and unshaved faces gave them a rough, distressed appearance.

"Bout time they get this down here!" Birdie said in a loud voice, drawing the attention of those around him.

As a Fema worker passed by, Birdie took the opportunity to verbally assault the worker, in a harsh tone with unfounded accusations.

"Yea, y'all took care of all the white folks, now ya'll can come down here for us black folks," Birdie said.

The worker ignored Birdie's comment and took comfort in the guardsmen that were on hand to provide security.

"Easy, brother, we don't need to bring the man's attention on us," Sweet cautioned.

"Lousy bastards!" Birdie cried, "Killed almost everyone of us!"

THE CITY BENEATH THE SEA

One of the men ahead of them in line turned around on hearing Birdie's remarks.

"What you looking at!" Sweet snarled, "Better mind ya business!"

The man turned back around, not saying a word, not wanting a confrontation.

"We're the only one's left!" Birdie said, saddened by the loss of the rest of the gang, who he had formed a close friendship with.

"I know, little brother, our time will come," Sweet promised. "But for now, we just have to stay low, bide our time."

Birdie nodded his head in understanding, regaining his composure.

THE CITY BENEATH THE SEA

CHAPTER FORTY-TWO

A line of cars stretched for miles, as residents waited in line to return back to New Orleans and to their homes. The checkpoints set up by guardsmen in an effort to cull the curiosity seekers and looters was responsible for the long lines and wait. The guardsmen were checking identifications, only residents with proof of residency were being allowed back in the city.

Sitting patiently in their rental car, and inching along with the traffic. Donald, Stan and Janelle saw the roadblock up ahead.

"Looks like they're checking IDs," Donald said. "Does everybody have one?"

"Yes, made sure we saved that," Janelle said, as she began digging in her purse."

Donald pulled up to the young guardsman who was checking proof of residency.

"Morning folks," the guardsman said, greeting them with a smile. "I need to see some sort of proof of residency."

"Sure," Donald said, handing him their identification.

"These are my parents," Donald explained, "they live in New Orleans, I'm their son. I came down to help them settle in, that's why I have a New York address."

"Ok folks," the guardsman said, after only a quick glance of their IDs. "Be careful, lots of power lines are down, and debris," the guardsman cautioned, as he handed Donald back his ID's.

Driving off past the checkpoint, they experienced very little traffic, the checkpoint being the bottleneck in the return home. As Donald drove through Metairie, they saw wind damage, which they found to be extensive. But it was not until they crossed the 17th Street canal bridge that the true impact of the catastrophe was realized.

THE CITY BENEATH THE SEA

Having been evacuated at night from the darkened city, they were unable to appreciate the magnitude of the devastation until now. Watching the reports on TV did not compare to the first-hand account of a city knocked to her knees.

The dark brown line on the buildings and houses, was an indicator where the encroaching water reached its height, with some marks etched as high as the shingles of roofs. The light brown dust and mud that now covered everything under the mark, created a surreal image. Adding to this brown colorless landscape were the dying plants; silent victims of the salt-water intrusion which spared no living vegetation in its path, from grass to massive oaks, all lay dead or dying.

"Wow! Seeing it on TV doesn't put this into perspective," Stan said, looking around at the devastation. "It's a lot worse than I thought."

Driving past the familiar landmark of the St. Louis Cathedral, Donald headed toward his parents' house. A few civilians milled about, but mostly it was military, city, and state police, some carrying automatic weapons. A visual reminder of the state of affairs in the city.

"It feels funny to be back," Janelle said, looking around at a city she now barely recognized.

"Yea, last time we were down this street, the police were looting the liquor store," Stan said, reflecting back on his exodus experience.

"Really!" Donald said, as though shocked by the revelation.

"Why does that surprise you?" Stan asked his son. "New Orleans has got some of the most crooked cops in the country."

"I know they've got problems," Donald said, still finding it hard to believe police could be so blatant.

"That's like saying Paul Prudome is a little overweight," Stan argued, "We've had problems with the police force for years. Most of the city police don't even live in the city. They commute, so how can they have a vested interest in a city they don't even live in? Most of them take the path of least resistance, do the bare minimum, take their time to respond to calls. Biding their time, padding out their pensions while the city continues its spiraling decline into the cesspool it has become, taking countless lives with it."

"I didn't know it was that bad," Donald confessed.

"Every year it becomes worse than the previous one," Stan continued. "We have the highest murder rate in the country. Black men killing other black men for drugs, while the police do little to stop it. I bet if the young brothers were killing white folks, they would stop it."

"I don't think race has anything to do with it," Donald said, disagreeing with his father.

"Open your eyes, son," Stan said, surprised at his son's naiveté. "You think if we were a group of whites trying to cross the bridge, we would have been beaten and turned around?"

Pondering his father's point for a moment, Donald was unable to make an argument to counter his dad's; for the fist time in his life he was speechless.

Driving slowly down the street, avoiding the many potholes as she went. Melanie headed toward Sherry's home, observing the destruction as they went.

"A lot of doors are kicked in," Melanie said, seeing the shattered frames that once held them secure.

"We don't know if the National Guard opened them looking for bodies or if it was looters," Sherry said, bringing into question the immediate assumption that the shattered frames were kicked in by looters.

"I know they went house to house looking for bodies," Melanie agreed, "but I thought they only went to the really flooded areas. They would spray paint on the outside of the house, indicating if there was anyone inside. Without any markings, I would lean toward looters."

"I hope you're wrong," Sherry said, "but I know you're right. I wish we had some men folk with us, I'd feel much better."

"I know what you mean," Melanie agreed, feeling the same anxiety her friend felt; returning to her neighborhood was like coming to a ghost town, not a living soul appeared to be anywhere in sight.

As Melanie drove up to Sherry's house, the watermarks began to tell the story before she even got out of the car. Reaching half-way up the side of the house, the prospect of salvaging any of her property began to quickly fade away.

Fighting back the tears, Sherry slowly climbed the front steps of her home with Melanie close behind her. The door stood open, the shattered frame stood witness to the violent force exerted on it. Entering her home for the first time since her hasty departure several weeks earlier, Sherry began the heartbreaking tour of what was once her home.

A light brown film covered everything below the watermark. The walls were black with mould and a strong decaying, rotten smell filled the air.

In this sea of devastation, something unusual caught Melanie's attention. Scattered about on the floor were hundreds of lottery tickets.

Walking from room to room, Sherry no longer made any attempt to hold back her tears as they flowed from her freely. Bending over occasionally to pick up a broken memory of her past, only to cast the once valuable artifact to the floor again, as though only now being able to accept its destruction.

"Everything!" Sherry cried, "Everything's gone!"

Regaining her composure, Sherry headed for the closet. Pulling down several boxes, she finally found what she was looking for.

THE CITY BENEATH THE SEA

"Bertha! She's still here!" Sherry cried with excitement.

Opening the box, Sherry displayed her nine-millimeter pistol to Melanie. "This is Little Bertha, a little bitch, with a lot of attitude!"

"Don't point that thing at me!" Melanie said, feeling uncomfortable around guns.

"Don't worry," Sherry said, "I never load it," she informed her cautious friend. But as she lowered her arm to her side, her words were soon contradicted, as the pistol discharged into the floor, scaring both women.

"Well almost never!" Sherry said, the first to recover from the unexpected discharge of the unloaded gun.

Sherry quickly removed the clip and cleared the chamber, only now was she able to say with confidence that the gun was unloaded.

"Sorry about that," Sherry said, sheepishly embarrassed by the whole incident.

"Well, let's check out my house," Melanie suggested, but stopped to ask her friend a question.

"Before we go, I've got to ask you something." Melanie said, unable to suppress her curiosity.

"Yes, I'm sure it's unloaded this time," Sherry said, as she put the pistol in her purse.

"No, not that. What are all these lottery tickets on the floor for?"

"Had them on the table, when the water came up they must have floated about, then when the water went down, they were scattered on the floor," Sherry reasoned.

"You play a lot?" Melanie asked, not being a gambler herself.

"Sure do, one day I'm going to hit the jackpot! I'm going to buy a big house, a fancy car and not worry about anything again," Sherry said, giving her an insight into her dreams and fears.

THE CITY BENEATH THE SEA

"You know the odds are not in your favor," Melanie said, trying to enlighten her friend as to the miniscule chance of her winning the lottery.

"You know, I know that, but there's something pretty magical about the lottery," Sherry said, expressing her fascination with it. "Someone's life somewhere, is magically transformed overnight. As far as the odds, I don't know exactly what they are, I do know what the odds of winning are if you don't have a ticket."

Sherry and Melanie smiled broadly as they exited the house, closing the door behind them.

Leaving Sherry's house, Melanie drove down the few blocks to her home. Having seen the condition of Sherry's home, she did not hold much hope that anything would survive in hers. As she drove, when not engaged in conversation with Sherry, her thoughts were on her possessions and all the items that were not replaceable.

"I never realized how uneven the city was," Melanie commented as she drove, observing the water line on the houses as they went. The dips and valleys of the city streets were hardly noticeable, but the watermarks on the houses removed any doubt of the different terrain elevations   "What do you mean?" Sherry asked

"Here on the same street, you have some people who had four feet of water in their house and for some the water barely crossed the threshold." Melanie pointed to the houses which she sited as examples.

"I never realized that," Sherry admitted. "I kinda wish I'd bought on higher ground. I don't have flood insurance, it was never zoned as a flood zone. I never dreamed this could happen. What happened to all the millions they spent on levee protection?"

"Probably wound up in some politician's freezer," Melanie said, while the two women shared a laugh at the corruptness of Louisiana politicians, not knowing how true their statement had been.

"Don't worry too much about flood insurance," Melanie said, "When everything is said and done, I think they will have to take into account the levees failing."

"I hope so," Sherry said, her tone one of concern.

Arriving at Melanie's house, the same scenario began to repeat itself. After Melanie hastily departed, the water had continued to rise unabated another few feet.

"I was hopeful for a while," Melanie said, as she and Sherry climbed the steps of her porch. "I guess it took a little longer than I thought to secure the breaches in the levees."

As Melanie walked through her home, it wasn't long before she realized the hopelessness of salvaging anything. What the water hadn't damaged, mould and had mildew finished off.

"What now?" Sherry asked, shaking her head at what had turned out to be a mirror image of her home. "Looks like we're both up the bayou without a push pole."

"Looks like we go to the Community Center I work at," Melanie said, having evaluated all her options in her head. "They've set it up as a shelter."

"Well," Sherry sighed hard, not relishing the thought of another shelter, but knowing her options were limited. "It's better than anything I can think of."

"Oh," Melanie said, as they headed towards her car. "You won't be able to take Bertha in," she explained to her friend. "You might want to put her in the glove box."

"Alright," Sherry agreed reluctantly. "I hate to let her out of my sight again, I thought I lost her once."

Sherry opened the glove compartment and placed the pistol and clip inside.

"She'll be ok, I promise."

THE CITY BENEATH THE SEA

CHAPTER FORTY-THREE

Driving into his father's driveway, Donald saw the brown, dead landscape; an aftermath of the salt-water intrusion, which had spared no living thing. Everything that was once green or sported color on the previously well-landscaped and manicured lawn now lay dead or dying.

The watermark on the house gave some hope to what had first appeared a hopeless situation, as it did not appear to have reached too far into the house.

Stan was the first to reach the porch and entered the house, followed closely by Janelle, then Donald.

Entering the house, no one was prepared for what they saw, though the water had done little more than wet the linoleum floor.

What could have been a relatively happy return home, spared from the fury of the storm and the ravishes of flood waters was not to be. The otherwise unscathed home was destroyed by the depravity of man. Looters or vandals had stolen everything they could carry, what they couldn't carry they destroyed, evident with Stan's big screen TV, which had been thrown to the ground and shattered.

"It doesn't look in too bad a shape compared to some of the others we saw," Donald said, trying to put the best possible spin on the situation.

"I guess when I shot that fellow, they came back and got even," Stan surmised.

"Shot! Shot what fella?" Donald said, surprised by the revelation.

"Somebody broke in while your mother and I were still here," Stan explained. "He took a shot at me, he missed, I didn't."

"Did you kill him?" Donald asked, trying to understand what went on.

THE CITY BENEATH THE SEA

"Don't know, he ran off when the guard showed up."

"So the National Guard got a description of him and are looking for him?" Donald asked, thinking he now understood what happened, but didn't.

"No, they came to take my gun," Stan explained.

"Took your gun?" Donald repeated.

"Son!" Stan finally said, "Keep up! I hope you don't repeat everything the Judge says to you."

"No."

"Good," Stan said, then continued. "Well the guard showed up and confiscated my gun, I later learned they did that a lot after the storm."

"We were so scared the rest of the night, not knowing if they would come back or not," Janelle said, reliving the incident.

"It must have been a long night," Donald said, empathizing with his parents.

"It was," Janelle agreed, "God was watching over us that night."

"Too bad he wasn't watching the levees," Donald said, identifying them as the catalyst of their problems.

"Watch your mouth, son," Janelle said, surprised by her son's comment. "You're not too big for me to turn you over my knee."

Donald smiled and began to roll up his sleeves.

"Where do you want to start?" Donald asked, looking over the enormity of the task they faced to return their house back in order.

"Let's just each pick a spot and we'll work our way to the middle," Stan suggested, and everyone else agreed.

"Sounds like a plan," Donald said, picking up a broom, and the three of them got to work cleaning and straightening up.

THE CITY BENEATH THE SEA

Outside the Community Center, two eighteen-wheelers were on location distributing ice, MREs(meals ready to eat) and water to the waiting people, which now formed a line halfway down the block.

Parking her car on the side of the center, Melanie and Sherry walked to the entrance and disappeared inside.

Once inside the Community Center, the place was abuzz with activity. Volunteers moved about in the orchestrated symphony of organized chaos. Seeing a volunteer heading towards her down the hall, Melanie stopped her.

"Excuse me," Melanie said, bringing the woman to a halt. "Could you tell me where I can find Jessica Larose, the director?"

The volunteer pointed her arm towards the gym. "She's in there."

Walking into the gym, Melanie saw that the recreation center had been transformed into a shelter. The basketball court was covered with cots, but volunteers continued to set up more. Possibly anticipating a large turn out from people like themselves, returning to their homes only to find them uninhabitable.

In the distance, Melanie saw Jessica and headed towards her. Seeing Melanie approach, Jessica met her half-way giving her a big hug.

"Jessica, good to see you!" Melanie said, ecstatic to see her friend and co-worker.

"You too! I was worried about you."

"This is Sherry, a friend of mine," Melanie said, "How can we help?"

"You can come up with a plan on how to distribute generators," Jessica said. "In less than six hours, they're coming in, and I don't have a clue as to how we're going to distribute them."

"No problem, I'll get right on it," Melanie said.

THE CITY BENEATH THE SEA

"Sherry, you can come with me," Jessica said, taking her by the arm. "We need to come up with some sort of register to know who is in here."

"I'll be glad to help," Sherry said with a big smile, feeling useful for the first time in quite a while.

THE CITY BENEATH THE SEA

CHAPTER FORTY-FOUR

"LaToya Williams!" the booming Pa system called in the Astro Dome, the announcement escaping no-one's attention.

"What the heck?" LaToya wondered, hearing her name over the PA.

Taking her two boys by the hand, she headed for the registration booth that had been set up inside the dome and acted as a multipurpose information center.

As she approached the booth, she noticed two white men in suits and two white ladies standing by the booth, as though waiting for someone.

LaToya reported to the booth passing the unidentified strangers as she went.

"I'm LaToya Williams, you called me?" LaToya asked.

"Yes, these people are here to see you," the attendant at the booth informed her, pointing to the two men and ladies she noticed when she walked up.

"Ms. Williams?" one of the men she had noticed asked, hearing her identify herself.

"Yes."

"I'm Pastor Fleming of the First Baptist Church of Houston. This is Deacon Foster and our wives, Betty and Clair," the Pastor said, identifying himself and the rest of his party.

"Yes, sir?"

"Well, our church has taken upon itself to try to help the victims of Hurricane Katrina," Pastor Fleming explained.

"Thank you," LaToya said, not fully understanding what he was talking about.

"Ah, you're welcome," Pastor Fleming said, "Given the enormity of the task we realized we could not impact the lives of everyone, but we may be able to make the difference to the lives of one family."

THE CITY BENEATH THE SEA

"We received thousands of letters requesting assistance," the Pastor continued. "Each and every story tore at our hearts, but your story was a story of grit and determination," Pastor Fleming paused for a moment before continuing. "When we read your story, we knew you were the one."

"I'm sorry, Mister, you must have me confused. I never wrote a letter to you."

"No, you didn't," Pastor Fleming agreed, "The letter was submitted by a friend. We don't have her name only what I think is a nickname, Big Mama."

"Now if you and your boys will come with us, we want to take you to your new home."

"An apartment!" LaToya cried with excitement. "You rented me an apartment?"

"Well, not exactly, but we'll show you."

"Can I bring Big Mama?" LaToya asked.

"Sure, if you want to."

"Jamal, go get Big Mama," LaToya said, sending her son off to get Big Mama.

A short time later, Jamal returned with Big Mama.

"Big Mama, these people say you put me in for an apartment and I got it," LaToya explained. "I want you to come with us when we go."

"OK, baby, I'm so glad for you," Big Mama said, giving her a big hug.

"This way," Pastor Fleming said as he led the group out the Astro Dome.

Outside, a ten-person van waited to transport the group to their destination.

Inside, LaToya, the boys and Big Mama pondered LaToya's recent blessing.

"It's going to be so nice to be out of the Astro Dome," LaToya said, as the van headed to an as yet undisclosed location.

"I'm happy for you," Big Mama said giving the boys a hug. "You're overdue for a break in your life."

THE CITY BENEATH THE SEA

"Big Mama, I want you to come stay with us, I know the apartment may be small, but we can make do," LaToya said, "I'll not see you suffering in the Astro Dome."

"Ok, baby, but it's just until I can get back to the city," Big Mama said, "then I'm going home."

LaToya smiled at Big Mama's determination to get back in the city. After everything that had happened with the storm, she was still determined to go back to the city she loved.

In sharp contrast, LaToya couldn't care less about ever going back. New Orleans had been all she had known, but if she could somehow make a better life for her and her sons, she would stay in Houston in a heartbeat.

As the church van turned into a drive, LaToya's attention once again focused on her surroundings.

Parking in the driveway of a newly constructed home, Pastor Fleming and the rest of the church members exited the vehicle.

"Who lives here?" LaToya asked, confused by the unexpected stop.

"You do," Pastor Fleming informed her.

"What do you mean?" LaToya asked, even more confused than before.

"This is your new house," Pastor Fleming explained, "A gift from our church to you."

"Really?"

"Yes, really," Pastor Fleming repeated seeing the disbelief in her face.

"My God!" LaToya began to cry. "Thank you so much. I never lived in a house before. How much is the rent?"

"There's no rent," Pastor Fleming said, "You own it. It's yours, LaToya, the deed is in your name, free and clear. Let's go see your new house."

"Big Mama!" LaToya said, turning to her friend. "They gave me a house!"

THE CITY BENEATH THE SEA

"I see that, baby."

"Boys!" Pastor Fleming said, "Go see what's in the back yard."

The two boys ran to the back yard and screamed for joy with what they found.

"Mamma! Mamma! It's a swing set!" the boys cried out as they rushed over to the set.

Through her tears of joy, LaToya said, "This is the happiest day of my life."

Pastor Fleming lead the group to the front door, unlocking it, he handed the key to LaToya.

"I'll let you be the first to enter your new home," the Pastor said, as he stepped to the side.

LaToya slowly turned the knob, looking over her shoulder with a big smile as she entered her new home.

THE CITY BENEATH THE SEA

CHAPTER FORTY-FIVE

Outside the Community Center, Sweet and Birdie were once again in line waiting for food and water. As they waited, Sweet's keen eye spotted Melanie and Sherry walking up the sidewalk heading into the Community Center.

"Lookie here!" Sweet says to Birdie. "It's that chick off the bus."

"Yea, Melanie sent you flying off that bus!" Birdie said, with a smile, laughing under his breath.

"Nobody threw me off the bus!" Sweet said, as he snatched Birdie by the neck. "I tripped! You better remember that!"

Just as Sweet snatched Birdie by the neck, a guardsman witnessed the aggressive action and intervened.

"Is there a problem here?" the guardsman asked, an automatic weapon across his chest.

"No problem," Sweet said, releasing Birdie and eyeing the guardsman hard.

The guardsman also eyed the two men hard, burning their images into his mind. After a few moments, satisfied the situation wouldn't escalate, he walked away.

"How you know her name?" Sweet demanded after the guardsman had walked off.

"She said it on the bus," Birdie said, his lie not convincing.

"No, she didn't!" Sweet said, his tone harsh. "I'm going to ask you again! How you know her name?"

"She was a lady I had to see for my parole," Birdie reluctantly confessed as to how he knew Melanie. "She's a psychiatrist or something."

"Why didn't you tell me you knew her on the bus," Sweet asked, in a not-so-polite manner.

THE CITY BENEATH THE SEA

"Everything was happening so fast, I didn't have a chance," Birdie argued, trying to make a case in his defense.

Sweet gave Birdie a menacing look, so threatening that for the first time, Birdie actually felt nervous.

"That's crap!" Sweet said, expressing his disbelief, and disapproval with Birdie. "You know, Birdie, you're starting to worry me and I don't like to worry. Well, it looks like me and Melanie are going to have to finish our business together," Sweet said, smiling for the first time since he saw Melanie. "I hate leaving loose ends."

"What do you mean, Sweet?" Birdie asked, knowing how unpredictable Sweet was. "You're not going to hurt her?"

"No one humiliates Sweet and gets away with it!"

Coming into the guest room where Stan and Donald were straightening up, Janelle was excited as she began to explain.

"I heard on the radio they're giving away generators at the Community Center." she said, excited at the prospect of getting one.

"Well, what do you think, Donald?" Stan asked his son, "How 'bout a generator?"

"Yea sounds good, it's not far away, is it?"

"Two or three blocks," Stan said.

"Then let's go before they give them all away," Janelle said, anxious to have some source of power in their home. Janelle led the way while Stan and Donald followed her out the door.

By the time the Kings arrived at the Community Center, a crowd had already began to form at the back door of the truck that was suspected of having the generators. The door was still sealed and the only thing preventing the crowd from pulling the generators out themselves were the armed National Guardsmen who were standing guard on the trailer.

Taking their place in line, Janelle noticed a familiar face emerging from the Community Center.

"Stan!" Janelle said, her tone excited. "You and Donald wait here, I've seen someone I know."

Janelle headed down the walk, in hot pursuit of Melanie who was leaving.

"Melanie!" Janelle cried, "Melanie!"

Hearing someone call her name, Melanie spun around to see Janelle running up to her.

"Janelle!"

The two women embraced.

"Where's Stan?" Melanie asked, happy to see her and looking forward to the possibility of seeing Stan again.

"He's over here with my son, Donald," Melanie said, "You remember him, don't you?" she asked with a coy smile.

"Oh yes, I remember."

"Come on," Janelle said, taking her by the arm. "I know Stan would love to see you," She brought Melanie back to the generator line.

"Stan, look who I found!" Janelle said, returning to the line with Melanie in tow.

"Melanie!" Stan cried out loud, excited to see her, he went up to her giving her a big hug.

"How are you?" Stan asked with a big smile.

"Fine."

"You remember our son, Donald?" Stan asked as Donald stepped forward and shook her hand.

"Yes, I remember," Melanie said, shaking his hand.

"Hi, Donald."

"Hi," Donald said, as their eyes met for a long stare before Stan interrupted the moment.

THE CITY BENEATH THE SEA

"We're here, hoping to get a generator. How did your house make out in the storm?" Stan asked, wondering what her status was.

"'Fraid I got flooded, but I can help you with the generator, I am in charge of distributing them," Melanie said, sharing both bad news and good news with Stan.

"Where are you staying?" Janelle asked.

"I'll stay here in the shelter."

"I just spent one night in a shelter and I know I didn't like it. You're coming home with us, we've got an extra room and would love to have you," Janelle said, far more insistent than Melanie had ever seen her before.

"Absolutely!" Stan agreed, still wanting to express his thanks to her for saving his life, in some meaningful way. "Stay until your house gets fixed."

"I couldn't really," Melanie said, trying to find a way to graciously turn down their offer.

"You might as well give in, once they get their minds set, it's hard to change them," Donald said, deep down a part of him wanting her to accept more than his parents did.

"Well, if you think I won't be any trouble," Melanie said, finally accepting their offer.

"You'd be doing me a favor. I could use someone to talk to after a while," Donald said, smiling a contagious smile, causing Melanie to grin widely also.

"Great!" Stan said, excited, "Then it's settled. Donald, help Melanie collect anything she wants to bring."

"Sure thing," Donald said, then turned to Melanie. "Lead the way."

THE CITY BENEATH THE SEA

CHAPTER FORTY-SIX

Inside the Kings' house, an amazing transformation had taken place. The once vandalized, dirty house, which at first glance anyone would deem not habitable for months, now projected a pristine image, reflective of the pride the owners took in their home.

At the large dining room table, the Kings and Melanie sat down to a candle-lit dinner. Prepared with a special degree of love and pride, Janelle had put together a meal that far exceeded anything anyone of them had had in quite some time.

"I'm glad we still got gas and water on," Janelle said, "Stan would have had to cook on the grill."

"Thank God for gas!" Donald said, poking fun at his father's culinary skills.

"Did anyone hear when we might be getting power back to this area?" Melanie asked.

"Been listening to the radio a bit," Stan said, sharing with them what he knew. "The system's pretty messed up, but they talked about restoring some power tomorrow."

"I hope we're one of them," Janelle said, "Our air conditioning got flooded, but it would be nice to run a fan."

"Our Yankee son isn't used to this heat," Stan explained, "and it hasn't been that hot."

"Just because I live up north doesn't make me a Yankee, Dad."

"Whatever you say, son."

"I remember you saying you live in New York, right?" Melanie asked, remembering that Donald mentioned it in the Astro Dome when he picked up his parents.

"Yes, that's right," Donald said, surprised and impressed Melanie had remembered what seemed to him to be such a minor detail made in passing. "You have a good memory."

"Well, thank you," Melanie said, flattered by the comment. "What do you do in New York?"

"He's a partner in one of those rich white law firms," Stan said, interjecting the answer before Donald could.

"Ok, Dad!" Donald said, appearing to be a little annoyed by the way his dad presented the facts. "Yes, I'm an attorney."

"That's nice," Melanie said, appearing to be generally interested. "Civil or criminal?"

"You know, you're the first person who ever asked me that," Donald said, surprised again by her question. "Most people when I tell them I'm a lawyer never ask or know to ask what area of the law I specialize in."

"I thought I wanted to be a lawyer before I became a social worker," Melanie shared with the Kings.

"Donald always wanted to be a lawyer and come back home and help his people," Stan said, frustrating his son even more bringing him to the point of boiling over.

"Would you like to take our conversation on the porch?" Stan asked Melanie, obviously trying to get away from his parents.

"Sure."

As Donald and Melanie retreated to the privacy of the front porch, Stan and Janelle were left to talk alone.

"Why did you keep taking shots at him?" Janelle jumped on Stan as soon as Donald was out of earshot.

"I was hoping he would get aggravated enough with me that he might retreat to the porch with Melanie," Stan explained in a whisper. "I guess it worked."

"You crafty old fox, " Janelle said, with a laugh.

"Well, this old fox still got one or two moves even you haven't seen," Stan said, very proud of himself.

THE CITY BENEATH THE SEA

"Is that right?" Janelle said, starting to challenge his assertion, but deciding to let him have his moment.

Sitting on the railing of the front porch, Donald and Melanie looked out into the darkened neighborhood. What was once a well-lit street with light coming from every resident's home, now sat shrouded in darkness, as though the grim reaper somehow held a grip of death on the area, refusing to release it. The only sign of life in the entire block was the glow of the candles coming from inside the Kings' house.

"So what made you want to become a social worker?" Donald asked Melanie, initiating the conversation.

"I wanted to help people," Melanie began to explain, "try to make a difference. I know that sounds corny and all, but it's true. The black community is deteriorating, so many of our young people are on drugs, so many black men in jail. Young women pregnant with no husbands, the young men call it hit and run, like it's funny to father children and abandon them. Well, I could go on and on and bring us both down," Melanie said, catching herself before she talked too much about a topic she felt so passionate about. "So why did you want to be a lawyer?"

"Well, at first I guess for the same reasons you did," Donald admitted to Melanie. "Funny, until now I actually forgot that. I got so caught up in the money, the success, I guess I lost perspective." Finishing his comments, Donald stared out into the darkness, as though pondering his own words.

"Well, I'll tell you what I tell my kids," Melanie said, preparing to give Donald some advice. "Life's about choices, don't keep piling up bad choices on top of bad choices."

"You a social worker or psychiatrist?"

"Sometimes I have to be both," Melanie said, with a smile. They sat in silence for a while, in their own thoughts.

THE CITY BENEATH THE SEA

"Look at that!" Melanie said, excited by what she saw in the darkness.

"What?" Donald asked, puzzled by her sudden excitement.

"A firefly! I haven't seen fireflies in years! Come on!" Melanie said, running off the porch and into the front yard, trying to catch the firefly.

Donald soon followed, also grasping at air trying to catch the elusive little fly.

"I got one!" Donald said, being the first to catch one.

"You did not!" Melanie said, not willing to believe he could have caught one before her.

With his hands clasped together, he held them in front of her.

"See!" Donald said, keeping his hands firmly clasped together.

"Show me!" the skeptical Melanie demanded, wanting proof.

"If I show you, he'll get away."

"If you don't show me," Melanie reasoned, "how do I know you're telling me the truth."

"Hey, I'm a lawyer, remember."

Melanie just looked at Donald for a moment, allowing him to evaluate his choice of words.

"Ok, bad example," Donald acknowledged his mistake. "Tell you what, come close."

Melanie followed Donald's instructions and moved closer, closing the distance between them to only a couple of feet.

"Closer."

Melanie moved even closer to Donald, as he cupped his hands in front of them. As she drew near, their eyes meet. They looked at each other, neither one able or willing to break the stare. Slowly, their heads began to lean in towards each other. Their lips closer, almost touching, their eyes closed. At the last possible moment before their lips touched, Melanie pulled away.

THE CITY BENEATH THE SEA

"It's late, I think I'll turn in," Melanie finally said, putting an end to the moment. "Good night, Donald."

Melanie walked back to the porch and into the house, leaving Donald with only the company of the fireflies.

"Goodnight," Donald said as she headed into the house, then grabbed his head in frustration, staring into the star-filled sky.

Many more days and conversations would pass between Donald and Melanie, but none would ever come close to surpassing this night.

THE CITY BENEATH THE SEA

CHAPTER FORTY-SEVEN

A flag-draped coffin sat next to a tomb, in the once flooded cemetery. A light brown dust now covered the area up to the now familiar watermark. Many police officers were present in dress uniforms, with black armbands, as they put to rest one of their own.

Quiana stood silent, with Timmy by her side, she tried to find strength as she stood next to the coffin of her deceased husband. The black veil only partially concealed the tears that slowly streaked down her face.

The twenty-one gun salute startled both Timmy and Quiana, as it resonated around the cemetery, giving notice to all that a hero was being given such a great honor. Slowly, and with great reverence, the Honor Guard began to fold the flag that once covered Les's coffin. As one of the officers brought the flag to Quiana, she struggled to fight back tears. She felt herself getting weak and leaned on Kirra for support, as the flag was handed to her.

Quiana watched as though she wasn't really there, as though it was all a bad dream and she would wake up at any minute, but as Les's coffin was lifted into the tomb and slid into place, she realized it was real. A husband, a father, a servant of the community, gone forever.

LaToya and her boys watched as the flag that covered the coffin was slowly removed and folded with the greatest of respect.

The grieving widow then accepted the flag. LaToya was just a little taken back by the fact that the widow was black. Next to her side, a young boy close to the age of Jamal stood holding his mother's hand.

"That's what he meant when he said Jamal reminded him of his son!" LaToya reasoned.

THE CITY BENEATH THE SEA

As the funeral ceremony concluded, the crowd slowly passed, one by one in front of the widow, paying their respects.

Mourners offered their condolences, while Quiana tried to remain strong, but deep down, all she wanted to do was crawl next to her husband and die. She felt empty, as though someone had reached inside of her and ripped out everything she had. Now a hollow shell of what she once was, she struggled not only to find a way to go on, but just to make it through the day.

Timmy stood stone-like, still unable to accept and comprehend what had happened to him, slow to find a way to accept the fact he would never see his daddy again.

The funeral that had drawn LaToya's attention was not the only one taking place. Since the city had reopened, so had the cemeteries, and family members began the interning of their loved ones.

In the distance not too far from where she stood, LaToya observed two coffins side by side, the only double funeral she ever remembered seeing.

Hanging back, LaToya waited, hoping to speak to the widow, not wanting to feel rushed. But as LaToya watched the crowd slowly dissipate, she noticed a white couple hanging back, like her. They were waiting to speak to the widow, creating a dilemma for LaToya.

LaToya tried to wait the couple out, hoping they would give in first, but they seemed more determined than she was as the line to the widow ended. LaToya finally gave in, as she began to approach the widow.

As LaToya approached Quiana, she extended her hand to shake hers.

"Thank you for coming," Quiana said as she grasped LaToya's hand.

Not recognizing LaToya, she began to inquire about her presence at the funeral.

THE CITY BENEATH THE SEA

"Did you know my husband?" Quiana asked, then waited for a reply.

"No, ma'am, I didn't," LaToya admitted, the answer only confusing Quiana more.

"Then why are you here?"

"Ma'am, in the days that followed Katrina, my boys and me were trapped in the dome. After a day or so, a few buses arrived to begin transporting the people out. But there were too few buses and too many people. The crowds were pushing and shoving trying to secure one of the few seats on the bus," LaToya began to tell her story.

"This is where me and the boys were, when a fight broke out and panicked the crowd," LaToya said, tearing up as she vividly remembered the events of that day. "They pushed me to the ground. Luckily, my boys were close enough to the rail. I wasn't so lucky; I was being trampled, I couldn't breath. I thought I was going to die. Then like an angel from heaven, your husband's hands lifted me up, saving my life. That's why I'm here."

Quiana embraced LaToya giving her a big hug. "Thank you for sharing this story with me," Quiana said, a tear forming in her eye.

"I just wanted you to know," LaToya said, "I just wanted you to know what kind of man your husband was."

"Thank you," Quiana said. "But I already knew."

"God bless," LaToya said, hugging Quiana one more time before leaving.

Quiana observed how Paul had conspicuously hung back, wanting to be last. Quiana had not seen him since the storm. Having heard the reason why he was not with her husband when he was shot only added salt to an already festering wound. Quiana found it hard to accept Paul's excuses for leaving, and could now only view him as a coward who abandoned not only the city when it needed him, but he also abandoned her husband. The result may not have been any different if

THE CITY BENEATH THE SEA

Paul had been there, but by choosing the path he chose, no one would ever know.

Quiana saw Paul begin to approach her, while Gina hung back. Taking Timmy's hand, she tried to walk away, trying to indicate to Paul she did not want to speak to him. But Paul was determined, he carried not only the disgrace of a deserter from the police department, he also carried the guilt of his partner's death, which was becoming increasingly hard to live with.

"Quiana!" Paul said, chasing after her.

Quiana tried to ignore him, but he was too determined.

"Quiana, don't walk away, it's killing me what happened to Les!" Paul yelled, almost in tears.

"What do you want, Paul?" Quiana screamed, letting her emotions fly. "Forgiveness? The only person you stood a chance of getting forgiveness from is in that coffin!" Quiana yelled. "He trusted you! He loved you like a brother! And you left him to get killed!" Quiana said, her lip trembling with her anger.

"You were supposed to be watching his back! He trusted you with his life, and so did I! Quiana screamed. "I guess we both were fools."

Even through her anger, Quiana still was able to find some unshed tears.

"Forgiveness!" Quiana said, "I'm not your priest, Judas!"

"I'm sorry!" Paul said, as tears began to stream down his face.

"Sorry doesn't bring back my dead husband, does it?" Quiana said, as she walked away, as Timmy looked up at Paul saying nothing, but tears flowed from his eyes for the first time.

Standing near the two coffins, Stan fought to retain control of his emotions, as the priest concluded the ceremony, momentarily interrupted by gunshots from the twenty-one gun salute, honoring a slain police officer not far away.

Two people, whose deaths could have been prevented if the politicians they trusted had done the right thing! Stan thought, focusing his anger not only at the nursing home workers who left his mother, he also blamed the men and women who had collected money to maintain the levees, but which never made it to the levees.

As the King family slowly passed the coffins, Donald noticed Melanie standing near a tree not far away. As the services concluded and hugs were exchanged, Donald walked over to Melanie, who had begun to walk away.

"Melanie!" Donald called out.

Hearing his call, Melanie stopped and turned, waiting for him to catch up.

"Thank you for coming, but you didn't have to stay back," Donald said, trying to understand her motivation for doing so.

"I wanted to give you a moment, I don't do well at funerals," Melanie confessed, "Ever since my father, it has been so hard, just brings back too many memories," Melanie explained.

"I completely understand," Donald said. "I appreciate you coming."

"Well, I'll see ya," Melanie said, and walked away.

"See ya,"

THE CITY BENEATH THE SEA

CHAPTER FORTY-EIGHT

As the midmorning sun shone down on the Community Center, only a couple of the Guards that had been sent to provide security still remained. Giving only a token presence, but projecting the subtle reminder that more were not far away.

Passing the guardsmen, Donald climbed the steps of the Community Center, still dressed in his suit from the funeral as he entered the building.

Walking down the hall, Donald didn't hesitate; he knew where he was going. A short time later, he stood outside of Melanie's office. Only now did he wait, he hesitated for the first time showing signs of uncertainty. As though finally mustering up his courage, Donald knocked on Melanie's door.

"Come in," Melanie answered from the other side of the door.

"Hello," Donald said, as he entered.

"Donald!" Melanie said with surprise. "Hello yourself, I didn't expect to see you so soon after the funerals. Have a seat."

"How's the Center going?" Donald asked as he took a seat.

"About the same, we're housing more people now," Melanie explained. "Many people came back when the FEMA trailers started coming in. The trailers arrived only to face another bureaucratic nightmare of trying to get permits to hook them up. On top of all that, many of the trailers' keys were locked inside. They're having to get locksmiths to open them. More delays, will this nightmare ever end?"

"You sound worn down," Donald observed. "What you need is someone to take you out for a good meal. K-Paul has opened back up, I've made reservations for seven."

"Yea, but I've got so much work."

THE CITY BENEATH THE SEA

"And I'm all dressed up with nowhere to go," Donald said, but seeing little response from Melanie, he began a different approach. "Blackened redfish, hush puppies, steak, wine," Donald said, stimulating her senses.

"You don't play fair!"

"I'm a lawyer, remember?"

"Ok, I give in," Melanie conceded.

Just then, they were interrupted by a knock on the door.

"Come in," Melanie said, inviting the unknown intruder into her office.

As the door slowly opened, an elderly black woman entered.

"Ms. Melanie, I'm sorry to interrupt," the old woman said in a pleading tone.

"Ms. Barnes," Melanie said, recognizing the woman. "It's no bother, come on in, what can I do for you?"

"Well, a bunch of us finally got some of our mail today," Ms Barnes began to explain the purpose for the visit. "I've been going through some of this insurance papers, I can't make head or tail of this legal mumbo jumbo, best I can tell, they're saying they won't pay because I was flooded not because of the Hurricane. I don't know what to do," the old woman concluded and began to cry.

"Let me try to sort this out, Donald," Melanie said, "I'll meet you in front of K-Paul's at seven."

"I tell you what, I'm about done at my dad's house," Donald explained. "I've got some time, let me help around here with some of the legal questions."

"You would do that?" Melanie asked, surprised by his generosity.

"Anything that keeps me out of the house," Donald said, smiling from ear to ear.

Donald turned to the old lady to introduce himself.

THE CITY BENEATH THE SEA

"Ma'am, My name is Donald King, I'm a lawyer," Donald explained to the elderly woman. "I specialize in mumbo jumbo, let's go somewhere where we can sort this out."

"You don't look like a lawyer?"

"I've been through a hurricane," Donald explained, "my horns got knocked off."

This brought a big smile to Melanie as Donald led the old woman out the door.

Outside a residence in the garden district, Sweet and Birdie lay in wait. Using the bushes to conceal their location, they patiently waited for the owner to come home.

After what seemed like hours, their patience was rewarded when a car drove into the drive.

Crouching down even further behind the bushes, Sweet and Birdie waited for the man to exit his vehicle.

As the middle-aged man exited his car, he was totally unaware of what was about to happen to him. Going to the trunk, he opened it and began to remove his groceries, when a gun was shoved into his face.

Frozen with fear, the man dropped his bags, as the two men grabbed him and pulled him to the side of the house.

"Give me your money!" Sweet ordered the trembling man.

Not waiting for the man to comply, Birdie took the wallet out of the man's pants. Opening the wallet, Birdie removed several hundred dollars.

"Shit! Look at all this!" Birdie said with a big smile.

"Please, that's all I've got!" the man cried, but his pleas fell on depth ears.

Sweet reared back with the pistol and struck the man in the head, sending him to the ground bleeding, dazed and crying.

THE CITY BENEATH THE SEA

"Now we've got it!" Sweet said, referring to the man's original plea.

Sweet took the wallet from Birdie and began going through it.

"Get the keys!" Sweet ordered Birdie.

Birdie knelt next to the dazed man and removed the keys from his pocket. Sweet, meanwhile, removed the man's license from his wallet.

"Lookie here, Mister, I got your license! I know where you live. I know who you are. If you call the police, either me or some of my friends will come back here," Sweet told the injured man. "Do you understand?"

The dazed man nodded his understanding.

"Let's get the hell out of here!" Sweet ordered Birdie. "You drive!"

Birdie jumped into the driver's seat while Sweet rode shotgun. Backing out the drive, they headed down the road, burning rubber as they went.

"Where to, Sweet?" Birdie asked, as he sped down St. Charles Street.

"We got some bread finally, time to satisfy my sweet tooth," Sweet said, "Since the only places open are in the Quarter, let's go there."

"You think the guy will call the cops?" Birdie questioned, as he headed for the quarter.

"Hell yea! He's got to report his car for the insurance," Sweet explained to his young neophyte, "but he won't do it right away. I scared him pretty bad, he'll wait a day or two. By then, we'll be ready to dump this car and do it all over again."

"You're the man, Sweet!" Birdie said with a big smile.

Melanie waited outside K-Pauls for Donald to arrive, but she did not have to wait long, as Donald walked up to her.

THE CITY BENEATH THE SEA

"You been waiting long?" Donald asked, surprised she had beaten him there.

"Not long."

"Good," Donald said, as he opened the door for Melanie and they went inside.

Sweet and Birdie approached K-Pauls just as Sweet's sharp eye spotted Donald and Melanie going inside.

"Did you see that?" Sweet asked, pointing to the entrance of K-Paul's.

"See what?"

"That chick from the bus!" Sweet said, his tone elevated and excited. "She just went into the restaurant with some dude!"

"What you want to do?" Birdie asked, not sure to what extent Sweet would go to get even with Melanie. Deep down he knew there was a point he would not cross, not with her. *She was always been decent to me.* Birdie thought. *Maybe Sweet will just scare her,* Birdie reasoned.

"Make the block, we'll wait for them to come out and we'll follow them," Sweet ordered Birdie as he headed down the block.

Inside K-Paul's, Donald and Melanie sat at their table perusing the menus, unaware someone was stalking them outside.

"Mm, it all sounds so good," Melanie said, excited to finally be eating at a restaurant again.

"This is what I miss most about the south, the food," Donald said, "They don't have the same flavor for food in New York."

"I know what you mean," Melanie agreed. "I traveled up north a few times, the food was always disappointing."

As they talked, their waiter arrived at their table.

THE CITY BENEATH THE SEA

"Hello," the young cheerful gentleman said upon his arrival at the table. "My name is Michael, I'll be your waiter, have you decided yet or do you need more time?" Michael asked, as he removed a pad from his apron.

"Melanie?" Donald said, posing her name as a question of whether or not she was ready to order.

"I'll have the blackened drum," Melanie said, handing the menu back to the waiter.

"Same here," Donald said, handing his menu back to the waiter also. "And would you bring us a bottle of your white house wine?"

"Certainly, I'll put your order in and get the wine out right away."

The waiter left allowing Donald and Melanie to continue their conversation.

"Were you able to help Ms. Barnes this afternoon?" Melanie asked, not having been able to check up on him at the center.

"Yes, as a matter of fact I was," Donald said, a sense of pride and accomplishment coming over him. "Her and about half a dozen of her friends."

"I'm sorry."

"I'm not!" Donald said, "It's the first time in a long time I felt good about what I do."

"Well, don't get too attached, you'll be leaving soon," Melanie cautioned.

"Not necessarily," Donald said, "I've decided to stay a while. The residents down here are going to need an attorney to help them with the insurance companies."

"What about your practice?" Melanie asked.

"I guess they'll just have to buy me out. I don't belong up there, funny it took a catastrophe to make me realize it."

The waiter arrived with a bottle of wine and opened it, pouring each of them a glass.

THE CITY BENEATH THE SEA

"A toast!" Donald said, lifting his glass as Melanie did the same.

"To new beginnings," Donald said, gently touching Melanie's glass.

"New beginnings."

THE CITY BENEATH THE SEA

CHAPTER FORTY-NINE

On the street, Birdie and Sweet waited in their car not far from the entrance of K-Paul's.

"Damn!" Sweet said, "It's been an hour! How much are they going to eat?"

Just then, Melanie and Donald exited the restaurant and began walking down the street.

"Here we go!" Sweet said, stirring Birdie into action as he started the car.

Arriving at Melanie's car, Donald was observed getting into the passenger seat.

"Ok, what's the surprise?" Donald asked, as Melanie slowly pulled away from the curb.

"I'm not telling."

Melanie began to drive out of the French Quarter heading for the wharfs. After a short drive, they arrived at a dark secluded area of the wharf, next to the Mississippi River. Turning off her lights, she parked.

"I've got to tell you," Donald said kidding. "I'm not the kind of guy you can just take parking."

"Yea, right!" Melanie said, not believing a word of it.

Melanie exited the car into the night. There was virtually no wind, the night was calm, cool, and very dark without the moon to assist it.

As Donald followed Melanie's lead, he too got out the car and realized why Melanie had brought him here. Thousands and thousands of fireflies flew about, magnifying what they had experienced the other night ten-fold.

"Look at all the fireflies!" Donald said, sounding like a little kid at Christmas, unable to contain his excitement. "There must be millions!"

"They won't survive long," Melanie cautioned, "As soon as they start spraying for mosquitoes, they're going to disappear."

THE CITY BENEATH THE SEA

"How did you find this place?" Donald asked, amazed after all the years he had lived in the city he never knew or even heard about the place.

"My dad used to take me here when I was a kid," Melanie explained, "He worked the docks down here, this was the last place he took me before he died." Melanie took a moment as the memory of her father brought a tear to her eye. "I used to come here every so often after he died, but never saw the fireflies again. I gave up thinking I ever would. Then the other night when I was with you, and we saw the fireflies, it made me think of this place again."

"Thanks for sharing this with me," Donald said, as he slowly took Melanie by the waist and pulled her close to him, taking a long moment looking into her eyes, the fireflies providing their only light. As he leaned in to kiss her, lights appeared in the distance, closing in fast. The car approached, then screeched to a halt. Sweet and Birdie jumped out, brandishing their pistols.

"Hello, hello!" Sweet said, "Remember me?"

Donald was confused, but Melanie was scared, she recognized Sweet from the bus.

"I think we've got some unfinished business," Sweet yelled.

"We don't want any trouble," Donald said, trying to evaluate the position they now found themselves in. With two armed opponents, the chances of Donald being able to disarm both without one getting a shot off was not good.

"Shut up!" Sweet yelled, "No one's talking to you! You! Open your mouth again, I'll put a bullet in it!" Finishing with Donald, Sweet once again turned his attention to Melanie.

"Now, lady, what you going to do to make up for the insult you inflicted upon me?"

Donald recognized the voice he had heard on his parents' porch.

THE CITY BENEATH THE SEA

Melanie was scared; she was trembling and began to cry.

"Ok, Sweet, that's enough," Birdie said, "let's go!"

"Shut up!" Sweet barked at Birdie, "We go when I'm ready! Keep your gun on the dude. Me and the lady here need to talk."

"No, Sweet!" Birdie said, his tone determined. "I thought you just wanted to scare them. I can't let you hurt her. She has always been good to me."

"You can't?" Sweet said, repeating the words Birdie had told him with a surprised inflection. "You better do what I say!"

Birdie turned his gun away from Donald and pointed it at Sweet. "I mean it, Sweet!"

Sweet's expression changed.

"Ok, brother," Sweet said, knowing he would have to somehow pacify Birdie since he had the jump on him. "I was just fooling, we'll go."

Birdie pointed his gun back at Donald. Sweet raised his gun and shot Birdie.

Donald leapt at Sweet, knocking the gun out of his hand. The two fought in front of the headlights of the car.

Even though Sweet was not formally trained in the martial arts, his raw street fighting skills were extraordinary, making the two men evenly matched. Each began delivering kicks and punches to the other, neither one able to immediately get the upper hand.

As Donald and Sweet fought, Melanie rushed over to Birdie; she cradled him in her arms.

"I'm sorry," Birdie said, then died in Melanie's arms.

Gently laying Birdie on the ground, Melanie began to search around in the darkness for Birdie's or Sweet's gun, but couldn't find them.

Donald landed a hard punch and kick to Sweet's midsection, sending him to the ground. To Donald's surprise, Sweet came up with a straight-edged razor, swinging wildly, changing the whole dynamics of the fight, causing Donald to retreat.

As Donald was backing away, he tripped, landing on his back. Sweet, taking advantage of the situation, dived on top of him, but Donald was able to catch his razor hand, stopping it in mid-air.

Pushing the blade closer to Donald's face, the stronger Sweet inched closer and closer to his target.

Donald knew he wouldn't be able to overpower Sweet, but he didn't give up, delivering knee kicks to Sweet's ribs, which had little effect. Donald stared at the blade of the razor, he knew he was about to die.

Suddenly, there was a blast of gunfire, surprised by this, Donald looked at Sweet, who was equally as shocked. A surprised look came over Sweet, as he turned to see Melanie holding the gun that had shot him, then he fell over, dead.

Donald got up; walking over to Melanie, he took the gun from her trembling hands.

"Is he dead?" the shaking and trembling Melanie asked.

"Yes," Donald said, "but because of you, I'm not. Where did you get the gun?" Donald asked, "That doesn't look like the guns they had."

"It's Little Bertha," Melanie said, "she's a little bitch with a lot of attitude!" Melanie said, repeating the words Sherry had said the first time she saw the gun. "It belongs to a friend of mine."

"Thank you, Little Bertha!" Donald said, grateful she was there to save him.

THE CITY BENEATH THE SEA

CHAPTER FIFTY

During his return to New Orleans, William had filled countless body bags, and confiscated numerous weapons. Only now did he realize the futility of weapon confiscation, as he saw how criminals were still able to obtain weapons, regardless of his efforts.

It was time for the city to begin to heal, and like New Orleans, it was time for him to begin to heal. He had to face the demons that had tormented him for so long. Somehow, he was going to have to put them to rest.

William slowly crossed the streetcar tracks, a reserved, reluctant look on his face. Carrying a large book in his hands, he climbed the steps to the top of the levee, leading to the Moon Walk that overlooked the powerful muddy waters of the Mississippi River. He had forgotten how beautiful and how peaceful it was; he used to spend hours sitting on the levee, but this was the first time he had been back since Frank died.

The tragic events of Katrina had forced him back to the city and resurfaced the suppressed memories he had fought so long to keep locked away. William knew he would have to somehow come to terms with what had happened five years ago, and finally put the demons that haunted him to rest

Slowly descending the Moon Walk steps, William stopped momentarily as he reached the step Frank died on, then he continued down until he reached the water.

Kneeling down, he opened the book he had closely guarded for five years, and removed the bloody rose that had been pressed between its pages. Gently, he placed the treasured rose into the brown water, as the current carried it off immediately.

Just as the rose moved on down the river, William knew it was time for him to move on also. A new beginning, one free of fear of discovery. William had decided to retire from the military and pursue another career where he would not have to live a lie as to who he was. Life was too precious and too short; he would be happy, and after everything was said and done, wasn't that what was important?

Paul entered the locker room of the NOPD, he was dressed in his police uniform as he headed toward his locker.

Having been reinstated due to the severe shortage of police officers after Katrina, many opposed his reinstatement regardless of how desperate the city was for trained officers.

Despite the opposition, Paul was reinstated, though never assigned a partner. The Captain said it was because of personnel shortages, but he knew different. He heard the whispers, he knew the gossip; the truth was no-one wanted to work with him. Many viewed him as a deserter; when they needed him the most, he ran, and his partner was killed. Few took the time to learn or even ask the whole story; besides, embellishing of the facts made for a better story anyway.

Opening his locker, a photo of Les was taped to the door. Few knew the reason, some viewed it as a penance of guilt. The real reason was Paul wanted to be constantly reminded of his friend and the ultimate sacrifice he made for the city.

Paul knew nothing he could do could ever change the past, but he was committed to be the best cop he could, and in the event circumstances should ever threaten his loved ones, he would prepare for the worst, and hope for the best.

THE CITY BENEATH THE SEA

The doors to the Algiers police station were pulled open, as five men, one white, and four African Americans entered the building.

All five men wore suits and a no-nonsense look on their faces as they walked up to the desk sergeant's desk.

"My name is Mason Grayson," Mason said, identifying himself to the desk sergeant. "I'm with the Justice Department and I need to see Sherriff Ferrell."

The desk sergeant picked up his phone and dialed a number. Waiting only a moment, someone on the other end picked up, evident from the one-sided conversation which pursued.

"Ah, Sir," the desk sergeant said sheepishly. "I have some men from the Justice Department here to see you," he explained. "No, Sir," the desk sergeant continued, "but I can ask. What is this concerning?" the desk sergeant asked, relaying the question Ferrell had posed.

"It's of a personal nature," Mason said with a smile.

Repeating Mason's reply on the phone, the desk sergeant returned it back to its cradle.

"He's on his way," the desk sergeant said, curiosity beginning to overwhelm him.

The desk sergeant was not the only curious set of eyes trained on the five strangers from the Justice Department. Many of the officers who just happened to be in the office at the time watched and waited as the purpose of these men's mission would be revealed.

A short time later, Sherriff Ferrell came limping down the hall from his office.

"Sherriff Ferrell," Ferrell said, as he walked up to Mason, extending his hand as he introduced himself.

"Mason Grayson," Mason said, grasping Ferrell's hand. "I'm with the Justice Department, these four men are with the FBI," Mason explained, as the four men showed their credentials.

THE CITY BENEATH THE SEA

"What can I do for you?" Ferrell asked.

"You can put your hands on the desk and spread your legs," Mason said. "You're under arrest for violating the civil rights of over a hundred New Orleans' residents."

"What the hell are you talking about?" Ferrell demanded. "You can't come in here and arrest me!"

"We can and we are!" Mason said, as two of the FBI agents turned Ferrell around and began to pat him down, removing his service revolver from his pants.

"You have to do this here?" Ferrell asked, beginning to become aware of his men watching him.

"'Fraid so," Mason said, feeling no compassion for a man who showed so many others none, and it was no accident he specifically requested African American agents. Nothing would humiliate Ferrell more than being handcuffed by African Americans, and Grayson knew it.

As one of the FBI agents produced a pair of handcuffs, Ferrell began to object.

"That won't be necessary, I'll come with you," Ferrell said, trying to demonstrate the fact that he was co-operating.

"Sorry, policy," one of the FBI agents said, as he fastened the cuffs securely to Ferrell's wrists.

"What law did I break?" Ferrell demanded, up until this point never believing he ever done anything wrong.

"You're being arrested under 'Color of Law'," Mason began to explain. "Kind of ironic don't you think? The Color of Law."

"What's that?"

"Title 18, U.S.C. Section 242 Deprivation of Rights Under Color of Law," Mason began to explain. "This statute makes it a crime for any person acting under color of law, statute, ordinance, regulation, or custom to willfully deprive or cause to be deprived from any person those rights, privileges, or immunities secured or protected by the Constitution and laws of the U.S."

"In layman's terms!" Ferrell said, not understanding all the legal terminology.

"In layman's terms," Mason began to explain. "You will be brought to stand trial in New Orleans, probably in front of some of the people you turned away from the bridge. In other words, you're screwed!"

The agents escorted Ferrell out of the station to the waiting patrol car, leaving a station of officers shocked at what they had just witnessed, and wondering if they would be next.

One year later, a very pregnant Melanie walked into the auditorium, which a year earlier had been covered with cots. Donald was teaching a group of kids Karate, leading them through their forms. Seeing Melanie, he turned the class over to his assistant, and ran towards her. Donald touched her very pregnant stomach.

"He's not punching and kicking yet, is he?" Donald asked, then gave Melanie a big kiss.

"Not today," Melanie smiled. "Come on, get changed, your parents are coming over. Your mama's going to help me pick out wallpaper for the nursery."

"I deal with crooked politicians, immoral insurance companies, floods, crime, now my parents," Donald stated, "Does anything ever come easy in the Big Easy?'

"Well, at least the fireflies stayed," Melanie said with a smile, as she took her husband by the arm.

"Let's go, hot-shot, your parents are waiting." Melanie led Donald down the hall.

OTHER GREAT TITLES BY
Ricardo S. Dubois

Ghost Squirrel
Swamp Witch
A Time for Miracles
Crossroads
The Treasure of Jean Lafitte
When Destinies Collide
Vengeance is Mine!
Southern Justice
Turnabout
The Mardi Gras Murders
City Beneath the Sea

Autograph copies available by contacting me at:
craftycajun@yahoo.com

www.ingramcontent.com/pod-product-compliance
Lightning Source LLC
Chambersburg PA
CBHW030527030726
47495CB00004B/880